"MY GOD," SHE GASPED, SHUDDERING. "IT'S A DUNGEON."

Gripping the stairway bannister with a trembling hand, she descended toward the bottom of the steep steps that led to the cellar room. Incredibly, she saw a saw-dust covered floor, black walls festooned with long straps, a black leather-covered bench with shackles and chains at the four corners and a large wooden rack that displayed whips, paddles, swords, a mace and a spear.

Then softly behind her she heard a creaking sound. Turning, she screamed in terror.

Swinging almost imperceptibly from a rafter by a hangman's rope and noose, the corpse was naked except for a black leather hood that covered the entire head. . . .

THE FINEST IN FICTION
FROM ZEBRA BOOKS!

HEART OF THE COUNTRY   (2299, $4.50)
by Greg Matthews
Winner of the 26th annual WESTERN HERITAGE AWARD for
Outstanding Novel of 1986! Critically acclaimed from coast to
coast! A grand and glorious epic saga of the American West that
NEWSWEEK Magazine called, "a stunning mesmerizing perfor-
mance," by the bestselling author of THE FURTHER ADVEN-
TURES OF HUCKLEBERRY FINN!
    "A TRIUMPHANT AND CAPTIVATING NOVEL!"
        —KANSAS CITY STAR

CARIBBEE   (2400, $4.50)
by Thomas Hoover
From the author of THE MOGHUL! The flames of revolution
erupt in 17th Century Barbados. A magnificent epic novel of
bold adventure, political intrigue, and passionate romance, in the
blockbuster tradition of James Clavell!
    "ACTION-PACKED . . . A ROUSING READ"
        —PUBLISHERS WEEKLY

MACAU   (1940, $4.50)
by Daniel Carney
A breathtaking thriller of epic scope and power set against a
background of Oriental squalor and splendor! A sweeping saga
of passion, power, and betrayal in a dark and deadly Far Eastern
breeding ground of racketeers, pimps, thieves and murderers!
        "A RIP-ROARER"
        —LOS ANGELES TIMES

*Available wherever paperbacks are sold, or order direct from the
Publisher. Send cover price plus 50¢ per copy for mailing and
handling to Zebra Books, Dept. 2787, 475 Park Avenue South,
New York, N.Y. 10016. Residents of New York, New Jersey and
Pennsylvania must include sales tax. DO NOT SEND CASH.*

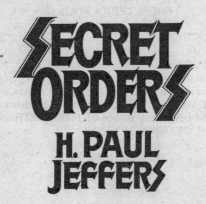

SECRET ORDERS

H. PAUL JEFFERS

ZEBRA BOOKS
KENSINGTON PUBLISHING CORP.

ZEBRA BOOKS

are published by

Kensington Publishing Corp.
475 Park Avenue South
New York, NY 10016

First printing: October, 1989

Printed in the United States of America

This book is dedicated to my friend and colleague

DICK LEVITAN

"If we believe absurdities, we shall commit atrocities."

—*Sarvepalli Radha Krishnan*

Part One: Judah

Chapter One

The House on Amos Street

"I never feel comfortable going to Jerusalem," said Daniel Ben Avram as the aging black Mercedes sedan labored uphill.

Wrenching his attention from the highway and shifting his smoky gray eyes to his young passenger, Amnon Dorot erupted with astonishment. "What a hell of a thing to hear from a Jew!"

Sliding back a blue baseball cap that had been slanting down to the bridge of his nose since they'd headed out of Tel Aviv into the glare of the rising sun, Daniel squinted against the white fieldstones littering the surrounding steep hillsides which looked like the blanched bones of the ancient prophets of Israel. "When I'm there I am painfully aware of the presence of the Holy Spirit," Daniel said. "And, therefore, of my grave shortcomings as a Jew, an Israeli, and a man."

"That's a rather harsh judgment on yourself," said

Amnon. "Considering the fact that you're only twenty years old."

"Nineteen, actually," said Daniel with a shrug. "Born on the fifteenth of May in 1948."

"Independence Day," exclaimed Amnon. "What an auspicious birthday!"

"It makes it difficult for any of my family or friends to say they forgot," said Daniel with a smile as his wary blue eyes scanned the tops of the rough hills looking for signs of the hostile Arab forces that had occupied the high ground flanking the lifeline corridor that connected Tel Aviv with Jewish West Jerusalem since the 1948 war, as many years as Daniel's life. It was along this road in fierce fighting at Latrun in a military operation codenamed "Maccabee" in the War for Independence that Daniel's father had been killed in action a week after his son's birth, never having seen him.

Now, on this April morning of 1967 cutting through the oppressive weight of that personal and Israeli history was the always cheerful rasp of Amnon Dorot, a slender man with a weathered face and curly salt-and-pepper hair who was a contemporary of Daniel's father and a hero in his own right, in his own secret way. "Have you ever met the General?"

"No, I never have," said Daniel, sitting upright and straightening his cap as he sensed the approaching closeness of the divided Holy City of Jerusalem.

"Ah, he is the best! A legend," said Amnon animatedly. "One of the original Zionists. Leader of the Irgun; some say he was its operational brains. One of the planners of the commando operation that brought Eichmann to trial for his atrocities. When

10

the history of modern Israel is written the General's name will run through it shining like a vein of gold."

"Which name? He's used so many!"

"This is true," chuckled Amnon.

"My father knew him," said Daniel quietly.

"There will be a brilliant chapter in that history for him, as well, Daniel," said Amnon solemnly as the Mercedes struggled upward. "Soon we'll come to my favorite spot on this road," he went on brightly. "The turn where you suddenly see the city. 'If I forget you, Jerusalem, let my right hand wither, let my tongue cleave to my mouth, if I remember you not.' You see. Daniel? I quote the Psalms! I, too, feel the presence of the holy spirit when I come to Jerusalem. As to those grave shortcomings of yours, you are unfair to yourself. You've got nothing to apologize for as a Jew, an Israeli, or as a man. The General could have had his pick of hundreds of very capable young men for this job. Out of them he chose you."

"What I don't understand is why we're having this meeting in Jerusalem. Seems to me Tel Aviv would have been safer."

"The answer is simple. The central figure in the case belongs in Jerusalem. For him to go to Tel Aviv would attract undesirable attention."

"Have you met him?"

"Yes."

"Do you believe his information?"

"I believe what he's told us is so important and so compelling that we would be fools not to follow up."

"Then why not follow up with a more experienced agent?"

"The General wants someone fresh but tough.

11

Someone not known because of previous actions yet full of potential. Top of his class at Kfar Sirkin. And, most important of all, someone who is young. All that spells Daniel Ben Avram."

From the start of schooling Amnon had been certain that Daniel Ben Avram would qualify.

For the sake of the memory of his father if for no other reason he would strive harder than any of his classmates in the special school that from the other side of its high barbed wire double fence appeared to be an appendage of the old airbase of Kfar Sirkin near the town of Petach Tikva on the agricultural plain 10 kilometers east of Tel Aviv.

Indeed, flight instruction was part of the curriculum for the student body whose numbers would be cut in half at the end of the six month term, from forty to twenty, with that number being reduced by half again over the next six months. But service with the Israeli Air Force was not the objective of the eighteen year old volunteers who'd boarded an old school bus bearing a sign proclaiming its destination as the Kibbutz Rosh Ha'Ayin, the first of many deceptions to come if Daniel Ben Avram were to be one of the ten survivors; "the chosen," as Col. Amnon Dorot called the graduates of what he referred to as his "little shul for secret agents."

Addressing the new class in his orientation greeting to them on their first evening at the school, he'd said, "Don't think of me as an officer or your teacher or your boss." With a widening, winning grin he said, "I prefer you to think of me as a *moyl*."

12

When the inevitable laughter subsided, he said with a chuckle, "I'm here to circumcise your innocence."

They'd laughed again but when they quieted he spoke gravely. "Believe me, the world you will be entering, should you make it through this process, is no place for the uninitiated. If you graduate from here you will become members of a secret brotherhood and leave here as secret warriors engaged in secret struggles on secret battlefields where the heroes are given secret medals and the dead are buried in secret graves."

That night they swore an oath to keep the secrets.

Before dawn as they were awakened to begin learning them, their *moyl* was already cutting, culling, sifting, weighing, and gleaning.

At the end of the year, as he'd expected, Amnon took the salute of Lieutenant Daniel Ben Avram—first in his class: first at languages, speaking English without an Israeli accent; first in codes; first in tactics; first in planning, surveillance, posting and gathering messages, opening and closing letters, tapping wires, planting bugs and finding them; best scores on the firing range with pistols and rifles, as near to perfection as anyone could be with the Uzi; tops in concealment of weapons; number one with explosives; unmatched in identification of the enemies of Israel; and unequaled in that highest of all qualifications for success in the secret life he had elected to enter—motivation.

Accordingly, when the General had asked Col. Amnon Dorot for a recommendation of a fresh graduate of the school for an extraordinary assignment, there'd been no hesitation in naming Daniel.

The stone house on Amos Street was barely visible behind a high bricked wall, overhanging towering trees, and a thicket of obscuring evergreens through which curved a gravel path that crunched underfoot in loud proclamation of their approach to three slate-topped concrete steps. A small wooden porch creaked with their weight and a heavy oak door with a peephole winked at them before the door swung open.

"Right on time, Amnon," said a tall man with a military bearing who opened the door. Daniel knew him by the name of Ezer. "Hello, Daniel," he said, stepping aside to admit them. "Go right into the first room on the left. The one with the double doors."

The doors closed behind them as Daniel and Dorot entered. And locked, Daniel noted as his eyes became accustomed to the abrupt change from sunlight to the dim parlor. Spacious with a high ornate ceiling and heavily draped tall windows, the room was furnished with sturdy tables and thick cushioned sofas that appeared to date back to the pre-British Mandate era when Jerusalem was occupied by the Ottoman Turks before the First World War. Having been seated in the facing couches and drinking tea from an ornate silver service on a low table between them, three men now stood.

"General," said Amnon crossing the room with a soldierly stride, "here is your man."

Clearly the eldest of the three, the General was a tiny man with silver hair, a ruddy pudgy face and a

14

potbelly straining the buttons of the vest of a double-breasted suit which was the same shade as the tan camouflage army uniform that the General usually wore. "Shalom, Daniel," he said, coming out from between the couches with outstretched hand. "We'll be using only first names," he whispered as he held onto Daniel's hand and turned to introduce him to the others. "Gad, whom you may know, and our guest, Pierre."

"I do know Gad," said Daniel with a nod. "A friend of my father's. It's been a long time, sir. Shalom."

A colonel in the army assigned to a special branch of Israeli intelligence services, sandy-haired and green-eyed with a suntan like burnished saddle leather, Gad Horev was the tallest of the men in the room and a veteran of all of the most famous of Israel's commando actions. "Shalom, Dan."

"Shalom, Pierre," said Daniel as he turned to the third man, slender and elegantly attired in a blue suit and white shirt with heavy gold cufflinks and a wide red, white, and blue striped tie.

Pierre replied in a heavy accent as French as his name, his shirt cuffs, and his tricolor tie. "Shalom, Dan. It's a pleasure to meet you. You are so young! So good-looking. Like a film star! But, of course, the man for this undertaking must be, mustn't he?"

"I suppose so," said Daniel, not knowing what was expected of him, then suddenly realizing that he recognized this elegant stranger.

An official in the Jaffa Road offices of the French government, his name came back to Daniel as Pierre AuCoin who had been very helpful in arranging a trip to Paris for Mrs. Ben Avram and her son on the occasion of the boy's sixteenth birthday, cutting through the red tape that France's consular officials in Tel Aviv had seemed determined to put in the way. Something to do with passports and visas, Daniel recalled.

Invited to sit beside AuCoin, he now wondered if the Frenchman remembered him. And, as people in the same profession as the novice Daniel Ben Avram were wont to do, he speculated on whether the dapper Pierre AuCoin was in the same line of work as all the men in the curtained parlor of the house of Amos Street—if Pierre were a brother in the world-wide fraternity of Free World secret services. In Israel, it was Mossad. In the United States, the CIA. In Britain, MI6. In Egypt, the Mukhabarat. South Africa's was BOSS, the Bureau of State Security. In France, it was called the S-deck, short for an unpronounceable organization that because of DeGaulle's troubles over Algeria spied on the French as much as France's enemies and was a direct descendant of the Deuxieme Bureau that not only failed miserably in coping with Nazi agents but often collaborated with them before France collapsed in the face of Hitler's armies in 1940.

Although the smooth-faced AuCoin did not appear to be old enough to have been active in the war he did seem to Daniel to possibly have been involved in S-deck activities in the immediate postwar years when the French intelligence services had fragmented politically concerning relations with Israel, some of its members being pro-Israel and many siding with the Arabs. Judging by his presence

16

in this room with the General, Gad, and Amnon, Daniel reasoned, AuCoin must have been of the pro-Israel faction. Unless, of course, he reasoned further, AuCoin was pulling some kind of frog dirty trick involving double cross and disinformation.

Apparently unconcerned about this possibility and delicately balancing a teacup and saucer as he sank back in the comfortably encompassing sofa opposite Daniel and AuCoin, the General said, "Pierre, please brief Daniel completely and thoroughly as to your purpose in being here—all the details of fact and surmise. For Daniel's life will most certainly depend on it." .

Chapter Two

The Frenchman's Story

"I was born in 1930 in Paris," began Pierre after a sip of tea.

Dear God, thought Daniel, is he going to tell his life story?

"My parents were Communists. During the war they were active in the Underground. So was I, as much as a teenager could be. Mostly I acted as a courier, delivering messages that I had memorized. It happens that I have an exceptional memory. This applies to faces as well as data. Throughout my lifetime I have been blessed, perhaps I should say cursed, with an ability to recall the faces of people I've met in the most casual circumstances—waiters, motorbus operators and busboys, hotel chambermaids, everyone! I never forget a face."

"What an extraordinary ability that is," interjected Daniel, thinking that if it were so, why hadn't Pierre remembered his?

"It is exceptional," the Frenchman said as he leaned forward to put down his cup. "Take you, for instance! You probably don't recall it, but I remember you! It was a few years ago. You came to my office with your mother, I believe. A very striking woman! There was a problem with visas or some such. Do you remember?"

Grinning broadly, Daniel nodded. "As vividly as if it were yesterday, sir. It was three years ago, by the way."

"Well, well, well," chuckled the General. "What a small world. And what a facility you have, Pierre." With a building amusement he wagged a finger at Daniel. "Seems your cover is blown already!"

"I merely wish to make the point that I do have this trick of the mind," said Pierre. "It is important that you believe it because it's this memory for faces that is at the crux of the matter, isn't it, General?"

"Absolutely, sir. So pray continue."

"A face that has been impressed on my mind since I was fifteen years old is that of a Nazi officer—and not just an officer but an SS colonel!"

He paused a moment, then quietly continued, "You may wonder what was so striking about his appearance as to leave such a vivid memory. There was nothing unusual about his face, except that it was the face of the man who got me tortured."

Daniel exclaimed, "Tortured? How? Where? Why?"

"Let Pierre tell the story in his own way and in his own time," declared the General. "There's no rush."

19

"Thank you, General. As I was saying, I was a courier for my parents' Underground cell in Paris. I might add that although I was fifteen I was still quite small and boyish, looking much younger. It was after the war that I sprouted. Therefore, being so young-looking, I suffered from that curse of children—being so easily overlooked. In my line of work at the time this was a definite advantage. I flitted around Paris like a butterfly. No! A moth. Butterflies are always noticed. Moths never are. Yes, I was a moth. The perfect cover for my errands. That is until I ran into this SS officer. Literally ran into him. Bowled him over by striking him, quite accidentally, with a bicycle!"

"Oh, hell," muttered Daniel, suppressing a grin.

Grimly, Pierre said, "That is the precise word, Daniel. Hell! For that's what my life became at that instant. Immediately, the son of a bitch had me arrested."

Indignantly, Daniel demanded, "On what charge?"

"The SS never needed a charge, son," asserted the General.

"Well, I suppose he could have made a case for reckless driving of a bicycle," smiled Pierre. "I did make quite a mess of the colonel's trousers. Ripped them from boottop to hip. Tore his coat, too. Anyway, I was arrested on his orders and had every expectation of being shipped off to a concentration camp. Naturally, I was asked my name and, being a novice at fighting the Nazis, I gave it. My real name. Which, of course, was the same as that of my parents, who were on the Nazis' wanted list."

"So they tortured you to find out about them?"

"Yes, Daniel, that is exactly what happened."

"This SS colonel participated?"

"Oh, no, he was out of the case by that time. He had nothing to do with the actual torturing of me, though he had a great deal to do with the torturing of others. Shall I go into that at this time, General?"

"That's an aspect on which Daniel will be briefed by others, Pierre," said the General with a wave of his hand. "From you at this time we're only interested in your subsequent encounters with this SS officer. The next time was . . ."

"After the war."

"And where was it?"

"Again in Paris. The date was late 1945 or early 1946. The place was Gare de l'Est. He was boarding the Simplon Orient Express, which at that time was operating daily from Paris to Trieste and Belgrade, and three times a week to Istanbul via Sofia."

Amnon asked, "Which one did he take?"

"The Istanbul train. But I do not believe he would have traveled beyond Trieste. Had he, he would have found himself behind the Iron Curtain where no Nazi in his right mind would have ventured even if he were traveling with the finest documentation. I made that journey in 1950 and even then with my genuine French passport I was harassed. The locals and the Soviet NKVD agents collected all the passports and carefully scrutinized them. Then they searched every compartment. They even removed the light bulbs and searched the sockets for contraband. My guess, and it's only a guess, is that the SS officer I

21

saw boarding the Orient Express traveled to Switzerland where he undoubtedly slipped into the Nazi escape route, by then well established."

"If you spotted this Nazi," said Daniel, "why didn't you point him out to the authorities at the train station?"

With a shrug Pierre said, "I tried but by the time I found a gendarme and brought him to the platform the train had departed."

"Move ahead to your next encounter," said the General.

"New York City. April eighth."

Amnon asked, "What year?"

"Why, this year, of course."

Bolting off the couch, Daniel exclaimed, "Two weeks ago?"

"It was at the Brooks Atkinson Theater, a preview performance of a delightful little musical, *Sing, Israel, Sing,* for the benefit of Jewish charities."

"Now hold on, Pierre," scoffed Daniel. "Are you saying you saw this ex-SS officer, this ex-Nazi, at a performance of a Jewish play being given for the benefit of Jewish charities? You must have been mistaken. Your memory for faces has to have failed you at last."

Patiently, Pierre said, "It was the same man."

"Did you look for a policeman?"

Gently stroking the arm of the sofa, Pierre said, "And just what would I have said to a policeman had I been able to find one in the crush of Broadway theaters letting out? 'Officer, come quick, I just spotted a Nazi?'" Raising his hands as if in supplication, he said, "I had no proof that the man I saw was a Nazi. Save for my memory of his face."

"Did you follow him?"

"Of course not."

"Well, what the hell did you do?"

"I came here."

Chapter Three

The General's Story

"We are quite certain that the SS officer whom Pierre has had an affinity for encountering with such coincidental regularity over the years is this man," said the General, producing a file folder and an eight-by-ten photograph from a desk drawer. "Col. August Grenier, as he looked in 1941."

The black-and-white picture appeared to have been softly focused in the taking and made even fuzzier in what probably had been multiple duplications over the intervening 26 years. It showed a tall and slender man with fair hair, dressed in the black uniform of the SS. Stiffly posed, the officer stood outdoors before what appeared to be a concrete-block warehouse.

As if he'd read Daniel's mind, the General said, "The building behind him is the crematorium at Theresienstadt. You will learn more about that camp from a man who was there. But before he comes in, I want to brief you on what we know about Grenier *before* his service at Theresienstadt."

Among the many stories about the General that Daniel had heard was that he had been a brilliant student of the Torah by age ten and a distinguished professor of Judaism and the religions of the world when he was barely into his twenties but that he'd abandoned the academic world to devote himself to the cause of Zionism, being a revolutionist. Through his military career he laid the foundation for Israel's secret services and the special branch whose sacred and sworn duty was to track down and bring to justice the enemies of Jews, past and present.

But as Daniel listened to him in the small upstairs room of the house on Amos Street, the General became again the lecturing university professor aflame with his subject.

"Grenier was born in Bavaria in November 1900 and was raised a Roman Catholic. As a youngster he was quite devout and given to mysticism so that he appeared to be destined for the Jesuit priesthood. He was obsessed with puzzles, of which God and the settled order of things were uppermost. He consumed the music of Wagner. Then came the First World War and an end to any dreams he may have had of the Jesuitical life. Serving as an officer, he came under the influence of army right-wing elements and as a result was fiercely anti-Communist after the war. Like so many Germans he was increasingly embittered by the punishments imposed on Germany by the victorious allies. Whatever it was that might have propelled him into the Jesuits had become twisted and now pushed him closer and closer to the fanatics and hate groups that flourished in Bavaria. He read all the literature, and was especially influenced by a tome called 'Spiritualism,' *'Der Spiritismus'* in the German. It's shot full of theories about the transmigration of souls. At this time, the handsome young Grenier met and came under the spell of an anti-Semitic multimillionaire eccentric art collector, Helmut von Graubatz. From this wealthy patron and sadomasochistic pervert, Grenier learned a great deal about art and secret pleasures of the flesh. In his years with the SS, Grenier put that knowledge of both to use, collecting a rather substantial trove of confiscated art treasures and becoming one of the most brutal of all the SS in the camps. But I'm jumping ahead in the story! As you can see, Grenier's head was stuffed with the ideas of both von Graubatz and the book on spiritualism: black magic, satanism, notions about a super race, and all the legends and fairy tales about a lost advanced civilization called Atlantis. In 1923, at the urging of von Graubatz, he joined a Bavarian outfit known as the Free Corps. After that it was a short step into the fledgling Nazi Party where von Graubatz introduced him to another like-minded and frustrated ex-army officer, Heinrich Himmler. When 1925 came and a special bodyguard was formed to protect the Nazi leader, Hitler, Himmler was put in charge of his local unit and made Grenier his deputy. That elite guard was called *Schutzstaffel*, the SS. In Grenier's mind they were Black Knights, a cadre of Teutonic warriors marching to a Wagnerian beat."

*　　*　　*

"There are many striking similarities in Grenier's dossier to the life and career of his boss and hero, Himmler," said the General as he reached for a glass of water, the abrupt gesture shattering his spell as professorial storyteller and returning him to his military persona, declaring, "I met him once."

Astonished, Daniel gasped, "You met Himmler?"

"No," laughed the General. "Grenier."

"How on earth . . . ?"

After a sip of the water, the General was neither the legendary Zionist nor the lecturing professor but an amiable and ruddy-faced portly gentleman of advanced years with a personal yarn to spin. "It was in Venice long before the war, well before anyone heard of Hitler. A professor of religion and philosophy of our mutual acquaintance was sponsoring a colloquium on the subject of Satanism. What a contrast! The devil being talked about while we were surrounded by the immense splendors of that magnificent city with its grand cathedral of St. Mark. There we were, feasting on the banquet of *La Serenissima* with the Prince of Hell as the main dish! It was quite bizarre, believe me."

"Fascinating," said Daniel, not knowing what else to say.

"I'd been invited to discourse on the Jewish viewpoint. Grenier was there with his grotesque mentor, von Graubatz, and a Baron Rudolf von Sebottendorf, the Grand Master of a Bavarian group calling itself the Thule Society. This was a fraternal lodge that appeared to me to be stuck in the Middle Ages, filled with all the ancient bigoted notions about Jews as the killers of Christ and the instru-

27

ments of Satan. When it came time for Sebottendorf to speak to us he ranted and raved about an international conspiracy of Jews and Freemasons. Grenier, being in the shadow of his Grand Master, was rather quiet during the formal sessions, as I recall. What I remember vividly, however, even after all these years, is something he said to me at dinner. I can still quote him exactly. 'You being a Jew will not understand this,' he said, 'but every German has one foot in Atlantis and one in this world where he will build a new order of society.' Without Jews, he meant. There is one other item I remember about Grenier from Venice. Dangling from the gold chain across his vest was a tiny golden swastika, the symbol of the Thule Society; years ahead of Herr Hitler's use of it as the emblem of his Nazi New Order."

While the General's Cupid's bow lips stretched into the tight and nervous black-humored smile of a man thinking "If only I'd recognized then what I learned to my regret later," a cold finger of horror was stabbing down Daniel's spine, making him shudder.

The professor again, the General asked, "Now where was I?"

"Grenier joining the SS."

"Because Grenier had been smiled on by Himmler, Grenier became one of Himmler's inner circle. This was an unofficial group known as the Order of the Teutonic Knights, based loosely on the secret medieval society of the same name. Candidates for membership had to prove pure noble German

28

ancestry for eight generations on both sides of the family. Considering his own rather humble roots, Himmler was a little more liberal with his updated version of the Order. There were also close approximations in the organization of the Order of Teutonic Knights to the Jesuits. This appealed greatly to Grenier, of course. The Order's principles were absolute obedience. An oath was required. Grenier raised his hand enthusiastically.

"Another icon from Germany's past for Himmler was King Heinrich I the Fowler. Indeed, Himmler had ideas that he was the reincarnation of that monarch. He had the ancient bones disinterred and moved to a cathedral near Himmler's residence where he staged annual processions and rituals. One of the hallmarks of the old king was a hatred for Slavs. Therefore, Himmler placed the persecution of Slavs high on his agenda. And his agenda was the SS's. And, of course, it was Grenier's. That's how he came to be at Theresienstadt, sent there by Himmler in 1942."

With a sigh as he reached for water again, the General said, "This is the time for you to hear from someone else, Daniel. Would you prefer to take a break? Rest a little first? Freshen up?"

"No, please," said Daniel urgently. "Let's go on."

Chapter Four

The Rabbi's Story

"I was sent to Theresienstadt in December 1941, just a few weeks after the camp was established in Czechoslovakia some 40 miles from Prague," said the rabbi. All in black, he was an old man with a worry-furrowed forehead and a long and wavy gray beard. Tufts of gray hair poked out around his homburg and ringlets of gray were at his temples. He sat on the edge of a straight-back wooden chair, ramrod erect and stern as a Biblical prophet or, thought Daniel, one of the teachers of the Torah who had labored in vain in hopes of turning Daniel Ben Avram into a scholar. "Do you know about this place called Theresienstadt, young man?"

Blushing with embarrassment at having to admit his ignorance of the details of this particular death camp of the Holocaust, Daniel muttered, "I'm sorry, not much. It was some kind of Nazi showplace, wasn't it? A concentration camp built for show for the benefit of the Red Cross?"

"The Paradise Ghetto," said the rabbi, spitting the words. "It was put on show once! This was at a time when the International Red Cross was invited to see how well Jews were being treated. It was a sham and a hoax. For weeks before the visit the place was spruced up. 'The Great Beautification,' it was called. '*Verschonergunaktion.*' When the visit was done, it was back to the old ways.

"Listen, boy, and I will tell you all. For you must understand Theresienstadt if you are to appreciate the character of the man in that photograph whom we in the camp knew as 'the devil in the mask.'"

His lecture was not professorial like the General's. Rather, it was punctuated with a marvelous array of facial expressions of amusement, astonishment, disgust, and dismayed amazement accompanied by rolling eyes, darting tongue, curling lip, wild hands and arms, poking fingers, and punching fists.

"Once upon a time the Czech village named Terezin was indeed a showplace. A lovely little village of quaint stone houses and clean streets with a population of maybe five thousand people.

"Then came the war, the Nazis, and the SS. Then came the prisoners. In time, more than thirty-three thousand Jews died there. Maybe ninety thousand more were sent from there to die elsewhere. When I arrived there were fifty-three thousand! At the end when the Russians came to liberate us there were seventeen thousand.

"There had been fifteen thousand children. Only

one hundred survived.

"This is where the devil in the mask comes in. This beast, Grenier. He arrived at about the time I did. Maybe it was early in 1942. Oh, I remember him very well.

"He took special interest in the teenage boys' house. It was his private pool of candidates for his special experiments.

"I hope you have a strong stomach, Daniel, for this is rough stuff that I am going to tell you about; what this animal did to those boys.

"Have you ever heard of *vril?* Spelled v-r-i-l?

"No, I expect not. So I will give you a little lesson about vril. It was supposed to be 'the one great fluid of life' and if you could store it up you could become a person with enormous mental and physical abilities.

"There was a society in Berlin, the Vril Society, made up of people who believed this drivel. Grenier was a member of the Vril Society. He and his cohorts sought to connect themselves with supernatural beings at the center of the world. They practiced techniques which they believed would strengthen their mastery of this divine energy, this vril stuff. They did this in the expectation that the world would one day be transformed and the creatures from the center of the world would emerge and form an alliance with the vril people and so dominate the earth.

"Grenier believed all this but he gave it a twist of his own. You see, he became convinced that he could create vril. He thought he could concoct a potion of the stuff. But to do it he needed to draw off the vital fluids of young male Jews. Somehow in his perverted way of thinking he came to the idea that through the suffering of Jewish boys he could create vril. To do this he would use electricity, connecting the wires to their private parts and then forcing them to masturbate.

"At the moment of ejaculation, he turned on the current.

"In the teenage Jewish boys of Theresienstadt he had an abundant source for his experiments, which he always conducted while wearing a leather face mask. Did I tell you about the mask? He had a black leather mask that covered his whole head. This is what he wore while he turned on the current to collect what he called the 'vital fluids' of these tortured and screaming boys so that he could, somehow, concoct this *vril*.

"He was a madman, like all the Nazis.

"I prayed that the Russians would get him. But they didn't. He was long since gone by the time the Russians liberated the Paradise Ghetto.

"God only knows what happened to him."

Chapter Five

The Historian of Hell

It was late in the day now and through the wind-tossed trees outside the window of the upstairs room of the house on Amos Street winked a streetlight.

The lecturer who had come in after the rabbi was a man known well to Daniel because he was a public figure. Famous around the world as "The Historian of Hell," Yehuda Wasserman had become the visible, outspoken, and eloquent spokesman on behalf of the cause of justice and the memory of the millions of Jews who had been consumed by the Holocaust.

Slouching his lanky frame into a corner of a sofa with his pointy chin cupped in the palm of his left hand, he stared with narrowed green eyes raking Daniel Ben Avram from his wavy sandy blond hair to the steeled toes of his Israeli Army combat boots. "Kind of new at this, aren't you?"

If there were such a thing as an avenging angel, thought Daniel uncomfortably, this would be his look. "Totally."

The green eyes shifted questioningly to the General.

"Don't worry," said the General. "He's the right man."

"What is it you want from me?"

"Everything you know about Grenier. The wartime files. The Nuremberg dossier. The postwar period. All about escape routes, et cetera, et cetera. How the apparatus worked. And all you know about August Grenier at that time."

"Blessed little, I'm afraid!"

"Anything will be helpful."

"His medical files, confiscated when the Russians liberated Theresienstadt, were turned over to the Nuremberg prosecutors, although, of course, SS Stormbannfuhrer August Grenier never stood in the dock.

"He'd slipped away from Theresienstadt well before the Russians arrived by disguising himself as a priest. God only knows where he got the cassock and collar.

"It's surmised that he traveled on foot with ordinary refugees streaming to the west rather than be taken by the Russians, reached Prague and then somehow got to Vienna and on to France, where he was seen in late '45 or early '46 boarding the Orient Express in Paris.

"The description given by the man who saw him at that time fits. A slender man of slightly above average height with a medium build. Fair-haired.

"The medical file shows that he had considerable dental work consisting of upper left and upper right bridges. In a slight accident in his laboratory at Theresienstadt he sliced off the tip of the little finger of his right hand, clearly the most identifiable physical anomaly that we know about. There was also a small sickle-shaped scar on his right shoulder.

"He had a mellow baritone voice and was known to entertain his fellow officers with nearly professional renditions of famous songs from operettas and show tunes. The theater was of great interest to him before the war. We presume it still is, given evidence that he was seen recently attending a Broadway musical.

"How he got to New York is a mystery to us.

"One established escape route for the SS bigshots on the run was through Switzerland where there were plenty of sympathetic types from several friendly nations, mostly South American.

"We've found one document that might have been Grenier. It's an application with a passport-size photo for a transit visa in the name of a Dutch priest, one Father Leyden, who bears a slight resemblance to Grenier. The visa was for Portugal. We have no information that Father Leyden used it.

"Nor do we know for sure if Father Leyden ever left the country. It's quite possible that the priest was a ruse and that Grenier was planning to travel under a different identity.

"There was an intelligence report from a friendly government that an individual who might have been Grenier was in Italy in 1946. In Venice, to be exact, attending an art exhibition and auction and apparently quite interested in buying a painting, only to be outbid."

"I've been told," said Daniel, "that Grenier knew a man in Venice long before the war, a fellow who ran some kind of symposium on Satanism."

"As far as we can determine," smiled Wasserman, "Grenier was never in contact with that gentleman after the war. The Italian in question was, in fact, a British agent before and during the war. He also worked for the French and the Americans. But not, as far as we know, for the Russians. The little intellectual get-togethers he staged were part of his cover. Had Grenier been to see him again, the British and Americans and probably the rest of the world's intelligence brotherhood would have descended on Venice thicker than the pigeons of Piazza San Marco." With a widening grin, he added, "Of course, I'd've gotten there first."

"I can see why you'd swoop down on Venice in hopes of grabbing him, but why the others?"

"Herr Grenier carries with him a treasure trove of information that would be of great interest to the intelligence circles on both sides of the Iron Curtain. In fact, our interest in laying our hands on him goes beyond his war criminal status. Though that's our chief motivation in wanting to locate him."

"What you're saying is that Grenier hasn't been seen since he boarded the Orient Express in Paris more than twenty years ago. That is, until two weeks ago in New York."

"If he were seen then."

"You doubt it?"

"Dubious is my middle name, Daniel. That's why you're here. It's why you'll be traveling to New York. To erase the doubts."

Chapter Six

Secret Orders

"You will leave for New York tomorrow morning," said Amnon Dorot in the clipped cadence of the army officer he'd been since he was Daniel's age. Wearing only green army-issue underwear, he sat with bare feet propped atop a rattan table littered with the remains of their lunch and squinted against the glare of the high sun reflecting from the flaked turquoise of the Mediterranean Sea and the tourist-dotted white sand of their beachfront Tel Aviv hotel room. The briefing had been going on for two days. "I will drive you to the airport. You'll be traveling commercially on an El Al flight to Rome. From there it's Alitalia to Paris. Then Air France to London and from London to New York via British Overseas Airways."

"Why all the hopscotching?"

"This is the itinerary that Mr. Goldstein would use."

In a large travel wallet on the bed was all that was needed to turn Daniel Ben Avram into Joshua Goldstein, the youngest son of Sidney Goldstein of Goldstein Sons and Associates, international dealers in religious items and artifacts, especially ancient Judaica, with offices in Tel Aviv and New York. This legend had been made real with a passport, driver's license, four credit cards, and documents verifying that Joshua had been in Israel on business related to the Dead Sea Scrolls.

"There's damn little that I know about religious items and artifacts," said Daniel, "including, I'm ashamed to admit, ancient Judaica. I've never even been to Cumran."

"It doesn't matter. Once you clear customs and passport control at Kennedy Airport you become someone else—a hopeful young actor of Italian–American ancestry from Howard Beach, a community on the outskirts of New York City—Danny Dacapua."

"Who came up with that?"

"Our only link to Grenier's identity is the fact that he was present at a charity theatrical event. The reasoning is that you may have to mix with the showbiz crowd until you can get next to Grenier. Presto! You're an actor. We think it's more likely that an Italian budding actor would be able to approach Grenier than a Jew-boy thespian. Besides, haven't you ever noticed that many Italian youths look Jewish and vice versa? Take a look at yourself in the mirror, Danny, and you'll see that you look as much like a paisan descended from the slopes of Mount Etna as you do a grandchild of the diaspora with

40

roots in Mount Zion."

Looking into the mirror above the dresser and deciding he needed a shave, Daniel saw nothing that was Italian and grunted, "How can I act like an Italian-American when my folks are from Haifa?"

"That makes you a Haifa-nated Jew," cackled Amnon.

"What's the rest of the story that goes along with the identity of Mr. Danny Dacapua. What plays have I been in?"

"None. You're a budding actor. Like the majority of the actors in New York you make your living waiting tables in restaurants. Be an actor! Improvise. Nobody's going to check."

"Grenier might."

"If he does, he'll find all he's looking for. It's all been fixed. You're in the files of Actors' Equity, the performers union, and your photo and résumé are sprinkled liberally amongst New York casting agents. But if he does check up on you, then he's given us pretty compelling evidence that he's our man, right?"

"Suppose so."

"Look, you'll have plenty of time during your trip to the U.S.A. to memorize all this, so don't worry."

Now, on the eve of Daniel's becoming Mr. Goldstein to go to New York to take on the identity of Danny Dacapua, Amnon was confident. "You're going to do fine. The General wouldn't've chosen you if he didn't have total trust in your abilities. And I wouldn't have recommended you. Now, is there anything else you wish to go over, New York plans-wise?"

41

"Nothing," said Daniel, throwing himself onto the bed. "I've been over the New York aspects a hundred times."

His contact in case of a dire emergency, and *only* in a dire emergency, he'd been told, was a telephone at the Israeli consulate on Second Avenue. "Use a pay phone. Ask for Mr. Mogen. Go to the automat at Third and Forty-second and wait. A man in a straw hat with a blue band will ask you if you have any change for the sandwiches. You tell him you've just used your last quarter. He says, 'Just my luck.' And the two of you leave, separately. You first, turning downtown. Mr. Mogen will catch up with you. Otherwise, if there is no dire emergency, and you wish only to report that you have located and confirmed the identity of Grenier, you call the special phone number you've already memorized, say only the codeword *Judah* and wait for orders."

"If I'm that close to the bastard why don't I just shoot him?"

Leaping to his feet, Amnon wagged an angry finger. "You don't take any action! That is for others. Your job is to locate this man and identify him. Nothing more. Understood?"

"Clearly."

"Good."

Chapter Seven

Looking for Judah

As he climbed the wide steps, which were flanked by lions, of the New York Public Library, a vast and imposing temple such as Solomon might have built, Daniel Ben Avram felt like a schoolboy again, as if he were going to look up something for a paper he'd been assigned to write for a class. "Excuse me, please," he said as he approached a pretty young woman at a counter beneath a sign that said INFORMATION. "Can you tell me where to find back copies of the *New York Times*?"

"Second floor," she said with a smile. She pointed a pencil to her right and a flight of marble stairs. "Or the elevator if you're really lazy."

"Thank you very much," he said, striding toward the staircase.

"Ask at the periodicals counter," she called after him.

The issue of the newspaper he wished to see, he

explained to a matronly woman at the desk was April 9 of this year.

"Fill out a slip."

"Pardon?"

"You have to fill out a request slip. One of these."

Taking the form to a table, he pondered the required information—the name of the periodical requested, the date, and his name and address.

Carefully, he printed:

DANNY DACAPUA

The address was a problem. His was the Hotel Lexington. Would the woman at the desk permit the loan of the *Times* to someone whose address was a hotel?

"Probably not," he muttered as he drew from his coat pocket a book of Hotel Lexington matches bearing its phone number and address.

On the slip he jotted 511 LEXINGTON AVENUE.

Returning it to the woman at the desk, he asked, "Is there someone who can show me how to work the microfilm machine?"

"Oh you won't need a machine. It's too soon for that issue of the *Times* to be on film."

Worried, he asked, "Does that mean you don't have that particular issue available?"

"We have it. It's just not on film. Unless someone else is using that issue, of course. Then you'll have to wait." Turning away, she retreated into rows of shelves then came back carrying the paper. "Here you are," she said with a forlorn smile. "It's a little dog-eared. But readable."

To examine the paper, he chose a chair at an occupied table. "Always blend in with your surroundings," Amnon had taught him at Kfar Sirkin. A slouching man to his left was intently studying a book on computers. The middle-aged woman to his right was leafing through a bound collection of 1951 *Newsweek* magazines. A pimply youth opposite him had a pile of books and was hunched over and scribbling notes from one on the history of music. "Join a crowd," Amnon had taught, "but always notice who's around you."

Turning to the theatrical pages of the *Times*, he saw immediately what he was looking for; a lengthy item with the headline *Israeli Musical Benefits Jewish Charities*.

What he had not dared to hope to find accompanying the article was a photograph. Yet there it was, a group of men and women in evening attire smiling for the camera around a pert and obviously pleased woman wearing a tiara and holding one end of a check. At the other end was a balding elderly gentleman.

The caption noted, "Mrs. Elaine R. Ruderman, Director, Combined Jewish Women's Charitable Organizations and organizer of last night's gala benefit performance at the Brooks Atkinson Theater of *Sing, Israel, Sing*, receives $500,000 donation from Mr. Peter Helder, financier and renowned art benefactor. Check is on behalf of the Helder Galleries which held an auction of art works and matched the funds collected."

Flushed with excitement, Daniel wanted to shout, "Peter Helder? Is that your name? The hell it is, you cunning bastard! You're SS Stormbannfuhrer August Grenier!"

"There's no doubt about it," he said aloud and exultantly, almost yelling with delight as he returned the newspaper to the desk.

"Beginner's luck," he chuckled fifteen minutes later in his hotel room, wondering if he should write that in the small black looseleaf notebook that lay before him.

He'd bought it that morning at a Woolworth's store to serve as a journal of his mission at Amnon's orders. "You must keep a meticulous accounting of all that you do, Daniel," he'd stressed in the briefing in the Tel Aviv hotel. "Our object in this mission is not only to locate, identify, and bring Grenier back to Israel for trial," he explained, "but to accumulate a detailed record of how we achieved this so that it may become a part of the permanent record of the court."

Now, here he was about to make the first entry detailing a breathtaking surprise and a stunning success on his first day functioning on his own as an agent, finding August Grenier's picture right off the bat, just like that, out of the millions of faces in the City of New York.

Like a sudden burst of cold water when hot was expected in taking a shower, caution drenched him and he wrote:

Saw newspaper photo of man named Peter Helder. Resemblance to Grenier is amazing.

Too amazing to be merely a coincidence, I believe. But will check further.

Beginning at the Helder Galleries, he decided as he closed his journal and locked it in his suitcase. "Now, where in this big city shall I find the Helder Galleries?" he muttered, picking up the weighty Manhattan Yellow Pages telephone book.

Turning to the listings for Art Galleries, he found an advertisement.

The Helder Galleries
Contemporary, Abstract, and Avant-Garde
Picasso, Pollock, Nevelson,
Antoni Tàpies
Mark Tobey. Arshile Gorky
Madison Ave. at 80th

In windows along both sides of Madison Avenue as he walked casually north of Seventy-second Street he found in beauteous and copious array the contemporary works of George Grosz and Peter Orlando; the American master George Luks; abstract expressionism by Milton Avery and Leonard Baskin; the modern work of Jasper Johns and Rauschenberg; the Old Master Breughel; and the Impressionism of Monet—all too rich for him were he to decide to take home a souvenir of his first operation.

The day was as splendid as the pictures, fair and warm with Madison Avenue so lush with colorfully attired strollers that it was worthy of being painted, the kind of early spring weather when going coatless was in order for anyone not wearing a shoulder harness that holstered a Walther PPK automatic pistol.

Near the northeast corner of Eightieth Street, the Helder Galleries occupied the first two floors of an elegant brownstone townhouse.

Dare he go in? What would they think, these keepers of great works of art displayed for the inspection and, they hoped, purchase by the wealthy, if someone his age—a mere teenager—walked in? Might they shoo him outside with a stern suggestion that if he wished to look at art he couldn't possibly afford to buy he would do better for himself and them if he went around the corner and bought a ticket of admission to the public Metropolitan Museum of Art?

"The secret of not being yourself," Amnon had lectured to the chosen, "is in *believing* you *are* the person you are not. It was the American novelist F. Scott Fitzgerald who said, 'It isn't being rich that counts. What matters is that people think you are rich.' With an outlook like that, Fitzgerald would have made a sensational spy!"

A small plastic sign above a doorbell button said: PLEASE RING FOR ADMISSION.

He pressed the button twice.

A stately, slender platinum-haired woman dressed in black opened the door. "May I help you?"

"I hope so," he said, stepping forward. "I'm looking for something quite bold and modern. Not for me. It's to be my gift to my wife. Well, that is, she'll be my wife next month. This is to be my wedding gift to her. Now, you'll have to help me, because I'm not the expert in art. Dara is. That's my fiancée's name. Can you assist me? Dara always says the place to go in New York for the kind of art she adores is the Helder Galleries. This is the Helder Galleries?"

"Yes," said the woman, swinging the door wide open. "Do come in, Mr. . . . ."

"I'm Josh Goldstein," he said, stepping past her, "of Sidney Goldstein Sons and Associates. We're international dealers in religious items and artifacts. Downtown."

"How interesting," the woman said, turning away and picking up a catalog. "Perhaps this will assist you."

"Thank you. That'll be a big help. But I was wondering if I might speak to Mr. Helder."

"Oh, I'm sorry, Mr. Goldstein, but Mr. Helder's not in."

"Do you know when he's expected?"

"It could be at any time."

"Well, suppose I have a look around. Maybe he'll return soon. Is that okay?"

"You are certainly welcome to wait, Mr. Goldstein, but it could be hours. Perhaps he won't come today at all. He's a man of many interests, you see, and has a full schedule every day. Being a busy man yourself you must appreciate how it is. Would you care to leave your card?"

Patting his chest and feeling the leather straps of his holster rather than a card case, he grimaced. "Afraid I don't have one with me. Why don't I take your catalog and come back another time?"

"Your best chance of catching him, and it's only a chance, is late afternoon. Mr. Helder often drops in on his way upstairs to change for whatever social event happens to be on his calendar."

"Upstairs?"

"Why, yes," she said. "The floors above the galleries are Mr. Helder's home."

Drifting toward the door, he said, "That's very convenient, isn't it?"

Like a lid on a pot, a shelf of ragged gray clouds had slid over Madison Avenue by late afternoon and the temperature had dropped considerably. People on the sidewalks who had been so content to stroll and amble in the sun were now rushing past him as he smoked a cigarette and waited at a bus stop that afforded a view of the Helder Galleries a block away. Dozens of buses had stopped in the course of the four hours he'd spent watching, and he strolled away as each bus came and then drifted back to wait again unchallenged and apparently unnoticed.

At six o'clock the woman in the gallery came out, locked the door, and scurried away in the opposite direction.

At 6:30, Helder appeared.

Stepping from a taxi, he was accompanied by a young man as he dashed up the steps and into the gallery, locking the door behind them.

At 11:00 they emerged.

Dressed in black leather jackets, trousers, and black

50

boots, they hailed a taxi and vanished into the night while a scene from dozens of Hollywood detective films danced through Daniel's mind, but with himself in the starring role hailing a taxi himself and saying to the driver, "Follow that cab!"

But there were no cabs available for commandeering on Madison Avenue.

Tomorrow, said Daniel Ben Avram to himself, I must rent a car.

Chapter Eight

To the Edge of the Pit

The next day Daniel recorded in his book that within two hours he'd used his credit cards to purchase a 35-millimeter camera and a telephoto lens along with ten rolls of 36-exposure black-and-white film at Willoughby's on West Thirty-second Street and obtained a blue Valiant sedan for the weekly rate of $33, plus eight cents a mile, from the Alexander's rent-a-car on East Sixty-fifth. At four o'clock he parked the Valiant uncomfortably near a fire hydrant half a block down Madison from the Helder Galleries and settled back to wait with his camera ready.

At that moment in a booth at the back of Kelly's bar on Forty-sixth Street just east of Times Square, Peter Helder was slowly twirling the maraschino cherry in his half-consumed Manhattan and relaxing by tormenting the grumpy youth beside him with a dissertation on the life of the painter Amedeo

Modigliani. "If you don't pay attention to me, Greg," he said, "your life will turn out as his did, filled with poverty, neglect, drink, and disease. Of course, yours will not end with a legacy of great art!"

They had just been to the Museum of Modern Art looking at the Modigliani collection, so the artist was fresh in mind.

The day had been full for Helder.

He'd been on the go since waking up at seven o'clock, leaving Gregory in the Victorian brass bed that was the centerpiece of the room crammed with furniture of the period collected during a 1955 sweep of the antique shops of Charing Cross Road in London when there had been little on his mind except the opening of his galleries and the furnishing of the private apartment above.

In that chaotic six months he had opened the Helder Galleries with great fanfare and success and decorated each room of the duplex residence in the style of a different era. Victorian had been picked for the bedroom. The dining room was 18th century Italian with Spanish silver and Chinese plates. A provocatively eclectic mixture of Bauhaus and Danish modern was the decor of a library filled with rare books where he also displayed a collection of ancient spears and swords. Art Deco filled the living room. A variety of decorative as well as utilitarian items had been painstakingly assembled for a room beneath the galleries which he simply denoted as "downstairs" while the select few like Gregory whom he invited to inspect the unique space called it "Peter's Dungeon." In 1956 the spectacular results of his frenzied work at remodeling and furnishing the grand old brownstone had been featured in *Architectural Digest* and two entire pages in a special antiquarian section of the Sunday *New York Times*.

Except the lower room.

Now, eleven years later, familiarity had made his opulent and costly surroundings commonplace, the mere everyday things of a daily life that had grown fuller and fuller with the expectations and obligations that came with the territory for a man with his wealth, interests, and multiple identities.

Leaving Gregory to fend for himself, he had started the day in the guise of the meticulous owner of the Helder Galleries, descending from his elegant apartment to confer with the capable Eleanora Swaim. Given the title "curator" because he considered the term "manager" demeaning, the austere and willowy woman who always wore black had been waiting for him only a few minutes before he came down to discuss the details of the expected delivery that morning of seven important new works by the sensational young silkscreen portraitist named Kevin Gordon whom inhabitants of the Manhattan art world had followed Peter Helder's lead in calling the next Andy Warhol.

An hour later in a cab ride across Central Park to the Museum of Natural History the art dealer had become the witty and erudite guest speaker at the monthly breakfast meeting of patrons of the museum. His subject was American Art with special attention to the works of Charles M. Russell, William Harnett, Winslow Homer and Frederic Remington. "As you no doubt have discerned by my impossible accent, I am not a native American," he said to his beguiled audience. "I am Dutch. But believe me, my friends, a naturalized American from the land of Rembrandt cannot fail to appreciate Remington! The glare of the desert sun, the energy and beauty of the quarter-horse at full gallop across the grassy plains, the nobility of the embattled warrior-Indian, the dignity and strength of the rough-and-ready cowboy!"

Downtown at ten o'clock he metamorphosed into a savvy businessman and financier striding through the marble lobby of the Morgan Bank in a charcoal gray pinstriped double-breasted business suit and wearing a slate gray hat with slouched brim and a perky small red feather that had become his daytime sartorial trademark. Ascending in a private elevator for a conference with his personal banker, he was prepared to sign documents drawn up for the financing of the acquisition of a private collection of 19th century European landscapes which he had estimated to be worth $75 million. "Unframed," he'd added as a joke.

Lunch with friends at the Atlantis Club was next, at noon, followed by a steambath and rubdown at the New York Athletic Club and a phone call to his stock broker an hour before Wall Street's closing bell, buying Middle East oil shares because he was convinced the Arabs were about to attack Israel.

To appreciate the warm, fair, April weather he'd walked from the club's Park Avenue mansion to Adler's Foreign Books between Sixth and Seventh Avenues on West Forty-seventh Street to examine a rare set of the two-volume *Foundations of the Nineteenth Century.*

"A very unusual subject," commented the scholarly gray clerk in a voice that sounded as dusty as his books.

Helder replied, "Ah, you've read Gobineau?"

Smiling sheepishly, the clerk said, "I dipped into the books, waiting for you to come fetch them."

"The German philologists have always interested me," said Helder. "And since Arthur de Gobineau is an extension of their thought on the subject of racial superiority, I thought I'd best look into him."

"Naturally," said the clerk. "Shall I wrap him up then?"

"Please," said Helder, drawing his checkbook from his gray suit. "And I believe you're also holding for me a volume by Madame Helena Patrovna Blavatsky."

"Indeed so, sir," said the clerk in an apologetic burst.

In a cab going to his next appointment, Helder's attention centered on the Blavatsky. He'd read her work in several editions but this one was special because it had been autographed. A Russian expatriate countess, she had founded the Theosophical Society in New York in 1875 and dedicated herself to delving into spiritualism and the occult and the Gnostic doctrine that there were two worlds, one good and one evil. And that evil world, the Gnostics contended—and Madame Blavatsky concurred—had been created by the Jewish god, who was really the devil, responsible for all the evil in the world.

He flipped through the heavy parchmentlike pages of the leather-bound book until the taxi drew up in front of Museum of Modern Art where he found Gregory Hardin sunning himself in the sculpture garden.

Looking like a statue himself, a bored Adonis in flesh languidly half-reclining amidst the cold stones, Gregory was sun-bronzed and flaxen-haired wearing a tattering brown leather bomber pilot's jacket over a pale blue tee shirt and blue jeans. Looking up with pouting blue eyes, he was curt in his greeting. "You're late, Peter."

"I'm precisely on time," snapped Helder, glancing at his gold wrist watch. "You're just impatient."

Rising sullenly, Gregory muttered, "Why couldn't we just meet at the bar?"

"Because I feel an obligation to educate and uplift you. Come along."

As they wandered the museum, Helder paused before each painting because he knew Gregory understood none of them and hated being in the place. At last, after lavishing an especially long-necked Modigliani with much more attention than it deserved, he turned to the boy with a smile and announced, "We'll have that drink now, I think, Gregory! Come along. Look lively!"

Minutes later they entered Kelly's, a pick-up-for-pay bar, passing the alluring muscular hustlers lined up at the bar at a much too early hour for there to be enough customers for all of them, and settled in the booth in the back at about the same time that Daniel Ben Avram was illegally maneuvering his rental car into a spot with an unimpeded view of the front of the Helder Galleries.

Lunch for Daniel had been a corned beef sandwich carried out of a delicatessen on Lexington Avenue and hurried back to the car parked on Madison, praying that he hadn't missed Helder coming or going. He ate while reading the *New York Post* and an upsetting news item out of Cairo detailing an agreement between Egypt, Syria, and Iraq to merge themselves into a federal United Arab Republic. Bad for the Jews, he thought, washing down the corned beef with a Coke. Bad for Israel.

At six o'clock, the woman he'd spoken to yesterday in the Helder Galleries closed up, left, and walked directly toward the car, passing as he ducked behind the newspaper.

Half an hour later, a cab arrived and Helder and a young man dashed up the steps not knowing they were being photographed all the way.

It was almost eleven o'clock when they came out.

Photographed coming down the steps, they were shadowy and fast-moving in shiny black leather outfits but minutes passed with them standing in the excellent picture-taking light of a street lamp before they could hail a taxi.

Starting up his Valiant, Daniel muttered, "Driver, follow that cab!"

With heart-stopping panic he thought he'd lost them coming out of Central Park as their cab went through the yellow light at Central Park West but he pressed his foot to the accelerator, flooring it, and hurtled through the red light. Closing in on the cab, he stayed behind it on Seventy-second Street westward to the West Side Highway then downtown paralleling the Hudson River, an exit at Fourteenth and downtown again into an area with wharves and docks to his right and bleak red brick warehouses and meat packing plants on the left where, unexpectedly, the taxi stopped and its black-garbed passengers got out.

Easing to the right, Daniel glided the Valiant to a stop.

Adjusting the rearview mirror, he saw Helder and the boy merge with a group of similarly leathered men, talk with them animatedly, and then cross the sidewalk to a door, open it and enter.

Daniel had managed two shots but, sliding the camera under the seat, he felt certain that in the minimal available light the pictures would prove worthless.

After waiting a few minutes, he left the car and dashed across the street to the door Helder had entered and found in crudely lettered red across the orange-painted metal door:

THE PIT
Private Club
Members only admitted
Membership $10
PAY AT THE BAR

From behind him he heard one of the leather men

59

at the curb whisper, "He's cute but outta uniform."

A second was a singsong taunt. "Does your mama know you're out, kid?"

A third voice barked, "That's a leather bar, honey."

Flustered and feeling the blush of embarrassment rising in his neck, Daniel ducked his head and hurried back to the car as the voice of Amnon Dorot rose beratingly from his memory: "You must never rush a surveillance. It's like playing cards. Get to know your adversary. Study him. Learn his ways. Let him win a few pots. Then play your winning hand."

Poker-faced, Daniel waited in the Valiant for two hours before he was able to photograph Helder emerging from The Pit with the boy, hailing a taxi, and returning home.

With the mansion dark except for the floodlit display windows of the Galleries, Daniel packed his camera in its gadget bag and broke off the surveillance.

The next day at a shop on Eighth Street in Greenwich Village he used a credit card to buy a black leather motorcycle jacket, pants, and boots for $200 with a jaunty motorcyclist's cap thrown in for free by a flirty young salesman with the comment, "The image isn't really butch enough without it, darling."

That night, when Helder and the boy returned to The Pit, Daniel left the car, tipped his jaunty motorcyclist's cap forward until the hard bill nearly touched the bridge of his nose like Marlon Brando in the movie *The Wild Ones*, and with a thumb hooked in the belt loop of the leather pants, strode cockily across the street in combat-style black boots that creaked from newness. With a nod at the leathered knot of men at the curb as if he knew them, he gulped air in expectation of being challenged, grabbed the handle, yanked open the door, and descended.

Chapter Nine

The Brotherhood

Rock-'n'-roll thundered from the blackness below as a lone bare red bulb like the safelight in a darkroom cast his shadow ahead of him while Daniel Ben Avram slowly descended the narrow staircase. But by the time he'd reached the bottom he had become the aspiring young actor from Brooklyn named Danny Dacapua, with all the identity cards to prove it creating a bulge of the back pocket of his tight leather pants. And when Danny's eyes had adjusted to the dark at the bottom of the stairs and he'd taken a ten-dollar bill from his wallet and handed it to a burly bearded barechested bartender, he was given another means of identity in the form of a picture of a devil's pitchfork stamped on his wrist in black ink, a one-night membership in whatever brotherhood had convened in this dank and dim cellar.

In simplest terms in writing of this evening in his

journal, he supposed, he could describe The Pit as a saloon with a long bar, inch-deep sawdust over a concrete floor, sharp-edged square wooden tables and straight chairs. But this was more than what he expected of a bar.

Despite the glittering glassware, arrayed liquor bottles lighted behind the bar, the green felt rectangle top of a pool table illuminated by the light from a metal-shaded lamp dangling from the ceiling, lights splashed from a jukebox, and three pinball machines in a row against a wall, there was a feeling of being literally in a black pit.

There was also a dark undertow, a feeling that something sinister and threatening was at hand, an air of impending danger and suppressed violence in the overall impression of limited light as he felt himself surrounded by surly-looking sinewy youths and older men, all in black leather. With bared, sweaty, and oiled biceps, shoulders, chests, and bellies revealed by open shirts and coats and vests and the occasional buttocks exposed by backless pants, they leaned against the bar, sat sullenly in the hard chairs at the tables or stood with their backs against the black-painted walls, their fists curled around beer bottles and their eyes probing the shadowy recesses and pools of light like ravenous bats in a cave.

Delving the dark with his own hungry eyes, Daniel Ben Avram did not discover his prey, Peter Helder.

Then he noticed that some of the bats stirred to prowl to the back of the long narrow room where they disappeared through a door that appeared to be nothing less than the mouth of another grotto.

"What're you drinkin'?"

It was the bartender who'd taken his ten. "Oh, beer."

"Which label?"

"Doesn't matter."

"It's a buck," said the bartender, opening a bottle of Budweiser as his own eyes appeared to savor what stood before them. "Ain't seen you here before. Where ya been all my life?"

"I'm from Brooklyn."

"You'll get over it."

"Uh, what's, uh, in the, uh, back room?"

"Action."

"Action?"

Shaking his head, the bartender leaned forward and whispered, "S-E-X." Rearing back, he said, forcefully, "Try it, maybe you'll like it." Smirking, he added, "I know the guys back there'll like you."

Out of the deepest recesses of a mind that had been tutored by rabbis before it was given into the hands of a *moyl* named Amnon Dorot rushed a passage from the Genesis story of Sodom and the voice of a righteous man named Lot crying out in warning, "Daniel, get you out of this place; for the Lord will destroy this city."

Then, as clearly as if the *moyl* of Kfar Sirkin were standing next to him at the bar, it was Daniel Ben Avram, not Danny Dacapua, who heard the rasping voice of Amnon Dorot cutting through the babel of male voices of the brotherhood of The Pit. "Lot never worked for the Israeli secret service. Lot didn't swear the oath you swore. Lot didn't have the sacred honor and duty of tracking down the abomination called

64

August Grenier. You must not falter, Danny."

But falter he did, leaning against the black wall with its blacker portal to his right and beyond it . . . what? The blackest of all? The abyss? Barely breathing and with clammy, trembling hands and cold sweat beading his forehead, he waited, listening to the subtle rustle of soft leather; the hard clink and rattle and scrape of metal buckles; what sounded like the jingle of chains; muted voices, unintelligible; grunts, groans, growls; a sighed, "Please." A barked "No!"; the hard sting of a hand on muscle; a quick intake of breath; sighs of pain and pleasure.

Underscoring these bizarre emanations was a constant scuffing of numerous feet on concrete that evoked in his laboring imagination the idea that this was how it must have sounded as chastened Jews shuffled into the gas chambers in the Nazi death camps that Yehuda Wasserman had described in his book *The Fires of Satan* as a "silent, disbelieving parade passing before the watchful eyes of an unspeaking, knowing Black Knight of Death who was the omnipresent overlord of the Holocaust and the fueler and stoker of Satan's hideously efficient furnaces, the SS Stormbannfuhrer."

In the quiet cacophony of sounds beyond the black hole in the wall in this queer bar called The Pit, Daniel reminded himself that one of those Black Knights lived unpunished, thriving in his respectable new identity, relishing his wealth and power and influence in New York City in the year 1967 and indulging his every whim and wish, fantasy and perversion.

Changing easily from the expertly tailored suits of daylight business to the tuxedo of glittering Broadway evenings and then to the black leather favored by his brothers of The Pit, the ex-SS Stormbannfuhrer August Grenier, now known to the Jew Daniel Ben Avram as Peter Helder, moved from one warmly embracing circle of the like-minded people of his pampered life to the next, and the next and the next, passing smoothly and seamlessly from the fabric of one existence to another; from his awakening in his elegant town house above his opulent galleries surrounded by priceless beauty and art to his grotesque after-midnight hours of secret sexual indulgence—all in comfort and safety—undetected.

Until now, vowed Daniel, as he lurched through the doorway.

"Oh," grunted the shape he slammed into in the dark.

"Please excuse me," said Daniel. "It's so dark. Didn't see you!"

Laughing, the shape said, "That's the whole point."

"Guess so," muttered Daniel, stepping back through the door to let the shape go by.

Pausing in dim red light, Peter Helder blurted, "Say, I haven't run into you here before!"

The voice was deep, rich, mellow, and accented, easily believable as being Dutch.

Left dry-mouthed and shaken by the unexpected encounter, Daniel struggled into a smile. "It's my first time."

"A fresh face and no one's latched onto you yet,"

Helder said, raising a hand to gently finger the lapel of Daniel's jacket. "As new as this coat, eh?"

"Just got it yesterday," said Daniel, tight-throated with nervousness. "The whole outfit, as a matter of fact."

Helder's hand slid caressingly down Daniel's arm. "It becomes you. Italian boys and leather were made for each other."

"How'd you guess I'm Italian?"

"I never guess. I *know*." Raising his right hand from Daniel's sleeve, Helder tapped a finger under his right eye. "I have an unfailing eye."

So do I, thought Daniel exultantly as his own eyes settled on Helder's abbreviated little finger with its flat tip, the evidence of a mishap at Theresienstadt more than a quarter of a century ago. "My name's Danny Dacapua," he said, grinning.

"You *are* new at this," laughed Helder. "No one comes right out with his name in a place like this. That is, not with his whole name. And usually not with his real first name. Or did you know that and lie about your name? Are you, in fact, lying about everything? Are you as much the novice as you pretend to be?"

Reaching to his back pocket, Daniel blurted, "I could show you my driver's license."

Deflecting his arm, Helder chuckled, "Not necessary, Danny. I shall divine the truth about you while we have drinks and get to know one another. My treat. This is what's known in places like this as a pick-up. My name is Edward, by the way."

No it's not, thought Daniel. It's not even Peter. It's

August! SS Stormbannfuhrer August Grenier of Theresienstadt.

"As to proving who you are with your driver's license," said Helder blithely, hooking Daniel's arm in his and leading him toward a table for two, "those things can be forged, you know!"

Chapter Ten

Helder's Story

"While I was his *pick-up*," Daniel wrote in his journal at five o'clock the next morning, "I was not invited to his home as I had expected—and hoped—to be. I do not know if this was simply because Helder had gone to the bar with a boy named Greg, to whom I was introduced and had seen on two occasions earlier while I had the Helder Galleries under surveillance, or if Helder does not make it his habit to take a young man he'd just met to a home that must be filled with valuables. Perhaps it is because he was afraid I would rob him. Or perhaps he is cautious with all strangers until he can get to know them and trust them, given his past. I am convinced Helder is Grenier. Now more than ever. But I know that I have to observe him further. I know I must gather as much data about him as I can in order to make an airtight case. I have a date with him tomorrow night. He says he is going to take me out on the town."

No leather, Helder had advised. "Wear your best suit and tie. It will be an elegant evening. I intend to show you off."

Even before Eleanora Swaim's early arrival the following morning, Helder was up and out of his town house for yet another breakfast, the semiannual meeting of yet another charitable organization on whose board of directors he served. Then it was a meeting with a Sutton Place dowager concerning her desire to engage his consultation services in the acquisition of three Degas sculptures from a rather unsavory but sometimes surprisingly astute dealer in Monaco. Were he to accept the assignment it would mean spending two weeks abroad beginning in late May, quite a busy time for him, he informed the woman. "But I shall look at my calendar and get back to you as soon as possible," he promised her. At 11:30 he sat for his weekly barbering at the Gotham Hotel, a custom dating back to his days at the nearby Fuller Building. At noon, he was ready for lunch with the Atlanteans.

Once the extravagance of a minor railroad magnate, the Beaux Arts mansion on Fifty-second Street had become the home of the Atlantis Club in 1929 as the result of a mortgage foreclosure following the stock market crash, thus being saved from the ignominious fall of similar mansions in the depths of the Great Depression as bootleggers bought them and converted them into speakeasies and jazz nightclubs.

Although he took his noon meal at the Atlantis

Club as often as his busy schedule allowed, luncheon there on this date was never missed, for the day was April 30. Notable on the occult and mystical calendars of all like Peter Helder, it marked the ancient Celtic Feast of Beltane and the eve of Walpurgisnacht, the traditional German witches' sabbath. But there were two immensely personal events which occurred on the date that had become indelible memories, each connecting Peter Helder to Adolf Hitler. The former had taken place in Berlin in 1938 when Hitler had invited SS Stormbannfuhrer August Grenier to join him in the Fuhrer's box at a performance of Schumann's operatic adaptation of Goethe's *Faust* with its thrilling Walpurgisnacht scene. The latter he had learned of in Paris some days after the event: the suicide of Adolf Hitler in his besieged bunker in Berlin on April 30, 1945.

"How telling and appropriate that our leader chose that auspicious date to end his life," he had asserted without a glimmer of sadness to the able friends who were assisting him in arranging to reach Geneva on his way to America in the guise of a Dutch priest. "I drink to his memory," he'd declared, raising a glass of wine. "Seig heil!"

At the Atlantis Club's April 30 luncheon, however, there were no goblets raised openly in a toast to Hitler.

Between lunch and six o'clock, Eleanora Swaim required his full attention.

Then it was time to prepare for an evening with his new friend, the amusing and somehow mysterious Danny Dacapua.

In a snit, peevish, and pouting, Gregory was being

71

flagrantly insulting: "I didn't know you went for wops." Jealous: "I can't see what's the big attraction in him, frankly." And frightened of being dropped: "Should I pack my stuff?"

"Don't be ridiculous," Helder snapped as he peered past his reflection in his dressing mirror at seven o'clock with Gregory sulking on the Victorian bed. "He's an interesting fling; nothing more."

"Will you be bringing him back here?"

"Probably."

Bounding from the bed and storming from the room, Gregory railed, "Well I won't be here to get in your way."

"Tomorrow I'll buy you a present. To make up," Helder shouted after him. "Or maybe I'll kick you out on your ass, you ungrateful bastard," he whispered to himself in the mirror as he tightened the knot of his necktie. Fifteen minutes later in front of Grand Central Terminal, where they'd agreed to rendezvous, he threw open a cab door and waved an anxious-looking Danny Dacapua into the taxi. "Did you think I wouldn't come?"

Dressed in a blue suit with a white shirt and red tie, Daniel Ben Avram had been pacing the pavement and watching taxis for fifteen minutes thinking just that, but Danny Dacapua cheerfully said, "Not at all!"

Patting the boy's knee as he settled beside him, Helder said, "You look splendid. I hope you're hungry because we are going to a fabulous Italian restaurant, Via Margutta on Minetta Lane. Have you been there?"

"Once, I think," Daniel replied. "When I was a

little kid."

To his relief, Helder ordered for them.

"There's a quality about you, Danny, that is unique," he said as the waiter brought the antipasto. "It's something you have that is, well, almost European. Continental. Quite mature. Old World-ish."

"Well, my folks did come from the old country."

"Yes, I guess that's it. You are the embodiment of what the Americans like to make so much of. You know, the son of immigrants grows up to be not only better off than his parents but President of the United States. The American dream."

"Is that bad?"

"No, just American."

"You came from somewhere else, right? You have an accent."

"It's Dutch! I came here from the Netherlands after the war. Picturesque Holland. The quaint country with the tulips and the windmills and the little boy with his finger in the dike. Rembrandt!"

"And Anne Frank," blurted Daniel.

"Quite," said Helder coldly.

Stabbed with the fear that he'd slipped, Daniel rushed to contain any damage, explaining, "Our school put on the play about her once."

Calmly, Helder said, "Did you play the part of the boy she liked?"

Uncertain of himself and his distant memory of having seen a production of *The Diary of Anne Frank* in Haifa, Daniel said, "I wasn't in the play."

"A promising actor and you weren't in the school play?"

Still scrambling for credibility, Daniel replied, "That was before I realized acting was what I wanted to do."

"Before the theatrical bug bit!"

"Exactly!"

The main course came, a welcomed interruption.

"You know, I have many friends in the theater," said Helder boastfully as he dipped into the restaurant's famous cannelloni. "I can introduce you to them, if you'd like. Are you Equity, by the way?"

"Well, you have to be," Daniel said, certain of his footing and voicing a silent prayer of thanksgiving for Amnon Dorot's thoroughness. Reaching for his wallet, he said, "Want to see my card?"

"Not necessary," chuckled Helder. "I believe you."

Relieved, Daniel relaxed and turned the conversation away from himself with a bit of flattery. "You probably know everyone that's important in New York."

With a self-satisfied smirk, Helder said, "Just about everyone."

"Talk about achieving the American dream," exclaimed Daniel, amazed at the sycophant that he could become. "You seem to have done it yourself."

"That's kind of you. But how do you know?"

"Well, it's pretty obvious."

"What's obvious?"

"That you, uh, have, uh, money."

Helder barked a prideful laugh. "Indeed I do! I suppose having a lot of money *is* the American dream, when you get right down to the nitty-gritty."

"I guess you're a big tycoon of some kind. Wall

74

Street magnate or something like that?"

"Basically I'm an art dealer. The Helder Galleries? Have you heard of them?"

Blatant liar now, with a shrug, Daniel feigned ignorance. "Art's not exactly my bag. No offense intended."

"That's only because you don't *know* art," said Helder pompously. "You haven't been taught. Perhaps I should teach you. The Peter Helder crash course! You're not born knowing and appreciating art, you see. It's learned. Like everything else in life. I can educate you."

"Henry Higgins turning Liza Doolittle into a lady in *My Fair Lady*?"

"Something like *Pygmalion*, yes," grinned Helder.

"Where'd you learn about art?"

"In . . . Holland. Before the war."

"Why'd you come to the United States?"

"For the same reason everyone else comes."

"To start over?"

"Exactly."

They had progressed to dessert, with Helder again doing the ordering. "The cheesecake. And two cappucinos."

Picking up where they'd left off, Daniel asked, "Did you come here right after the war?"

"Shortly after."

"I guess it must have been rough, starting a new life."

"I was fortunate in having helpful friends," said Helder, then turning again to art, which carried them to the end of the meal. "Now that we've dined," he said, "let's see what's happening in all the little bars and clubs in the Village, East Side, West Side, and all around the town, where, I promise you, Danny, you will turn every head. And break the heart of every faggot in town who will know, because I shall tell them, that you belong to me."

The contrast between The Pit and the clubs they now visited was amazing. These were worthy of settings in sophisticated Hollywood musicals not gritty reminders of Brando in *The Wild Ones*. It was not rock-'n'-roll banging from a jukebox and shattering the eardrums but a dulcet-toned young baritone in a tuxedo vocalizing his renditions of hits by Judy Garland and Barbra Streisand and playing a placid medley of Cole Porter and George Gershwin on a piano. There were no bare-chested bartenders with warnings of being raped in the back room. In these subdued spots solicitous waiters in black tie flitted between tables covered with white damask linens and small flickering candles with low flames that seemed to float at the bottoms of tiny pink frosted glass holders, bestowing a flattering and benign glow on the pink faces of whispering mature men and clean-cut youths wearing suits and neckties.

More and more as he drifted and explored Peter Helder's glittery and gay evening world, Daniel's thoughts riveted to the purpose that had brought him to Helder's side. Again and again he reminded himself that amidst this seductive secretive society of homosexuals might be revealed the conclusive and damning evidence that the wealthy, elegant, erudite, influential, and convivial table-hopping gentleman with the expensive suit, erect bearing, distinguished gray hair and the tip of his little finger missing was far from being the charmer he seemed to be.

Observing him so at ease with so many men like himself and introducing Danny Dacapua to them all, showing him off and hoping to goad them into jealous outbursts, Daniel wanted to scream at them that this wasn't Peter Helder the art connoisseur. He longed to shout that this was the ex-Nazi and sadistic SS Stormbannfuhrer August Grenier who was wanted for war crimes and brutalities that were not just outrages against Jews but an affront to the civilized world.

Many times in the half-dozen elegant bars they visited Daniel witnessed men like Helder striking up conversations with young men at the bars, overheard them solicit the youths to their homes and saw them leave together, but Helder made no such invitation. Instead, he simply said goodnight at the door of a bar called Julius, coupling it with a suggestion that they meet again the following evening at The Pit, adding with a wink, "Wear your leather."

Seething with frustration, Daniel stormed into his hotel room and threw himself onto the bed to spill his thoughts into his notebook. To get this close to Grenier was why Daniel Ben Avram had come to New York but he was yet to be with him except in public. If there was any conclusive evidence that Peter Helder was the despised Grenier it would never be found unless Danny Dacapua was admitted to Helder's home. What might Danny find that Daniel would recognize as incriminating? A worn and fading old photograph like the one Daniel had been shown at the house on Amos Street? Letters?

77

Documents? An object of such compelling importance that Helder had to keep it all these years? A journal like the one Daniel was diligently inscribing in his hotel room?

Or could there come an offhand but damning remark? Such a lucky slip would never be made in the guarded talk of bars where others might hear it. The privacy of the mansion was required. Seclusion. Safety. A place with inhibitions set aside. The quiet security of Helder's elegant fortress. On his own turf.

The intimacy of the bedroom was needed, where in the loose and languid ease of familiarity Helder might lapse and lower his guard, at last. And his mask.

"I must get him alone," Daniel wrote, underlining "alone."

It was not bar talk that was needed but pillow talk, he said to himself as he wrote, "Tonight, if he doesn't invite me to his place, I'll suggest it."

And to hell with the *moyl* of Kfar Sirkin and his warning about going slow.

But as it turned out when he kept his rendezvous with Helder at The Pit and accompanied him to several similar bars nothing so daring was required. At four in the morning when the last bar closed, Helder abruptly turned to him and said, "Would you care to come home with me?"

"Sure," said Danny Dacapua with a nonchalant shrug while within him Daniel Ben Avram joyfully cried, "God be praised! At last!" At long last he'd been provided the golden opportunity that had been hoped for in all the planning by the General and the briefings by Amnon that had gone into Operation Judah.

Finally, he was going to step inside Helder's mansion. And, no doubt, into his bedroom where it would be ascertained if the man with the mutilated finger also bore a sickle-shaped shoulder scar.

But first, Daniel discovered, Peter Helder could not let pass an opportunity to show Danny Dacapua the splendors of his mansion.

The tour took nearly an hour as Helder discoursed on his fabulous collection of art and antiques, ending in the Art Deco living room where he sat beside Danny on a pliant couch, pressing close and whispering, "I've been patient long enough. Now I must kiss you. Do you mind?"

With his body rigid with anxiety and revulsion and his head ringing with Biblical admonitions concerning abominable sins, the boy whose father had died a hero along the Jerusalem Corridor while defending Israel against Arab enemies who'd wished to strangle the infant nation at its birth, the teenage volunteer who had graduated first in his class in all subjects at the Kfar Sirkin agents' school and the young man who'd sworn an oath to do whatever duty demanded to bring August Grenier to justice . . . laughed. "Of course I don't mind."

As it happened, he trembled noticeably.

"My, you are a shy and nervous one," sighed Helder.

Gulping for breath, Daniel said, "Shall we go upstairs to the bedroom?"

"Not yet, Danny," exclaimed Helder excitedly. "Not just yet! There is one other room I want you to see. I wasn't sure until now if I should dare show you. But now I'm certain it will be all right. I can trust you. It's quite special. To me it's the most interesting one in the house."

Caught off guard, Daniel forced a compliant smile. "It must be something if it's better than all the rest."

"It's downstairs," said Helder. "Below the galleries . . . in the cellar."

Chapter Eleven

The Curator

To say that the view from the terrace of Eleanora Swaim's eighteenth floor apartment in a modern tower rising above historic Brooklyn Heights was spectacular was to understate the facts, for spread out below was the grandest man-made panorama in the world. From the Statue of Liberty to the left, to the graceful and stately curving stretch of the Brooklyn Bridge immediately in front, to the distant spider-webbed span of the Fifty-ninth Street bridge on the right sprawled the majestic skyscraper bluffs of Manhattan and the chugging and swirling hubbub of tugs, cargo ships, oil barges, perky sail boats, millionaires' yachts, and garbage scows plying the East River. But, as Eleanora liked to say when a visitor to her apartment was gasping at the sight for the first time, "A view is something you look at once. Then you simply have to get on with your life."

This did not mean Eleanora didn't enjoy the scene.

Rather, it was her way of saying without boasting that her employment by Peter Helder as his Curator kept her much too busy to waste time gaping from the terrace or her bedroom window affording the same view. When she did take the time to look out it was not in the evening when the buildings across the river were most impressive because they were gloriously alight but in the morning when she had her breakfast of decaffeinated coffee and butterless toast alone in her kitchen as the rising sun gilded the facades and set the millions of windows ablaze, a spectacle she would have captured with great gobs of garish oils on canvas if she knew how to paint. But she was not an artist, she liked to say to her many friends. She was a woman who *knew* art.

In seventeen years of employment at the Helder Galleries, beginning as an assistant to Mr. Helder's first curator in 1949 directly upon receiving her degree in Fine Arts from Vassar, her morning routine rarely varied; rising at six, leaving her apartment at seven, arriving at the Galleries a little before eight, two hours ahead of their opening for business.

For the first five years as an assistant to the curator who was a closeted homosexual who possessed a breathtakingly encyclopedic knowledge of art, she had dwelled modestly in a studio apartment on East Fifty-second Street only five blocks from her employment, Mr. Helder's art gallery then being established in the Fuller Building at the northwest corner of Madison Avenue and Fifty-seventh Street. Entered through a carved Rockwood stone portal and, she believed, one of the most glorious lobbies in the most architecturally competitive cities in the world, the first six floors were of black Swedish granite and had become the preserve of numerous galleries. Peter Helder had leased two rooms on the second floor.

Strolling to and from the Fuller Building, Eleanora had passed through the heart of New York's world of art galleries. Sprinkled like gems eastward on Fifty-seventh from the anchor of Tiffany's at Fifth Avenue were the ACA gallery, long established as the showplace for the foremost American artists of social consequences; Nicholas Acquavella's quietly exclusive second-floor displays of the Impressionists; the pleasant Artzt gallery of contemporary American works; Terry Dintenfass's representational paintings and sculpture displayed with flair in tidy basement rooms; Paul Drey's very sedate fourth-floor shop restricted to museum pieces for the very serious collector; David B. Findlay's array of the Paris School; Galerie St. Etienne's expressionists and primitives including Grandma Moses; the Midtown; Betty Parsons with her eye for abstractions; the 19th and 20th century French art of Utrillo and Monet at the Schoneman; masterworks shown only by appointment at Jacques Seligmann's; and the Knoedler, a century-old courtly firm housed in a mansion purveying Rembrandts, Raphaels, Renoirs, and Rodins.

While Peter Helder dreamed of emulating Knoedler by one day establishing his galleries in a mansion, he'd settled, temporarily, he vowed, for the space in the Fuller. Then, with bewildering speed and unprecedented early success, and with an influx of financial backing from an anonymous patron, he became one of the most important art dealers in the city, indeed, the world.

In 1960 with great flourish and hoopla he at last was able to acquire the Madison Avenue town house and open the Helder Galleries, two entire floors of mankind's finest works of art.

With the move of Mr. Helder to the mansion at Eightieth Street that year, the resignation of her immediate supervisor to join the staff of the Metropolitan, and her own elevation to the position of curator with a doubling of her salary, Eleanora had bought the Brooklyn Heights cooperative apartment and from that moment devoted herself to the Helder Galleries and their owner.

Of course, leisurely walks to her job along Fifty-seventh Street basking in the glories of her surroundings became a thing of the past replaced by a thirty-minute ride on the subways from Brooklyn Heights to her stop at Lexington Avenue and Seventy-seventh Street and then a short two-block pedestrian hike to the mansion, arriving around nine o'clock.

Although she was a tall and attractive woman with the features and bearing of a fashion mannequin, she was a person of propriety who dressed according to her keenly honed sense of place and purpose. Knowing that the men who came into the galleries might easily be distracted by her beauty and that women could be deflected by her fashions from the art she wished to sell to them, she always wore her hair swept up somewhat austerely and an unobtrusive yet stylish black dress with a high neckline and a rope of pearls that reflected her status but were no more diverting than the uniform of an attendant in an art museum.

While being current with the personalities and the gossip of the art universe in which the clients of the Helder Galleries orbited, she was a woman of discretion. Never from her lips would slip a juicy tidbit for the snoopy society columnists concerning who was seen with whom at the gala opening of an exhibition, what stunning and expensive painting had been purchased by a certain wealthy gentleman for a woman who wasn't his wife, what work had been bought by a matron of the arts for a boy a third her age, nor which young notable bachelor-around-town and scion of Fifth Avenue millions had breezed in at noontime one Friday still dressed in the evening clothes of a Thursday night binge and holding hands with a handsome young teenage film actor and pubescent girls' heartthrob to buy a Picasso lithograph for their secret love nest on Christopher Street in Greenwich Village. "Judgment of art is my specialty, not the vagaries of humanity," she once said to a reporter who had tried to pry a scandal from her.

This laissez-faire attitude she especially extended to her brilliant, attentive, generous, ever-solicitous, considerate, charming—and mysterious—employer.

The mysteries which most intrigued her concerning Peter Helder's professional life were two: his years prior to 1949 and his abrupt ascension to the heady stratosphere of the New York art establishment with enough financing to create one of the most important addresses in the world of art. She knew he was Dutch yet when he spoke of Europe he was more apt to discourse on Paris, Rome, Geneva, Vienna, Prague, and Berlin than Amsterdam or the Hague.

While he was a member of the National Arts Club, the New York Athletic Club, and The Brook, as exclusive a men's club as there was in New York, he was most likely to be reached, if absolutely necessary, at the Atlantis Club, of which Eleanor knew nothing save its unlisted telephone number. Her conjecture was that it was through the Atlantis Club that he'd obtained the extraordinary backing that had enabled him to vault from two rooms on the second floor of the Fuller Building to the Madison Avenue mansion.

On these subjects Helder was, in 1967, as inscrutable as he had been in all the years she'd been his employee.

Mystifying about him personally was his peculiar private nightlife that was as radically different from his open and professionally oriented social whirl of black-tie testimonial dinners, nights at the opera, charity theatrical events, and art exhibition openings as a Rembrandt portrait of a Dutch elder was from an Andy Warhol silkscreen of Marilyn Monroe.

Good-looking young men featured in this veiled nocturnal existence, she could not have failed to notice. Indeed, she had been introduced to a few of them; charming, all. Several she'd simply encountered. Most she'd merely glimpsed leaving the mansion by way of the residence steps. Their presence, the fact that Helder was not married and apparently never had taken a wife, led her to presume that he was homosexual.

This neither surprised nor shocked her, given the abundance of homosexuals in the artistic and theatrical circles that were so much a part of Peter Helder's public life. Nor did she make anything of it when she was delayed in leaving work in the evening and occasionally saw him on the way out of the mansion wearing black leather clothing, sometimes alone, often with one of his young friends, in pursuit of whatever pleasures leather and sex between men afforded him.

Because he was so open about himself with her and because he obviously knew that she was aware of all this yet never made so much as a passing reference to this secretive and mysterious aspect of him, she was puzzled—though not as mystified as she was about his pre-1949 life and his phenomenal post-1960 success.

There was a final mystery concerning him, perhaps the most unusual of all, and maybe the key to the others; a cellar room below the Galleries, entry to which was through a door at the rear of the exhibition space that could be opened solely by a brass key for which there was no duplicate unlike all the others which were kept in a drawer of her splendid Georgian desk.

At times when there were no clients in the Galleries, she sat at the desk and invented thrilling explanations for the secret room below. It was his private art collection, she surmised, consisting of masterpieces that museums all over the world coveted. Down there, she imagined, he kept a trove of contraband works that were the loot and booty of countless thefts, burglaries, and robberies by a ring of international brigands that Peter Helder master-minded. Once she concocted a scenario in which Peter Helder the art dealer emerged into the light with a vast number of his own masterpieces created down there at night and was promptly declared a modern genius of palette and canvas worthy of being displayed in his own galleries.

She had never seen him go down in the daytime but was certain he often descended at night, discovering on numerous occasions when she came to work in the morning that a switch next to the door for the lighting in the stairway which had been turned off when she'd left the previous evening was now on, apparently because he'd forgotten to switch it off. Because he never spoke about the room, she never inquired about it. But she had developed a daily morning habit of checking the switch.

Accordingly, when she arrived on the balmy morning after Helder had expressed his wish that his new friend Danny Dacapua visit the room, Eleanora glanced from her desk to the light switch and found it on. But when she approached to turn off the switch she discovered that the door was slightly ajar.

A singular event, it troubled her.

Not once since the move to the mansion had she found the door open.

Wondering if he might be down there, she pushed the door fully open, creating a sudden downdraft rushing past her.

Were she to switch off the lights, she reasoned, she might plunge him suddenly into darkness, if he were down there.

Listening, she heard nothing—except a very distant, very slight creaking.

An occasional weekend boater when she visited friends in the Hamptons who had a smart little sailing skiff, she formed the impression of the creaking as being very similar to the tug and strain of wind-tested rigging lines; quite a ridiculous leap of the imagination, she thought, in a mansion on Madison Avenue.

Calm reason prompted her to review the situation. The light switch had been off when she'd locked up the Galleries the previous evening. On this point her memory was vivid. Now it was on. Therefore, he had been down there during the night. While he often forgot to turn off the lights, never before had he left the door open. Why should he do so now?

Coldly, fear insinuated itself into her thinking. While Peter Helder was a robust and vigorous man, exercising regularly at the Athletic Club, walking frequently rather than taking cabs, he was a man in his sixties. The age when men like him suffered heart problems. The age when men like him dropped dead of heart attacks.

"Oh my God," she gasped.

Pushing the door wide open, she shouted down the stairway, "Mr. Helder? Are you there?"

There was no reply; no sound, save the creaking, slow now and barely discernible.

Edging to the top of the stairs, she called, "Sir?"

A horrifying vision came to her of him unconscious on the cellar floor, dying.

Gripping a banister with a trembling hand, as she descended toward the bottom of the steep steps most of the room slowly revealed itself to her.

Incredibly, she saw a sawdust-covered concrete floor, black walls festooned with long straps, a black leather-covered bench with shackles and chains at the four corners and a large wooden rack displaying what appeared to Eleanora Swaim as she reached the foot of the staircase to be ancient torture devices: whips, paddles, swords, a mace, and a spear.

"It's a dungeon," she thought, shuddering.

Then, softly behind her she heard the creaking, very slowly now.

Turning, she screamed in terror.

Swinging almost imperceptibly from a rafter by a hangman's rope and noose, the corpse was naked except for a black leather hood that covered the entire head.

Chapter Twelve

The Partnership

"Male caucasian DOA by hanging in basement of the Helder Galleries, Madison at Eightieth. Likely suicide, request homicide detectives," was the report from the 22nd Precinct to the Manhattan North Borough Command that had sent homicide investigators David Hargreave and Sheldon Lyman heading to the East Side. Had the death-on-arrival been judged a certain suicide by the first police officers to arrive on the scene after the frantic phone call from Eleanora Swaim, the possibility of murder still would have to be investigated. That was the law.

Coming out of West 100th Street and south on Central Park West they hit heavy morning rush-hour traffic. Frustrated, Detective-Sergeant Lyman drummed his fingers on the steering wheel of the unmarked police car and shot a sidelong glance at his partner and boss, hoping that Lieutenant Hargreave would give a decisive nod and let him hit the lights and the siren. But Hargreave was staring forward with his square chin pinched between a thick thumb and forefinger, patiently resigned to the slow going because he had long since learned when there was a need for siren and lights and when there wasn't.

"This is a hard thing for you youngsters to grasp, I know," Hargreave had said to Lyman the first time Lyman had turned on the lights and siren early in their partnership, "but the truth is, Shelly, that by the time we get to the scene the perpetrator of the crime will probably be halfway to Philadelphia. And the victim isn't going to get up and wander off. So, please, go easy on the speed without the lights and most definitely without all the racket. This isn't *Gangbusters*. Which, by the way, was a radio program long before your day."

"I've heard of *Gangbusters*. I'm not that young, David. And you aren't that old."

Twenty years separated their ages, which was not much by ordinary standards. But it was an enormous gap to a cop. By the policeman's way of measuring, David Hargreave at 45 was an elderly sage next to Sheldon Lyman's 25. In those twenty years Hargreave had learned all the hard lessons the hard way. In that score of years he had come to understand and accept what was required of anyone entertaining the idea of carrying the gold shield and the .38 caliber Police Special of a detective.

First of all, you had to love it. It had to mean more than anything else in the world—more than family, more than money, more than comfort. You had to feel the calling to a policeman's badge the way a Catholic boy was drawn to the priesthood or a Jewish boy was tugged to the study of Torah. You had to be a zealot. You had to believe.

Then you had to love it physically, the way a man loves a woman. You had to have a fervor for the weight of the cold steel of a revolver holstered at the hip or sheathed snugly below the armpit, the fit of the uniform, the dingy smell of cigar smoke in the squad room, the sweat, the burning of sidewalks underfoot, and the sagging of the seat of a worn-out patrol car beneath your aching butt at the end of a double shift.

You had to want it all—the rush of adrenalin at the start of a new case, the frequent boredom, the routines, the regulations, and the closer-than-a-brother-or-your-wife reliance upon a partner who shared all your values.

Most of all, you had to believe with all your heart in the good guys besting the bad ones and in the ultimate triumph of good over evil. If you didn't believe that evil existed and that there were evil people, born evil and living evilly, you had no right to be a cop.

So far in the year in which Sergeant Sheldon Lyman had been his partner, Lieutenant David Hargreave had seen nothing to cause him to doubt that Lyman had all the requisites and that in due course he would learn the beauty of restraint, such as not hitting the lights and siren every time they were beginning a case, as if they were firemen rushing to a conflagration. Usually a homicide was not a three-alarm blaze. All hands and hoses were seldom required. Mostly what was needed was what Mayor Fiorello LaGuardia had preached when he was

93

mayor of New York and Hargreave was a boy zealot dreaming about becoming a cop: patience and fortitude.

These thoughts occupied Hargreave while Lyman fidgeted anxiously over the impeding traffic, because he had come to a point in his life as a cop where a decision about the future would have to be made. In a few months he would face the choice of continuing on the police force or requesting retirement with a handsome pension but with enough productive years remaining to allow him to take an executive position with a private security agency offering him more pay than he was earning as a lieutenant.

Turning in his badge and gun at age 50 at the latest had been his plan for years, the objective being to spend more time with the wife who had endured the strains of 25 years of being married to a cop. But Nancy had died of cancer four years ago and now his plan of giving up being a cop seemed pointless, except for the appeal of a lot more money and much less stress and strain.

That point had been emphasized the previous evening by his daughter Sandra. The same age as Sergeant Lyman, Sandy was willowy and blond like her beautiful mother and just as smart, earning her living as an assistant district attorney. "You've paid your dues, Daddy," she'd pleaded as she heaped his dinner plate with a lamb stew made from her mother's special recipe. "The time has come for you to think about yourself for once. And, damn it, I'd like to see a lot more of you in the next twenty-five years than I did the last."

The remark had stung—the sharp slap in the face

of truth. That he'd shortchanged Sandy and her uncomplaining mother was an inescapable fact. Had it been Nancy saying it, he would have had an appropriate retort: "Nancy, my darling, you knew on our wedding day that it was my job that was going to be my wife and you my mistress." Sandra had made no concession. A part-time father had been imposed upon her. To mask his guilt, he'd replied, "As to retirement, my darling daughter, I'd be much more inclined to do it . . . if I had some grandchildren to spoil rotten."

"Oh, you are the clever one, turning the tables," she'd laughed, tossing her lovely long hair the way her mother used to and letting the subject of retirement drop.

In his mind, however, it lingered to plague him on his way to Madison and Eightieth to probe whatever dark and sinister deed that had been done there.

To investigators at all homicides, the scene of the crime is a curious mixture of the strange and the familiar. Surroundings are usually new, but the faces at the location are those of known associates, creating an atmosphere of familiarity. Underlying this feeling of new mixed with the old Hargreave found, was an uneasy realization that they were intruding into the victim's privacy and taking into their hands all of the intimate and secret details of lives that had unfolded within those walls. It was behind those doors, within the walls, in the closets, inside the bureaus and enclosed in locked desk drawers that a solution to a murder might be found, so into the murder victim's inner sanctum had to march a fraternity of professional snoops—forensic specialists; experts in the vast weaponry of crime, such as guns, knives, ropes and bludgeons; the Medical Examiner; crime photographers; fingerprint lifters; white-gloved men looking like janitors lugging vacuum sweepers to sift dust and carpet fibers for clues; and a brotherhood of detectives who brought with them all their years of education, training, on-the-job experience, instinct, and the most useful tool of all, their intuition.

In the horrifying dungeon beneath the splendors of the Helder Galleries, Hargreave's intuition screamed at him that the death of Peter Helder had not been the result of him tying a noose around his own neck and hanging himself. Although he had not a shred of evidence that this wasn't suicide, he knew in his policeman's heart that it was murder.

Of the uniformed policeman who had come in answer to Eleanora Swaim's cry for help, he asked, "Was there a note?"

"No, sir."

Of Eleanora he asked, "Do you know of any reason why Mr. Helder would take his own life?"

"None," she sobbed. "He was on top of the world."

Of Sergeant Lyman he asked, "What do you make of all this?"

"Suicide, cut and dried."

"No note. Suicides generally leave an explanation."

"He was an exception."

"Yeah, he was exceptional all right," said Hargreave, looking around the dungeon.

"What a shock it must have been for the woman," said Lyman.

"That's very good, Shel," smiled Hargreave.

"What's very good?"

"You have put your finger on it."

"I have?"

"The shock!"

"Well, isn't that what he wanted? To shock people?"

"Then how come there's no note? It seems to me that a guy who stages an elaborate suicide—naked, the black hood, and a chamber of horrors—would leave a message to bolster the effect."

"On that basis alone you're thinking homicide?"

"The woman says she knows of no reason why he'd do it," said Hargreave thoughtfully. "And, partner, *that* is a lady who'd know if something were driving her boss to suicide, believe me."

"Then I expect she'll have some ideas as to who might have killed Helder and made it look like a suicide."

"The lady's up in the galleries. Have a chat with her, Sheldon. Gently. Don't push her. She's upset. We can always come back. Meantime, I'm going to poke around Helder's living quarters."

Chapter Thirteen

The Library

The rumble of turgid music drew Detective Lyman up a spiral staircase to the fifth floor of the Helder mansion and into the library where Hargreave was seated in a deep leather armchair. Looking up from leafing through a small book in his lap, he smiled, "Ah, you found me."

"I just followed the noise," said Lyman, raising his voice.

" 'The Ride of the Valkyries' from *The Ring of the Nibelung* by Richard Wagner," said Hargreave, exaggerating the German composer's name—"Reecard VOG-ner."

Crossing the room to the blaring stereo, Lyman said, "Do you mind if I kill it?"

"Not at all. I put it on because it seemed to fit the occasion and the decor of this room. How did it go with Eleanora Swaim?"

"She's too shook up to be of any help," said Lyman

in the welcome quiet. "On one hand she insists that there is no way that Helder would have killed himself. On the other—"

"On the other hand," interrupted Hargreave, closing the book and rising, "she says that she just can't think of a single individual—nobody—who'd want to kill him."

"Right."

"I wonder how much she knew about her beloved boss' literary interests," said Hargreave, thrusting his book into Lyman's hand; an English first edition of *Mein Kampf* by Adolf Hitler. "Ever read it?"

"Hell no," grunted Lyman. "I'm a Jew."

"Ah! That was the mistake, you see. Very few people read it. And very, very few Jews." Taking back the book, he flipped it open and read, " 'By defending myself against the Jew, I am fighting for the handiwork of the Lord.' " Snapping it shut, he waved it in the direction of the room's surrounding bookcases. "If more people had read this crap and taken it seriously . . ." Letting Lyman finish the obvious thought himself, he said, "There's similar reading matter on those shelves. For instance, *New Templars' Breviary, The Psalms in German*. I found one by a Rudolf von Sebottendorf, *Bevor Hitler Kam*. My German's rusty but I believe that means 'Before Hitler Came.' He's got others by this Sebottendorf."

"That's a handful of books out of a very big library."

"True. He's got quite a collection of histories. But very narrowly focused. Mostly they're about kings, conquerors, emperors, dictators, and tyrants. He's got biographies of the German emperor Otto the

99

Great. There's Constantine and Justinian. Charlemagne. There's the German conqueror of Italy, Barbarossa. Napoleon. Shirer's *The Rise and Fall of the Third Reich*—Hitler again."

"I still don't get what you're driving at."

"Don't know that I'm driving at anything. I just think these books are interesting. There's one by Arturo Graf, *The Story of the Devil*. Something called *The Dawn of Magic*. There's a very old volume—1897—by Charles W. Heckethorn called *Secret Societies of All Countries*. Over there is Nesta H. Webster's *Secret Societies and Subversive Movements*."

"Okay, Helder wasn't exactly a light reader."

"Did you ever read a book called *The True Believer* by Eric Hoffer?"

"Nope."

"You should. It's an eyeopener. Hoffer's a longshoreman out in San Francisco. Big, rough, and tough. Self-educated. But what a perceptive and brilliantly illuminating mind the man has. 'The dock-walloper philosopher,' somebody called him. His books are best sellers. In *The True Believer* he pins down the truth about the crazies and the fanatics that seem to be blossoming everywhere these days."

"Is that what you think Helder was? Some crazy, some fanatic?"

"I'm not saying anything about Helder at this time, except that he's dead, probably murdered."

Crossing the room to Helder's collection of antique spears and swords, Lyman said sourly, "It does make you feel as if you've been thrust back into the Middle Ages, doesn't it? You know, Crusaders and

100

all that." Drawing a short, heavy spear, he grunted, "Look at this! Look at 'em all. This was some weird guy, Lieutenant."

"I've always believed that if you want to know a person, if you want to probe his heart and mind and soul, you should look at the things he surrounds himself with. *Si monumentum requiris circumspice.* The inscription is on a tablet in St. Paul's Cathedral in London. It refers to Sir Christopher Wren, who built the church. But it applies to everyone. 'If you would see the man's monument, look around.'"

Lyman chuckled. "Lieutenant, you are amazing."

With a shrug, Hargreave said, "A teacher I had in the tenth grade once said to me, 'Hargreave, choose an author as you choose a friend.' Judging by many of these books, the spears and swords, and that torture chamber downstairs, I'd say that Peter Helder chose some very peculiar friends. And, partner, I'm as sure as I am that God made little green apples that one of 'em murdered him."

Chapter Fourteen

The Cardinal

That the death of Peter Helder would be the headline of the evening and morning newspapers and the top story on the radio all day and on television newscasts at 6:00 and 11:00 had been obvious to Hargreave the moment he'd descended into the dungeon beneath the Helder Galleries and learned the identity of the hooded naked corpse still hanging from the rafter. At that instant he'd made a decision concerning the mask.

Now, more than an hour later as he cautiously parted the heavy curtains of Helder's peculiar and telling library and peered down five floors at the sizeable cluster of reporters and photographers he'd expected to be attracted to the front of the mansion by the violent death of a famous person, like bees to honey, he said to Sergeant Lyman, "The one thing we must not reveal to the press and the public at this time is the existence of the hood, that grotesque death mask. Pass the word, Shel, and make sure the Swaim woman understands that I don't want to hear a peep about it from her. If there's a back way out of this place, see that she uses it, 'cause I don't want her having to run that gauntlet of ghouls down there."

"What will you tell 'em?"

"Only that it's an apparent suicide, of course," said Hargreave, letting the drapery slip closed. "Emphasis on the word 'suicide,'" he said, drawing back the curtain again for a scowling second glimpse of the swarm below and a grunted, "Look at 'em."

Peering over Hargreave's shoulder at the milling crowd below, Lyman, a deep-sea fisherman on his days off, chuckled, "They look like sharks in a feeding frenzy." Spotting a bald head in the throng, he added, "There's trouble."

"Yeah, I noticed," said Hargreave grumpily. "Lomax!"

Lacking only a flashing red light on the roof and a wailing siren under the hood, Richard Lomax's olive green radio news mobile unit was crammed with everything required to keep him in touch with crime in the metropolis which another reporter, Mark Hellinger, had described as a naked city of eight million stories. Despite an early-morning reluctance to start, the unit was capable of sustaining high speeds which Lomax was never reluctant to attain in pursuit of the bare-bones tip from the police radios and what his intuition sensed was a good story.

Four of these radio receivers, known as scanners, crammed every inch of space below the dashboard on

103

the passenger's side of the front seat with tiny red bulbs winking like the lights of animated Times Square billboards until a cop's voice—flat and emotionless—crackled from one of them in the shorthand of secret-sounding phrases and code numbers whose meanings Lomax had long since deciphered and memorized.

Having been at work since before dawn for the all-news station that paid his wages, he had been cruising aimlessly downtown and listening to the scanners for some news item to hang his journalistic hat on for the day when the Manhattan North frequency blurted, "Male caucasian DOA by hanging in basement of the Helder Galleries . . . likely suicide . . . request homicide detectives."

It was the address that hinted at a good story.

Barreling uptown as fast as possible, he'd avoided the clog of the East River Drive in morning rush hour in favor of Third Avenue and Seventy-ninth Street to Madison. Arriving only minutes after the detectives, he waited with other newsmen corralled like horses behind hastily erected police barricades for the who, what, where, when, why, and how of what might be the big headline of the day.

From a uniformed cop they'd been told only that there'd been a death, that it looked like a suicide and that he hadn't the slightest idea who the victm was. Which was credible. But even if the cop did have a name he wouldn't have revealed it because of departmental rules and regulations, especially with all the brass hats around, considering the fashionable address. "You'll just have to wait and get all the dope

104

from Lieutenant Hargreave," the cop had said with a shrug.

So Lomax had retreated to his car. Balding, slightly overweight and straining the waistband of a brown suit badly in need of pressing, at this early hour he already looked as if he needed a shave. As he drank coffee from a thermos and chain smoked Camel cigarettes, he had radioed his station that there'd be no report from him until Lieutenant David Hargreave came out to brief them on what the hell had happened at the prestigious Helder Galleries.

"It's a dull newsday," chirped Freddie, the editor, "so let's hope it's a big name." It was the job speaking, not Freddie, who was a gentle and loving man—unless he was chasing a story.

"Like all the rest of us," muttered Lomax as he observed with fondness and amusement the familiar faces and figures of the disheveled and disgruntled members of the working press of New York City. Seeing them, he recalled an old friend and former journalistic colleague of his and Freddie's by the name of Alex Somerfield who'd invented the Sacred Order and College of Cardinals of the First Amendment. In idle moments over glasses of scotch at a reporters' saloon across Centre Street from Police Headquarters, Alex would say, "You and I are princes in this collegium, Richard. Each of us has been given the red hat of the Misfits and Malcontents. We are what Charlie MacArthur and Ben Hecht in their play *The Front Page* called a lot of lousy, daffy buttinskis. We skulk around peeking through keyholes. Chasing fire engines. Waking people up in the middle of the night to ask them insulting questions. Stealing pictures off old ladies of their raped daughters. For what? So a couple of million people who don't give a shit anyway will know what's going on. All because we think we know it all. Well, take it from me, Richard, we don't."

It was stuff like that, Lomax remembered, that had made Alex Somerfield a hit performing in an annual show put on by reporters who covered City Hall and the police beat and belonged to a genuine organization known as the Inner Circle. Given at a midtown hotel with all the political bigwigs in attendance and the proceeds of the price of admission going to the benefit of some charity, the Inner Circle Show was a black-tie banquet featuring a scathing roast of the politicians present, largely written by Alex, who always included a star turn for himself.

Because he seemed obsessed with Sherlock Holmes and held an investitured membership in the select, men-only order of Sherlockian experts known as the Baker Street Irregulars, his act inevitably involved dressing up like the famed sleuth. But this was only one of Somerfield's several unusual and outlandish eccentricities, such as suddenly dashing off on overseas trips, his fluency in Russian, and receiving more than a newsman's usual assortment of cryptic telephone messages, leading a few of the more imaginative initiates in their journalistic enclaves to contend that everything about the affable, portly, professorial, and decidedly un-Sherlockian appearing Alex Somerfield was a cover for his true calling as a spy.

Eventually Somerfield's passion for crime fiction as well as his occupation as a reporter had combined with his wit, perceptions, and ability with words in the form of a series of best-selling novels featuring not spies but a hard-boiled private detective who resembled Alex Somerfield more than Holmes and did his gumshoe work in the nostalgia-dripping New York of the 1930s when Lewis J. Valentine was police commissioner, LaGuardia was mayor, and there were nineteen daily newspapers vying for lurid stories like the one about which Lomax was waiting to ask the five W's and an H of Hargreave.

Having hit it big as a novelist, Alex Somerfield had given up the daily digging for stories and gone off to the seclusion of the Pennsylvania woodlands to write books, and now his old buddy and charter member of the Sacred Order and College of Cardinals of the First Amendment, Dick Lomax, missed him.

Telling himself that this story would have been right up Alex's alley, Lomax lit another Camel but a minute later he saw David Hargreave emerge from the Helder Galleries wiggling a long finger like a worm on a fish hook, luring the reporters to him.

A horde, they dashed.

Reading from his notebook in a flat voice, Hargreave said, "We have here the apparent suicide by hanging of Mr. Peter Helder, age sixty-seven, residence: this address, the owner of the Helder Galleries. He was a famous person, so you all can look up the details of his pedigree in your own files. Time of death: between midnight and five o'clock

107

this morning. The body was discovered by the curator of the galleries, Miss Eleanora Swaim, an employee of Mr. Helder's for some nineteen years, when she reported to work around nine o'clock. That's all I have for you."

His statement notwithstanding, now came the expected barrage of questions and his terse replies. No note had been found but the investigation was continuing. The last person known to have seen Helder alive was Miss Swaim the previous afternoon. Miss Swaim was quite understandably upset and because there was no reason to believe she had anything further to add to the facts she had been escorted home. As far as was known there were no financial irregularities or other difficulties connected with the Helder Galleries nor in Helder's personal life but, of course, the investigation was ongoing. As far as could be determined at this early stage of that investigation there was nothing to point to any reason for Mr. Helder's suicide. Then Hargreave asked a question of his own. "Who among us can ever really know what lies in the secret recesses of another man's heart and soul?" End of press conference.

Eight hours later before going home at the end of his shift, Lomax was looking for a fresh angle to advance his story—some new slant to leave on tape for tomorrow morning's rush-hour broadcasts. Deciding that it might come from the woman who'd found Helder's body, he looked for a listing of an Eleanora Swaim in the city's telephone books starting with Manhattan and then moving to

Brooklyn. Finding her listed, he now faced a choice between telephoning her or showing up on her doorstep. Having long since learned that it was easy to be hung up on, he appeared at the door of her Brooklyn Heights apartment as dusk was setting upon her spectacular view of Manhattan. Because she was so startled and unnerved by a reporter's unexpected visit, she admitted him and permitted him to interview her.

"It was horrible," she said, shuddering at the memory.

"I'm sure it was," he said sympathetically.

"It was that mask!"

Lomax had been slouched on a sofa with his tape recorder beside him. Now he was bolt upright. "Beg pardon?"

Rigid in a chair turned slightly towards the lights of the city across the river, she stared. Ghostly pale and trembling, she spoke softly into his microphone as if it weren't there and she were in a trance. "He had on this mask! Not a mask really. More like a hood. Covering his entire head. With a zipper for a mouth. And zippers to close the eyes. But even with that ugly leather mask I recognized him immediately."

"Why was that?"

"Well, you see, years ago he had lost the tip of a finger." She raised her right hand as if taking an oath. "The little one," she said, twitching hers. Suddenly leaden, the graceful hand dropped into her lap as she whispered, "And he was the only one who had the key to the . . . awful . . . lower room."

Tingling with excitement at the story he was

getting, Lomax coaxed. "What was so awful about the . . . lower room?"

With a sigh, she said, "I never dreamed he could have a room like that."

"Like what, Miss Swaim?"

"It was so black and gruesome and horrible," she sobbed. "It was a dungeon. A torture chamber."

Chapter Fifteen

The True Believer

"Sheldon," blared Hargreave on the phone, "have you heard the news on the radio?"

"Not yet, boss," mumbled Lyman, turning sleepy eyes toward his bedside table and his wrist watch which registered 5:30 a.m.

"You're still in bed, ain'tcha?"

"Guilty."

"I suppose you were up half the night tomcatting around?"

"As a matter of fact I was up half the night. But reading."

"Reading?"

"That book you mentioned yesterday. Eric Hoffer's *The True Believer*. I picked it up at the library on the way home."

"Well, stick a book mark in it, get your finger outta your ass, and get down here soonest. That Swaim dame spilled everything to Lomax and the whole ball of wax about the mask is all over the air waves. The goddamned genie's out of the bottle. I'm at the coroner's office, by the way."

"I'm on my way," said Lyman, reaching for the watch lying beside the Hoffer book that had kept him up too late. A square-faced, gold-cased Longines, it had been a gift from his father on high school graduation day. Since that moment he'd been without it only one week when it had to be repaired while ticking off the four years of his service in the Marine Corps.

Wearing the watch had not been allowed in Boot Camp but the moment he'd graduated at Parris Island he'd strapped it to his wrist and worn it every day of his duty as proudly as the uniform. Now it was registering the years of the naked and unshaven cop he saw reflected in the bathroom mirror. Today he would not be donning a policeman's uniform. He'd wear an ordinary suit—plain clothes for a plain-clothesman. But the pride of that uniform would be with him, just as the pride of having worn the colors of a United States Marine would always be with him.

While seeing in his mirror a man who was not as prime as he'd been when he was an 18-year-old Marine, he still judged himself as being in top condition. But there was no mistaking the wear and tear that was evidencing itself in his face, around the eyes, and at the corners of his mouth primarily. What once might have been a kisser on a Marine recruiting poster, he told himself mockingly, was showing its mileage; years made up of hundreds of thousands of seconds spent on patrol, in boring hours waiting for his cases to be called in courtrooms, in studying for the examinations that led to promotions and doing all the other things that had to be done to earn the gold shield of the detective.

Now what he was striving for was to be like his boss, although he did not expect ever to equal David Hargreave's amazing depth in things beyond police work—being able to toss off a pertinent quotation in Latin, for instance. Or knowing music and literature. And being aware of a brilliant old codger named Eric Hoffer who walloped the San Francisco docks in the daytime and then instead of staying up all night reading brilliant books, wrote them.

He was only a third of the way through *The True Believer* and there was no way of knowing when he'd be able to finish it now that Hargreave had his dander up, but he grabbed it off the bedside table and took it with him anyway as he dashed for the car to head downtown.

His progress halted at Times Square where a demonstration against the war in Vietnam had surged past police barricades into crisscrossing Broadway and Seventh Avenue from an island where there was an Armed Forces recruiting office.

Stuck, he raised his eyes to the moving news sign streaming around the triangular Times Building, its zipper of white lights spelling out the morning's main headlines:

U.S. DENOUNCES ANTI-WEST TONE OF SOVIET MAY DAY PARADE
AIR OF CRISIS GRIPS MIDEAST AS EGYPT MASSES TROOPS IN SINAI
MARTIN LUTHER KING CALLS FOR YOUTHS TO SHUN

113

"Shit," he muttered as he hit the switches for the red light and siren in hopes of clearing a way around the noisy mob that was blocking the so-called Crossroads of the World. But it was useless, he decided immediately, turning off the switches and picking up his radio to relay the bad news to his boss that he was going to be very late.

Nettled, Hargreave demanded, "What's the hang-up?"

"I'm stuck in the middle of a bunch of anti-Vietnam protestors."

"Great," said Hargreave disgustedly.

"True believers," Lyman said, switching off the radio. "In the flesh," he said to himself, mindful of the irony of coming up against exactly the people he'd been reading about for half the night in Eric Hoffer's book—*movement people.*

Pliant joiners and followers fueled by their frustrations and anger, they were eager to renounce themselves for a cause and in so doing find meaning and purpose in life. The movement provided an outlet for pent-up individual rage. But what was the cause of rage? What were they railing against?

Themselves, said Hoffer. Against their own lives, although they would be the last to recognize and admit it.

They donned the mask of the true believer to hide what really motivated them. Which is what this traffic-stopping antiwar protest was, Lyman decided.

114

It wasn't the war that these people really objected to. It was the possibility that they might have to fight it that brought them out. Or because they knew that their participation would infuriate their parents. Or because they hated their own country so much that they wanted to see America defeated and humiliated. Why? Was it because they felt humiliated and defeated themselves? What was it that inflamed the fury that stretched before him on a balmy May morning? Was Hoffer correct in suggesting that people who let themselves be swept up in movements did so because of a deep need for them to witness the downfall and disgrace of the righteous? What was there that made individuals submerge themselves in groups like this one raging in Times Square? Or the Nazis?

Was there any difference between these Americans in Times Square shouting "America out of Vietnam" and German youths who'd yelled "Heil Hitler" and sung "Deutschland uber alles?"

It was a subject he'd like to discuss with Hargreave, he thought.

If he ever got out of this mess.

After they wrapped up the Helder case.

Seeing an opening in the blockage, he eased the car through it and into Forty-fourth Street and sped toward Fifth Avenue with nothing on his mind now but the Helder murder.

With nothing to go on but Hargreave's word, he had accepted the Helder death as a homicide!

"Murder?" he grunted as he turned down Fifth. "Now who's the true believer?"

Chapter Sixteen

The Historian

When it came to fellowship, nobody surpassed Deputy Medical Examiner Dr. Hyman B. Turner either in his personal life or his profession. An affable man in his early sixties, he liked to socialize and was a member of several private dinner clubs where he was best known for his recitations of *The Face on the Barroom Floor* and the *Death of Dangerous Dan McGrew*. Short and bald, he had the face of an Old Testament prophet and a winning smile. As to his professional associations, he was listed in *American Men of Science* and *Leaders in American Science* as a fellow of the American Academy of Forensic Sciences, a fellow of the College of American Pathologists, a fellow of the American College of Cardiology, fellow of the New York Cardiological Society and thrice a Fulbright fellow in Forensics and Criminal Pathology at universities in Thailand, the Philippines, and India. Chief among his qualifications for assaying the deaths of individuals absent an attending physician were degrees in Anatomy-Electron Microscopy and Anatomy-Histochemistry, his M.D., being a diplomate of the American Board of Pathology in Forensic Pathology and a diplomate of the American Board of Family Practice; a professorship of Pathology at Columbia University College of Physicians and Surgeons; chairmanship of the National Association of Pathology Professors; and six years as an assistant M.E. at the city's morgue where the corpses he autopsied generally exhibited evidence of having met death violently and suddenly and almost always as the result of a criminal act.

To Detectives Hargreave and Lyman as they sat opposite him at dawn in his austere windowless cubicle of an office painted in hospital green he reported that such had been the case in the demise of Peter Helder. "In the plain language I know you prefer, David," he said, "somebody strangled him first with a leather belt, then strung him up with the rope."

Lyman said, "To make it look like suicide?"

With a tolerant smile the M.E. said, "Why else?"

Hargreave asked, "What's your evidence?"

"Ligature marks on the neck that could come only from a belt. There were no rope burns that result from the sudden constriction and downward pull of a dropping body. There is compelling evidence that he'd been dead several minutes before he was hanged. No broken neck, which you expect in a hanging, although you don't always find it. Then there were the fingernails. You see, if a person is being hanged and the neck isn't broken and the hands are not immobilized the natural reaction is a desperate clawing at the rope, even when it's suicide. Mr. Helder exhibited no such reaction."

"Evidence?"

"Had he, I would have discovered scratches on the neck, blood and shreds of skin under the fingernails. I didn't."

Hargreave asked, "Anything sexual?"

"The man was sexually active but hadn't been engaged in any acts in, I'd say, the twenty-four hours before his death."

"No signs of sadomasochistic activity immediately prior to his death?"

Slowly shaking his head, Dr. Turner said, "You're thinking about the hood as a bondage or S and M accouterment. No, there's nothing about the body that indicates any recent rough stuff. For a man of his years, in fact, there's hardly any damage to the body. He lost the tip of his right little finger years ago. There's a very old scar on his shoulder. Otherwise, his skin is flawless for a fellow his age."

"You won't be able to say the same for me when the day comes that I'm on your table, Hy," said Hargreave, rising to leave. "It'll take you an hour just to note the scar tissue on this corpus once it becomes delicti."

"My dear David," grinned the Deputy M.E., "who'd want to murder someone as lovable as you?"

"Doc, on account of that mask, today alone there's going to be about a hundred members of the Fourth Estate screaming for my scalp."

"So the M.E. proves your instincts were right,"

said Lyman in the car. "Helder was murdered. When are you going to tell the press? They'll be swarming all over the place when we get back to the office."

"Screw the press. We're not going to the office. You and I are going traipsing back through the life of Peter Helder in the hopes that along the way we'll find whoever it was that strangled him with a belt and hung him up to scare the bejesus out of Eleanora Swaim . . . and why."

Between the drawn shade and the glass of the door to the Helder Galleries were two paper signs.

In bold letters in red print on white cardboard:

CRIME SCENE—DO NOT ENTER. N.Y.P.D.

Below it was a small notice on Helder letterhead in Eleanora Swaim's careful penmanship:

BECAUSE OF A DEATH IN THE FAMILY WE ARE CLOSED UNTIL FURTHER NOTICE.

Unlocking the door, Lyman muttered, "Death in the family? Odd way of putting it, don't you think?"

"Not really," said Hargreave. "She probably thought of him that way. Just as you think of me as family. You do, don't you?"

"Sure do, Dad," chuckled Lyman.

"We're looking for Helder's appointment calendar and address book," said Hargreave. "You have a peek in Swaim's desk; I'll search upstairs starting with that gothic library of his."

Si monumentum requiris circumspice, thought

119

Hargreave as he sprung the lock of Helder's enormous antique desk with a heavy dagger-shaped letter opener with an ivory handle carved with what looked like interlocked and overlapping swastikas.

Immediately he found what he was looking for, the personal artifacts of Peter Helder's life: checkbooks, bank statements, a United States passport renewed in March 1966, and a large 1967 date book from Cartier covered in maroon leather to match the accessories on the otherwise bare desktop. Opening it to the previous day, he found numerous appointments neatly listed in ink: an early morning meeting of the board of directors of a charitable organization, the name of a woman with a Sutton Place address with *Degas sculptures* written next to it, an 11:30 appointment for a haircut at the Gotham Hotel, lunch at noon at the Atlantis Club, then "Conference with E.S. re: HG business" at 2:00 with an arrow drawn down the page to 6:00. Below this at 7:00 in pencil was printed DANNY and in smaller script, *Grand Central*.

"Ah, that's interesting," he said.

Leafing forward through the book he found many notations and on a page in the month of June a small envelope containing a pair of tickets for the Music Theater of Lincoln Center's opening on the 12th of its revival of *South Pacific*, all indicating that Helder was a man with his mind set on living, not on killing himself.

"So much for what the future held," said Hargreave, turning back to January. "Let's have a look at the past."

A busy four months unfolded in the pages—
numerous meetings and conferences with bankers
and brokers, several speaking engagements, monthly
gatherings of the bewildering number of artistic and
theatrically oriented groups he apparently belonged
to, weekly haircuts at the Gotham, dental appointments, notes of visits to book dealers and the obscure
titles he'd bought and the extravagant prices he'd
paid to add volumes to his exceptional library, and,
most interesting of all, masculine names written in
pencil in blocks of evening hours. And in a few
instances what appeared to be the places where he was
to rendezvous with those listed.

> Gregory, The Pit.
> Mark, Kelly's.
> Jim, Satan's Anvil.
> Anthony, Circles.
> Cal, the Jewel Box.
> Eddie, Stonewall.

Shown them when he came upstairs, Lyman
promptly declared, "These are all homosexual
hangouts."

"Check 'em," said Hargreave. "See what you can
come up with on somebody Helder had a date with
the night he died; name of Danny. It'll be night work
for you for awhile, but you're a night owl, aren't you?
And while you're sleeping after your evenings on the
town, I'm going to be seeing what I can turn up on
Helder generally. The man led a varied life. So while
you explore his netherworld of the night, I mean to

delve into the rest of it. After all, just because he went to gay bars it doesn't necessarily mean that somebody gay killed him, does it? Most murderers in my experience, indeed in all the history I've studied, have been straight."

Had there not been a Second World War and had David Hargreave not been inflamed with a sense of duty to his country he might have been earning his living as a scholar of history, but when the Japanese bombed Pearl Harbor he'd enlisted in the army intending to punish them. However, in the wisdom and vagaries of the military he was not wanted as a warrior in the Pacific. Rather, he was turned into a military policeman and eventually assigned to Patton's Third Army raging across Europe and into Germany.

There he'd come face to face with the appalling reality of the savagery of the Nazis, first at the Ohrdruf Nord concentration camp and then at Buchenwald where, like Patton, he'd been so sickened that he threw up.

In a letter to Nancy he'd written, "Honestly, words can't express the horror of those places. Of course, we'd all heard rumors about slave labor camps but nobody ever expected to find the horrors that awaited us as we liberated the places. They were death machines! Patton was so incensed that he had the mayor and his wife brought to see the first of the camps and they went home and hanged themselves. General Eisenhower has ordered as many of our soldiers as possible to see what the Nazis did. The scenes we witnessed are beyond the normal mind's imagination. No race except a people dominated by an ideology of sadism could have perpetrated such gruesome crimes. I trust that those in Germany who committed these atrocities will be tracked down to the last man and brought before justice. If it were in my power I would do the job myself, including putting the hangman's noose around their necks."

Besides his lasting outrage over the death camps, what he'd brought out of his service as a military police officer in the war was a liking for the work of law enforcement that eclipsed his passion for history.

Marriage to Nancy and an application to the New York Police Department followed his return, then the Police Academy and patrol duty while taking night classes in criminal justice at John Jay College. Soon he was rising in the ranks and then from the uniformed force into plainclothes. Then came promotion to homicide where he brought to the job all the instincts for digging into the facts, for rooting around in documents and following paper trails. He had a talent for interpreting what he unearthed which would have stood him well as an historian.

These talents for research he now brought to the task of writing the biography of Peter Helder. But, being a policeman, he started in a cop's way, searching the departmental files for a police record. "Not unexpectedly, the man's as clean as a hound's tooth, record-wise," he apprised his partner by telephone, waking up Lyman after his first night of exploring New York's gay scene. "How'd it go for you?"

"Fruitless," yawned Lyman, oblivious to the pun.

"Easy does it, no kicking over the traces in those gay joints; go gently there," Hargreave counseled, silently thinking, "No lights, no siren, Sheldon, please."

Fingerprints were next, requested from the FBI, in the event Helder might have a federal criminal history. When the report came back that there was no file at all on Helder, he was astonished, knowing that the FBI had prints on record for many reasons other than criminality, but immediately he remembered that Helder had been a postwar immigrant from Holland. More likely to have dossiers on him would be the Immigration and Naturalization Service.

At its offices on a high floor of 20 West Broadway downtown a gray-haired scarecrowlike bureaucrat fussed at the idea of opening a confidential file. Flaunting his badge as he glowered threateningly, Hargreave growled, "Now look, Mr. Immigration Man, if you think I won't go right over to Foley Square and get a court order, you got another think coming. I see the file on Helder now or later. So what's it gonna be? Cooperation or a writ?"

Choosing nonconfrontation, the cowed official pressed a button that buzzed open a door. "Go in that room and wait," he said, flicking his eyes toward a cubicle with a window and a stunning view of the Hudson River. Twenty minutes later—the revenge of the bureaucrat—he laid the file before Hargreave.

HELDER, Peter
Date of birth: October 12, 1900
Place of birth: Leyden, the Netherlands
Date of entry: March 15, 1946
Status: political refugee
Occupation: art dealer
Address in USA: The Atlantis Club
                Park Avenue
                New York City
Sponsor(s): H. V. Bork
            c/o The Atlantis Club
Disposition: resident alien status granted,
             3/15/46
Further action: see N file.

Returning the document to the pouty bureaucrat, Hargreave asserted, "Now I have to see Helder's N file."

With arching eyebrows, the bureaucrat snapped, "Had there been an N file I would have brought it."

"I see. Just what is an N file?"

"N stands for Naturalization. It would contain all the documents pertinent to the processes of requesting, qualifying for, and being granted United States citizenship. If there is no N file, the individual was never granted citizenship status."

"And without it being granted, what would happen?"

"When that person's visa expired, he would have to leave the country."

"Without a passport?"

"He would use whatever passport he had when he entered the country, the passport of his nativity."

"Is it possible that the N file in this instance has been misplaced?"

Snorting his outrage, the bureaucrat replied, "In my thirty years in this service, Mr. Police Detective, I have never seen it happen."

"Is it possible for someone who didn't get an N file to have obtained a U.S. passport?"

"Quite . . . IM-possible!"

Chapter Seventeen

The Man With No Past

"The guy has no N file yet he has a U.S. passport. How do you figure that, Sheldon?"

It was dusk and their paths were crossing in a coffee shop across 100th Street from Manhattan North noisy with cops at a change of shifts but the best place to brief one another on their daytime/nighttime investigations.

"It's probably some snafu," said Lyman, "a screwup at Immigration and Naturalization or the State Department."

"Well, I've shot off a rocket to Washington about it. I can only hope it doesn't get lost like Helder's N file," said Hargreave grumpily as he scrutinized Lyman's outfit. Clothed to blend with the Friday crowds in which he expected to mingle in Greenwich Village, he had on blue bell-bottoms, tan suede desert boots, a loud madras jacket and one of his old khaki

Marine Corps shirts open at the neck to reveal a necklace of small white seashells. Scowling, Hargreave said, "What peace march are you going to, you overage hippie?"

"What I worry about in this getup," said Lyman, twisting his beads and cracking a grin, "is that I'll have the make put on me by some undercover dude working an antiwar surveillance for the FBI."

"I gather there's been no sign of Danny."

"It's really too soon. I'm still the new kid on the block. The boys are still standoffish."

"I thought in that world the new kid was the immediate object of everyone's attention."

"I've met a lot of the boys."

"A handsome gallant like you? I'm sure!"

"But there's a lot of paranoia in the Village these days. I was only half-joking with that FBI crack, what with Vietnam and the civil-rights movement and the usual hassling of the gays by the guys from the public morals squad."

"Have you picked up any talk about Helder?"

"Plenty. Although nothing beyond what you'd hear in any straight bar around town since Lomax broke the story about the mask."

"The bastard has probably queered—sorry— *ruined* any chance we might have had of tying that grim little item to Helder's killer."

"What's next on your agenda, boss?"

"More digging into Helder's straight life. His murder aside, it's a damned interesting story. A postwar refugee—what we called back then a D.P., for displaced person—lands in New York apparently penniless in 1946 and nineteen years later is apparently as rich as Croesus. Maybe richer. I'd like to know just how much Helder was worth and who stands to benefit from his death. So tomorrow while you're sleeping off your night in the Village—alone, I trust, no FBI men under your covers—I will be swimming in a sea of lawyers and bankers."

The law offices of E.S. Rickards and Associates were a duplex aerie at the foot of Broadway overlooking the Battery, the harbor, and the Statue of Liberty. While primarily tending to the legal affairs of Wall Street firms and individuals, because of its founder's interest in New York's cultural community, the firm had a sizeable but select clientele from the artistic, entertainment, and broadcasting worlds.

Representing Peter Helder was the head of that department, John Hector McFarlane, whom Hargreave judged to be rather young-looking for his elevated position. He was, he also deduced from an assortment of medicine bottles next to a water glass and a silver carafe on a silver tray on a table behind his desk, an asthmatic. And from the pin in the lapel of his dark blue pinstripe suit, a Freemason.

To examine the last will and testament of Mr. Helder before it was probated, McFarlane advised Hargreave, an order from a court would be required.

"Obtaining a writ would take two days," Hargreave replied. "I was hoping we could circumvent the red tape," he smiled.

"Not a chance," said the lawyer.

Miffed, Hargreave snapped, "Then I'll see you in two days, Mr. McFarlane."

A brisk walk up Broadway and then along Centre Street were the offices of the District Attorney where Sandra Hargreave's window provided a view of an air shaft. Gathering bulging bundles of briefs for the impending opening of criminal court fifteen floors below her cubicle, she looked beautiful to her father. And startled. "Dad, what a surprise." And harried. "I'm in a rush!"

"Okay, short and sweet. Who do you know in the Registrar of Wills?"

"Stacy Cahn."

"Is she a good old girl?"

"Sure. Why?"

"Be a good daughter and take a second to call her and tell her your good old dad needs a favor from a good old girl."

A career as a fashion model seemed more appropriate for her, thought Hargreave as he waited while the tall and slender young woman with sculptured features, doe eyes, and shoulder-length raven hair searched to determine if Peter Helder were in the files. "It's a fairly old will," she declared, bringing a document to him at her desk. "Dated 1949."

In that same year Helder had opened his first gallery, Hargreave noted as he unfolded the legal-sized pages and scanned the boilerplate to get to the section of the will in which Helder spelled out bequests to beneficiaries. It read, "Now, therefore, I, Peter Helder, do hereby give, devise, and bequeath my Estate, both real and equitable, and wheresoever situate, to the Atlantis Club."

"Now that's interesting," mumbled Hargreave as

he turned to the signatures of witnesses at the end of the document, all listing their addresses as the Atlantis Club. "Doubly interesting," he muttered, flipping back through the boilerplate looking for the person Helder had designated as the executor of the estate. "H. V. Bork, President, the Atlantis Club," he read aloud. Remembering it as the same name Helder had listed as his sponsor in his file at Immigration and Naturalization, he said, "Triple interesting."

Looking up from her work, Stacy Cahn said, "Beg pardon?"

"Just talking to myself," he said with a smile. "Old cops do that, you know."

"You're not so old," she beamed.

Handing her the will, he said, "Thanks for this."

"Found what you were looking for?"

"Yes I did, Miss Cahn, but on this case it seems that whenever I find an answer to one question I wind up with a new one. Thanks again. I owe you one."

"Well, if I ever need a murder solved . . ."

"Don't hesitate to call me," he laughed, leaving.

The Consulate of the Netherlands, his next stop, was listed in the Manhattan telephone directory with a Rockefeller Center address. The request he had seemed simple enough; a search of government files in Holland for anything pertaining to Helder prior to 1946 and going back as far as possible.

"I'm afraid it will not be so easy, Mr. Hargreave," explained a tall platinum blonde with the name Helga ten Dorn printed on an identification tag pinned to the lapel of her navy blue blazer. "You see,

131

the records are incomplete because of the war. During the occupation of our country the Nazis took many of the files. The Nazis were hunting for Jews, of course, and the documents related to persons who were active in the Resistance; all those who were working against them."

"Which was practically the entire country, starting with your king," exclaimed Hargreave.

Pride in her countrymen's illustrious defiance of the Nazis shone in her eyes as she said, "Many records were destroyed in the war itself, as well. It made a lot of trouble for people after the war, of course; people who needed documents and couldn't find them. Many people were left with nothing to show of their past. Mr. Helder may have been one of them."

"Nonetheless, I'd appreciate it if you'd be kind enough to put through my request anyway. This is a murder investigation."

"Yes, I read it in the newspapers. How awful."

Lunchtime and the beckoning warm May sun created a carnivallike atmosphere in Rockefeller Center that prompted Hargreave to pause, peeling off his jacket and lining up behind other coatless men and women to buy two hot dogs and a bottle of Coca-Cola from a pushcart purveyor. Consuming them, he leaned against a wall in front of the splendid shaft of the RCA Building and peered past the gilt head of the statue of Prometheus gazing down with benevolent eyes at the festive New Yorkers swirling around and through the area at which there was no better place for eating lunch and which Hargreave believed was the true heart and the very essence of this city that he'd loved all his life and had been proud to serve by carrying a badge.

Finished, he tossed his paper napkins in a trash bin, returned the empty Coke bottle to the vendor, and began strolling east to Park Avenue and Peter Helder's frequent lunching spot, the Atlantis Club.

Chapter Eighteen

Pharaoh von Bork

Waiting in the awesome hush of the cool marble lobby of the mansion, Hargreave had a feeling of vague expectancy. When he had flashed his shield and asked a soldierly young doorkeeper dressed in a maroon coat with gold braid that was much too heavy for the season if Mr. H.V. Bork were on the premises he'd been answered with a curt, "You mean Mr. *von* Bork," the *von* sounding like *fun* as Hargreave handed him his business card.

"One moment, please," the doorman had said, turning to carry his card and his request up a long red-carpeted staircase.

Although he had returned promptly saying, "The President will be down directly," fifteen minutes had passed, the last five of them marked by Hargreave's rising anger at being kept waiting—and standing— in the chairless, cheerless white and gold lobby. "Another minute," he was saying to himself, "and I march up those steps."

At that moment there appeared at the top of the stairs a tall figure with a broad torso and spindling legs silhouetted for a moment and resembling a wandering eagle perching and turning his head down as if to peer with preying eyes at a morsel below. He descended slowly and softly, his long thin arms crossed before him. He wore a black coat and a stiff white shirt with a gray bowtie, and resembled nothing less than a mortician coming down to greet the bereaved. He did not offer a handshake as he said crisply, "I am von Bork. How may I be of help to you, Lieutenant Hargreave?"

"It concerns Peter Helder and it should be private," said Hargreave forcefully.

Entering a cavernous room that seemed to be littered with Egyptian furniture, sandstone statues of Pharaohs, and fanciful carvings of the half-man, half-animal gods of the distant kingdoms of the Nile, Hargreave had the feeling that he was reliving one of Sandra's attempts to uplift him by dragging him to the Metropolitan Opera's production of *Aida*.

Whether the artifacts of von Bork's office were genuine or museum-quality reproductions was beyond his telling but that they were a valid reflection of von Bork's consuming interest in Egypt was not in doubt. On a finger was a gold ring bearing a cartouche inscribed with three hieroglyphs, presumably his initials. Gold cufflinks were in the form of the funeral mask of King Tut. Framed photographs of him taken at the Pyramids of Giza, in front of the Sphinx, and amid the looming pillars of the Temple of Luxor hung among the brilliantly colored papyrus art of chariots, kings, and everyday peasant life which festooned the wood-paneled walls.

On an intricately carved Egyptian-style credenza behind a similarly made desk stood framed pictures of von Bork with both the grossly obese King Farouk and the square-jawed Egyptian Army General who'd deposed him, Gamal Abdel Nasser, President of Egypt.

"Excuse my ignorance, Mr. von Bork," said Hargreave as he dropped into an ornate wooden chair with lion paw feet, "but just what is the Atlantis Club? Some kind of geographical society or explorers' club?"

"We are a little of both and a lot more," said von Bork, settling behind his massive desk. "We are men with an interest in learning about and improving the world through the genius of mankind as reflected down through the ages in philosophy, politics, the arts, and sciences."

"Very interesting," said Hargreave.

"We believe that the fruitful evolution of mankind in the future relies on a thorough understanding of the tides of history," continued von Bork. "Therefore we undertake the cultivation of research in those areas. Each of us brings to the club a certain expertise or viewpoint. And each member has some special project. We have members who are deeply concerned about the environment and the deleterious effects of industrialization and the exploitation of natural resources. We have ardent conservationists worried about the world's diminishing wildlife and members who are deeply concerned about the finite nature of the earth's minerals and energy resources. Others are oceanologists interested in all things maritime. We are broad-minded men with interests running the gamut of human experience."

"This beautiful office of yours indicates that your interest is Egypt."

"All of the Middle East, actually."

"Quite a troublesome hot spot lately."

"Yes, Lieutenant, but I don't believe the work of the Atlantis Club or the crises of the Middle East brought you here this afternoon."

"Right you are," smiled Hargreave. "I'm in charge of the investigation into the murder of a member of your club, Mr. Helder."

Impassively sphinxlike until now, von Bork's face came alive with surprise. "Murder? The news reports said it had been a suicide."

"So it seemed at first. Now there's no question it was homicide."

"My word," he gasped. "Who would want to kill Peter?"

"That's what I'm hoping to find out. So, like you fellows here in the Atlantis Club digging into mankind's past, I'm looking into Helder's history. A very interesting story it seems to be, too."

"He was quite an impressive man, indeed," said von Bork, a sphinx again. "Being an art connoisseur, Peter Helder had been especially devoted to enlisting the Atlantis Club in efforts to keep Venice, Italy, from sinking into the sea and in preserving its artistic antiquities. He was quite an authority on Venice."

"I especially wanted to talk to you, Mr. von Bork, because I noted in Helder's records that you go way back with him. I believe you sponsored him into the country in 1946."

"I was honored to do so, sir."

"May I ask how it was you knew him then? You being here in America and Helder being in the Netherlands."

"I'd met him before the war," said von Bork as he lifted a hand-size blue stone in the shape of a beetle from amidst the desktop's array of small artifacts: an alabaster sphinx, a small coiled snake that looked like genuine gold, the god Horus in the form of the lithesome youth with a falcon's head in smooth onyx, and a dagger with the jackal-headed diety Anubis for a handle. "There was an Atlantis Club in Amsterdam of which Peter was a member. I was invited to speak to it in 1940. At war's end he contacted me to enlist my assistance in his coming to America. I was happy to do so. And he was grateful for the aid we here in the club were able to provide."

"He certainly must have been to have made the Atlantis Club his sole heir."

"I didn't know," said the sphinx.

"Yes, sir. I've seen the will."·

"How good of him."

"I imagine it should be a pretty big inheritance. From all that I've seen of Mr. Helder's possessions, he was very wealthy—the Helder Galleries, that opulent mansion over on Madison Avenue, the furnishings, his private art collection, that fabulous library of his. Yes, quite a wealthy man."

"By ordinary standards, yes," said von Bork, "but there are several of our Atlanteans who are many, many times richer than Peter."

"Atlanteans. Atlantis. Am I correct in assuming that those names are taken from the so-called ancient continent of Atlantis that supposedly sank into the Atlantic Ocean?"

"Correct, except that you could get into an argument with members of the club who contend that Atlantis was an island in the Aegean Sea. A few insist that it was in the North Atlantic. But it isn't the location of Atlantis that we are interested in. The Atlantis Club is rooted in the ideals of Atlantis."

"And they were . . . ?"

"They *are* the classic virtues, the perfection to which men are exhorted to strive to attain by all the religions and a few governments and which, we believe, the people of ancient Atlantis had already achieved before calamity overtook them. That is why, if you'll forgive me for saying so, Lieutenant Hargreave, you're on the wrong track if you suspect that a member of the Atlantis Club might be connected with Peter's death."

"I don't suspect anyone, sir. I'm just trying to get a homicide investigation cranked up and the classic way of doing that is by getting to know the victim. It was Aristotle who said, 'Know thyself.' If Aristotle had been a cop he would have said, 'Know thy victim.' Is it possible for me to get a list of members of the Atlantis Club? Current and past?"

"The current list is no problem. The past, however, could be. We date back to 1895."

"No need to go that far. How about to, say, 1946?"

"In other words, you want a list of all Atlanteans since Peter's arrival on our shores."

"Exactly!"

"It may take a day or two."

"I may not possess all the virtues, Mr. von Bork, but I do have one of them—patience."

"A necessity in your line of work, I'm sure."

"About the list of members—can you include their addresses? I guarantee they'll be held in strictest confidence."

"Whatever you wish, Lieutenant Hargreave."

Chapter Nineteen
Gods and Men

Hargreave whistled the Grand March from *Aida* softly while gods and their men paraded through his head; or should the proper order be men and their gods? he wondered as he stepped out of the stifling Atlantis Club with its stuffy pharaonic factotum and into the May afternoon with the air as fresh as it ever got to be in New York City in the latter part of the 1960s when all the present gods seemed to be under assault. Turning off Park Avenue he walked over to and up Madison to give Peter Helder's mansion one more going-over.

Even though he had bent departmental rules to allow her to have access to the Helder Galleries for work that she'd insisted could not wait a few more days, Eleanora Swaim shot him an icy look from her desk with its unobstructed view of the private entrance.

From such a vantage point, he believed, she could

not have been as ignorant as she'd insisted she was of her employer's secret life among comely gay boys and those who may not have been gay but hired out their muscular bodies to men like him. Yet there she sat staring daggers at him for intruding into Helder's life and hers, as though his presence were what had shattered her carefully structured existence and not the sudden revelation of what went on secretly in Helder's downstairs room.

As shocked and horrified as she'd been in being the one to discover the grotesque evidence of his life in that guarded netherworld that was probably anathema to everything she'd been taught to believe, she steadfastly clung to him. And worshipped him. Soon because of her, he expected, there would appear in the Fine Arts Section of the *Times* an announcement of a memorial service for him. And everyone who was anyone in his world of art, artists, and the patrons of the arts—and members of the Atlantis Club—would attend. Someone, no doubt, would rise to declare the establishment of an endowment, the creation of a foundation or the funding of a chair at some university in Peter Helder's honor. The beatification of another demigod of their closed and clannish world would be completed, just as the ancient Egyptians whom von Bork admired had enshrined theirs.

Opening the oak doors of the library, Hargreave wondered if Helder had a god. Or gods. If not, had there been a god in his past? As a boy growing up in Holland did he believe in the Jesus Christ of the Dutch Reformed Church? Had he believed in Father Christmas or Kris Kringle or whatever the Dutch called their version of Santa Claus? Did he believe the Christmas story at all? Might he have been a Roman Catholic? An altar boy?

"Know thy victim," said Hargreave as he ran a finger along the spines of the books on the library shelves and entertained the fascinating question as to why, if Helder had been a Christian in his youth, his mind had wandered so far from the catechism of the Christ of the Sermon on the Mount to these murky realms that surely would have required admission to a confessional box if Helder were a practicing Catholic. Here in painstakingly categorized and neatly ordered row upon row were soul-endangering subjects indeed: astrology, numerology, black magic, Satanism, demons and demonology, runes, spells, witchcraft, incantations, mesmerism, the Freemasons, occult practices and beliefs of secret societies and movements through the ages from the *hashshashin* of Arabia who gave the world the word and the practice of assassination, to the Thugs of India who committed murders in honor of the Hindu goddess Kali, to the Druids, and finally to the Nazis.

Clearly, Hargreave reasoned as he left the books and crossed to Helder's desk, the sinister chamber that Helder had built downstairs and where he'd been strangled and then hanged with his head enshrouded in a black hood was an extension of these dark books that were of such interest to Helder upstairs.

From the inside pocket of his jacket as he sat at the desk he drew a small brown notebook where he jotted items to be remembered about the case on which he was working. Usually these were in the form of questions to himself. Like a reporter's, they were Who? What? Where? When? Why? How? Regarding Peter Helder's death, four had been easily answered.

Sometime between midnight and dawn two days ago, Peter Helder had been strangled to death with a leather belt, a black hood had been pulled over his head and he'd been hoisted by a hangman's noose to the rafter of his secret sadomasochistic chamber below his art galleries to create the illusion of suicide.

The two questions that remained were the most important: who killed him? And why?

Instinct and experience whispered to Hargreave that he probably would not be able to answer the former unless and until he understood the latter.

"Know thy victim," he muttered again, pocketing his notebook. *"Si monumentum requiris circumspice,"* he said, tilting back in the chair and staring wonderingly across the room at the books.

Presently, not having been struck by a bolt of illuminating lightning that revealed the solution to this baffling crime, he left the mansion, noting that Eleanora Swaim had also departed, and walked six blocks east and five south to his own home—a third-floor walk-up apartment in a tidy brownstone near York Avenue on Seventy-fifth Street which he had shared with a wife in twenty-four years of her health and one of illness and dying.

Peeling off his coat in the room that used to be his daughter's bedroom and which he now called his den, he dropped wearily into a recliner Nancy and Sandra had given him for his fortieth birthday along with a color TV set opposite it.

He used the TV very little in his time off

preferring to read. "Meager and narrow," are what he would have said if asked to describe his own library, consisting of four bookcases of unpainted pine that he'd bought at one of the handy and inexpensive finish-it-yourself furniture stores that flourished in a city of apartments.

Staring at his books as he had gazed at Helder's, he could see how a stranger perusing the shelves would conclude that the reader of these books had to be a cop: *Penal Law and Criminal Procedure* in its black looseleaf binder for annual updating, *The Detection of Murder* by William F. Kessler and Paul B. Weston, *Arson* by Weston and Brendan P. Battle, *Handbook of Criminal Investigation* by Maurice J. Fitzgerald, *Plainclothesman* by Capt. Frederick W. Egen of the NYPD, Andreas Bjerre's admirable *The Psychology of Murder*, Virgil Peterson's *Barbarians in Our Midst*, LeMoyne Snyder's *Homicide Investigation*, and the old but still reliable *Murder and its Motives* by F. Tennyson Jesse.

The fiction? Just as illuminating! The old warhorses of the murder and mayhem genre: *The Complete Sherlock Holmes*, Dashiell Hammett, Raymond Chandler, S.S. Van Dine, James M. Cain, Graham Greene, Agatha Christie, Georges Simenon, Ellery Queen, and Earl Derr Biggers's Charlie Chan. Hargreave also had a growing collection of the newer practitioners of crime writing: Robert Fish, Ross MacDonald, Ed McBain and his gritty cops of the 87th Precinct Squad, Ian Fleming's licensed-to-kill secret agent James Bond, and Alexander Somerfield, a former crime reporter turned foreign correspondent turned mystery writer whose fictional hard-boiled dick sleuthed in New York in the 1930s.

Somerfield's latest, *The Fuhrer of 86th Street*, was waiting half-read beside Hargreave's bed, a yarn about a nest of Nazi spies working out of a restaurant in Yorkville's "Germantown" only a few blocks uptown from Hargreave's apartment.

In all of this literature what was required to prove murder? "Means, opportunity, and motive."

Picking up Somerfield's book, Hargreave asked himself, What was the motive in Helder's murder?

Was it as complex as Helder himself?

Would he find it in Helder's intricate daytime life of money, prestige, high society, the art world, and exclusive clubs?

Or would it be explained simply, unearthed by Sheldon Lyman as he voyaged through the dark passages of Helder's netherworld of the night?

Chapter Twenty

Stone Walls and Shadows

Cupping his hands to light a Marlboro cigarette in front of the all-night drugstore on the lusty northeast corner of Sixth Avenue and Eighth Street, Lyman peered across Sixth to where wide Greenwich Street ended and narrow Christopher Street began, a juncture of arteries that were as life-giving and sustaining to the Village as those of the human heart. It was Thursday night and the phenomenon which the news media trumpeted as the Sexual Revolution of the Sixties was in full swing. In a casual mixture of civilian and military garb Lyman was geared for it. Coatless, he had on tight bell-bottom blue jeans, a twisted rainbow-hued tie-dyed sash around his narrow waist for a belt and his Marine Corps short-sleeve tan shirt open at the neck to show his love beads. Hanging from his shoulder was a snakeskin bag about which the desk sergeant at Manhattan North had cracked, "Quite the fashion these days, I hear."

On Christopher Street stood the stonefront bar that had become his starting point during his nocturnal plumbing of Peter Helder's nighttime world in search of someone named Danny. One of the most popular of all the gay establishments he'd gotten to know, it was a long narrow room hazy with a mixture of tobacco and marijuana smoke, dimly lighted and with the bar down the middle. The crowd seemed very young, Lyman thought, and probably underage but enforcement of state liquor laws was not why he'd come to this bar whose name had come to symbolize what he'd encountered everywhere in the Village gay scene so far during his undercover investigation—Stonewall.

Immediately it had become clear to him that if anyone in the places he'd visited had known Helder or knew Helder's friend Danny, no one was admitting it. Hitting the stone wall of silence about Helder that had clearly been thrown up by the understandably frightened and nervous patrons of the gay bars as fast as the Communists had put the Berlin Wall, he'd become a listener hoping to pick up a lead on Danny by eavesdropping that direct questioning had failed to produce.

By now he was becoming a familiar presence in the bars and was able to size up a place in the first few seconds after entering, spotting among the known faces the new one who might not be so inhibited about Helder and Danny or who might be Danny. He'd become used to being scrutinized himself when he came into a gay bar and no longer feared, as he had at first, that he had "cop" written all over him. But

148

quickly he'd noticed that everyone was looked at when entering a gay bar. Being given the once-over was natural. The custom. To be expected.

Accordingly, turning to look at the newcomer himself had become natural for him. And as ordinary as it was for all the others to approach someone and strike up a conversation, it had become easy for him to exchange pleasantries, introduce himself and ask the name of the other and hoping to hear him say, "Hi. I'm Danny." He did not know if anyone had noticed that he differed from the other patrons of the bars in that he left them as he'd entered them—alone.

Except for its gay clientele, the Stonewall did not seem different from countless other joints and plenty of police hangouts he'd been in—raucous and noisy and brimming with the unbridled male conviviality of bellying up to a bar.

Far different and even more impenetrable were the cellars that were the riverfront leather saloons and S and M haunts that he and Hargreave had found listed in Peter Helder's calendar: The Pit, Circles, and Satan's Avil. Dark, dank, and dangerous-looking, these joyless black holes and their sullen ranks of black-clad men seemed to be the most likely shadows out of which would creep a killer capable of twisting a leather belt ito a garrot.

Opening late, they flourished only after midnight and required Lyman to change his clothing, converting the amiable, polite, gently spoken, and handsome young man of the gay Stonewall where he carried his Smith & Wesson Police Special in the fashionably correct but definitely masculine snake-skin shoulder bag into a surly, swaggering, and

149

leather-geared tough guy with his gun tucked into an ankle holster inside his boot.

"Another night with not a damned thing to report," he advised Hargreave by phone at six o'clock the next morning from his studio apartment on the upper West Side while Hargreave was getting dressed on East Seventy-fifth Street.

"Patience and fortitude, Shel," said Hargreave, his LaGuardian vocabulary stirred afresh after finishing Alexander Somerfield's nifty mystery yarn about a long-vanished New York. "The break will come."

"What's on your agenda today?"

"More of the same. Rooting around in Helder's past. I'll be checking in at the office first. I'm expecting a call from a woman at the Dutch consulate."

"Take your umbrella," Lyman added grumpily. "It's raining."

"I never carry the damned things," said Hargreave. "They either leak, get blown inside out, or wind up lost."

Had the weather not changed, he would have preferred to walk through Central Park to the West Side and perhaps all the way to 100th Street, but the rain was hard and steady and miserably cold, making the wearing of a hat and a raincoat and taking the crosstown bus a more sensible choice.

Certainly, the man who followed him onto the bus found it so.

Awaiting Hargreave at Manhattan North was a message for him to call Helga ten Dorn. "I have received an answer to my query from the Ministry of Interior in the Netherlands," she said, a sunny voice on a bleak morning. "They have nothing in the records regarding Mr. Peter Helder. I am sorry."

From Mr. von Bork of the Atlantis Club was a message scrawled in the handwriting of the desk sergeant. "The list you asked for can be picked up from the doorman after 10:00."

Slipping both messages into his notebook, he muttered. "That was quick."

In a pale blue envelope with the crest of the Atlantis Club in the form of the Roman god Neptune holding a trident, the list of names of the club's members since 1946 and their addresses was a document half an inch thick.

Curled and stuffed into a pocket of his raincoat, it was balanced an hour later by an envelope containing the flimsy sheets of a computer printout of records provided readily by Helder's Wall Street bank.

These Hargreave studied while being observed eating a lunch of a hamburger and french fries and a Coke in a crowded, noisy, and steamy Broadway coffee shop two blocks away from the next stop on his rainy odyssey through Helder's financial history.

"The transactions of our clients are held in strict confidence," said the slender fidgety youth to whom Hargreave was shuttled at the offices of a stock brokerage firm to which Helder had written numerous checks in large amounts. "But seeing that it's a police matter, I guess the usual rules can't apply."

"You guess right," smiled Hargreave.

"Mr. Helder was a major investor with our firm," the youth said. "The file will be substantial. It will take time to pull it together."

"I'll wait."

Two hours later, three inches of photocopied files of ten years of Peter Helder's stock transactions weighed on Hargreave's lap during a half-hour ride on the uptown bus in slackening rain.

By the time he got off at Seventy-fifth Street and Third Avenue the leaden skies showed breaks and there was a rising wind that caused Hargreave to walk with his head down to keep his hat from being blown off, a diversion that contributed to his not noticing, as he crossed First Avenue and passed a hatless man in a blue raincoat, that the man fell in behind him, a shadow on a sunless day.

Chapter Twenty-One

The Quick and the Dead

Walking across the sunny tarmac to board an El Al jetliner at Lod, Amnon Dorot could still hear the anxious voice of the General. "You must leave immediately for the United States, Amnon." Spread before him on his desk were two three-day-old New York tabloid newspapers, their front pages black with headlines about the death of Peter Helder:

THE CORPSE WORE
SADISTIC MASK

BLACK HOOD HORROR:
THE MYSTERY DEATH
OF ART DEALER

Glaring down at the unmistakable face of Colonel August Grenier in the form of photos of Helder accompanying the headlines, the General asked,

"When was the last time you heard from Daniel?"

"We've heard nothing," sighed Amnon. "He was running silent, sir. Orders were that he contact his control only to request the intervention of an action team to pick up Grenier or to send up a distress rocket."

"Apparently he wrote himself a new set of orders," said the General bitterly.

"Sir, you can't believe that Daniel did this," said Amnon urgently. "It's impossible for him to have taken it upon himself."

"What else am I to think? One would have expected him to notify us immediately of this," the General grumbled, slapping a hand on the newspapers. "How do you explain it?"

"I can't, sir. But I find it difficult to accept the idea that Daniel would take unauthorized action against this man."

"By God, do you realize what the repercussions would be if the Americans were to arrest Daniel for murder and then discover that he's an Israeli agent? The public would be outraged, and rightly so. Congress would be furious. And rightly so. President Johnson would be in an untenable situation. Even the leaders of the American Jewry would have to condemn us. Never mind that the son of a bitch he killed was a fugitive war criminal."

"There's no evidence that Daniel killed this man Helder," argued Amnon. "Nor that Helder was the Nazi Grenier."

"He was Grenier all right," thundered the General, glaring at the newspaper photos. "No mistake!"

"The resemblance is remarkable," admitted Amnon.

"If our man didn't kill him, then why haven't we heard from him? Why hasn't he sent up that distress rocket? Where is Daniel Ben Avram? You must go to New York, Amnon. You must find our man before the American police do. You have to locate him and bring him back to Israel. It is vital that the Americans make no connection between the death of this monster and the Government of Israel. Especially at this time. Not now when there are clear signs that our enemies are marshaling their forces for an attack. We are facing a grave crisis in which the support of the Americans will be crucial. Can you imagine how much we'll get if one of our agents is charged with murdering an American citizen?"

"Naturalized," said Amnon, a foolish legal nicety dismissed with an incredulous twitch of the General's angry mouth and a curt, "Leave for New York at once!"

In the hours while Amnon Dorot was flying toward Kennedy International Airport the New York newspapers made no mention of the Helder case on their front pages, carrying only small items adjacent to the obituaries that Miss Eleanora Swaim, Curator of the Helder Galleries, had announced that a brief memorial service would be held two days hence immediately after Helder's cremation at an upper West Side nonsectarian mortuary.

"I knew it would be so," chuckled Homicide Lieutenant David Hargreave as he clipped the item printed in the *Daily News* and placed it into his case notebook and filed the date and place of the service in his mental memo book with the intention of attending, in keeping with the old adage among cops that was made so much of in detective novels that the killer "just might show up at the funeral" and, presumably, give himself away, to which Hargreave said, "Fat chance."

A lack of expectations notwithstanding, he attended the noontime services, dragging Lyman with him in spite of the young detective's sleepless night in another vain search of the gay bars and S and M cellars for Danny. Positioned in the memorial chapel to see all who came to pay their last respects to Helder, Hargreave drew Lyman's attention to a delegation from the Atlantis Club. Four men in black suits led by von Bork, they sat tight-lipped as Eleanora Swaim was eulogizing her late employer. Hargreave looked at them and supposed that each was wishing Helder safe passage to Nirvana or wherever Atlanteans went when they died.

If it had been one of them who'd killed Helder, why?

Because their club was heir to his considerable fortune?

Was there bad blood between Helder and one of the members? Might there have been an estrangement so profound between Helder and one of them—or all of them—that his death had been required? A vendetta? Payment for a betrayal of some kind?

Why not?

Murder was almost always an act between people who knew one another. There were cases in police files of homicides in the cloisters of monasteries and seminaries. Why not within the tight brotherhood of the Atlantis Club?

Celebrities of Helder's other circles attended the service, Hargreave and his partner noted. Suave gentlemen and elegant women whose faces when adorning the society pages were usually alight with smiles, now were grim visaged and attired in black—the patrons and patronesses of the arts and the myriad museums, foundations, and charities which had counted Peter Helder among their benefactors and boosters. In their world of riches and rivalries, who might be capable of murder?

Much younger mourners had come, a few whom Lyman recognized from the bars. Would they remember him and perhaps begin wondering about him? he thought.

A smattering of the Fourth Estate had come, among them Dick Lomax looking for anything that might catapult the languishing Helder mystery onto the front pages again. Or, in Lomax's medium, on the air as the leading story every twenty-two minutes. He asked, "Anything new, Lieutenant?"

Hargreave replied, "No."

"Would you say that the hood indicates that Helder was a weirdo?"

Groaning, Hargreave said, "C'mon, Dick, stop fishing!"

"Can I report that you're at a dead end?"

"You can report anything you want to," smiled Hargreave. "And you usually do."

Leaving the mortuary and searching the somber faces of the mourners as they passed, Lyman asked himself, "Where's Danny?"

In that black throng and silently asking the same dark question was Amnon Dorot. "Where *was* Danny?"

In a different form he'd asked the question that morning at the registration desk of the Hotel Lexington. "Can you tell me if a Mr. Joshua Goldstein is staying here?"

Checking the records, the clerk had said, "The gentleman is on the books, sir. Room 1416."

"Is he in at the moment?"

"Try the house telephone, sir."

When there'd been no answer he'd gone up to the room. Knocking, he'd gotten no response. Trained to enter locked rooms, he did so. A deft searcher of other people's belongings and an expert interpreter of what he encountered, he found in the tidy room all the signs of peaceful occupation. Nothing in the room itself immediately indicated anything amiss.

Clothing Daniel had been wearing when he'd boarded the plane in Israel was hanging in a closet along with some new apparel. Receipts for these items were folded neatly into a notebook tucked into a pocket of his locked suitcase, pried open with Col. Amnon Dorot's Swiss Army knife as expertly as the door had been jimmied.

In addition to the receipts for the newly acquired clothing hanging in the closet were sales slips from a shop in Greenwich Village specializing in leather wear. No items of that nature were to be seen anywhere in the room, Amnon noted as he carried the receipts and the notebook to a desk. Conclusion? "He's wearing them." Odd stuff for a warm day in May, he thought as he peered at himself in the mirror above the desk.

As people do who sit at hotel room desks, he pulled open the drawers. Nothing of value, nothing instructive. Merely thin piles of Hotel Lexington stationery and a Gideon Bible. The metal oval-shaped waste basket under the desk was empty. Ash trays were clean, doubtless the work of a daily visit to the room by a maid who'd also made the bed, thus obliterating any clue as to when Daniel slept in it last.

Pointless, too, seemed an examination of the bathroom which the maid had tidied up even to the extent of mopping up water from the bathtub and the lavatory, leaving no clue as to their last use. But upon the gleaming white porcelain sink he found an array of Daniel's toiletries. A metal Gillette safety razor was as dry as a bone. Twisting it open and examining the double-edged blade inside, he found flecks of rust. The nozzle of an aerosol can of Rise shaving cream was encrusted with the lacelike leavings of long-dried white lather. Picking up a red-handled tooth brush, he gently stroked the bristles. Crushing them down, he noted crispness. And that they were also quite dry. Clearly, Daniel hadn't shaved and brushed his teeth this morning. Nor yesterday and maybe not the day before.

Returning to the bedroom and the desk, he turned his attention to the notebook with its neatly printed but cryptic entries, each on a dated page. The last, he observed, had been the night before Peter Helder had been discovered hanged with nothing on his corpse but a leather hood.

Suddenly he was swept by a sickening feeling that Daniel Ben Avram clad in his new leather outfit might have taken it upon himself to be the instrument of righteous vengeance.

Frantically flipping through the pages of Daniel's notebook that registered each day of Operation Judah since Daniel's arrival in New York, he searched for any indication that something had gone amiss, for any clue however slight that might point to a decision to ignore orders and all his training at Kfar Sirkin and become a cold-blooded murderer and an ignominy in the history of Israel.

What he found in the pages was all that he had expected and hoped to find—the detailed record of all the actions Daniel had taken, none pointing to a secret agenda of his own.

Of course, if you were planning your own private action, asked the *moyl* of Kfar Sirkin while he pocketed Daniel's notebook, you wouldn't write it down, would you?

Opening the desk, he took out paper and wrote, "Judah, I am here," signed it A.D., sealed it in an envelope and left it with the desk clerk who slipped it into the mail slot for room 1416.

Chapter Twenty-Two

Table Talk

Looking across the dinner table at his partner, Hargreave saw himself two decades ago: lean and fit, tough in both mind and body, ambitious. "These are the up-and-comers in the Department," the Captain of Manhattan North Homicide had pronounced, handing over the personnel files of those who had put in applications when the grapevine was buzzing with the news that there'd been a retirement and that Lieutenant Hargreave was looking for a new partner. On paper, Lyman was almost beyond belief. Brains, expert with all the firearms, great psychological profiles, aces on the exam for Sergeant, top-notch performance evaluations, commendations for heroism. Ex-Marine. Fire in the belly. Full of the requisite zeal.

Paperwork and red tape took two weeks to make them a team, though destiny, it seemed to Hargreave, had decreed it.

At the zenith of the arc between him and Lyman at the round table in the midst of the bubbling cauldron that was Luchow's restaurant sat Sandra looking like her mother twenty years ago. On a whim he'd telephoned his daughter and told her he wouldn't take no for an answer, that she had to join him and Lyman for dinner at the famous spot where nostalgia, noise, and German food were served in heaping helpings. Located on Fourteenth Street since the turn of the century, this was where Diamond Jim Brady had treated Lillian Russell to the sauerbraten with potato dumplings and steins of dark beer and they and the place had given a decade its name: the Gay Nineties.

A halfway point between Sandra's office and his apartment, it was also within easy walking distance of the Greenwich Village bars that had given new meaning to the word "gay" and which Lyman would be cruising again that night looking for the solution to the murder of Peter Helder.

Having dragooned Sandra into having dinner with him at Luchow's, Hargreave had then phoned Lyman, interrupting his sleep, and all but ordered him to attend, barking, "To hell with the case for a couple of hours."

But after a dessert of flaming pancakes flavored with lemon, cinnamon, and sugar, filled with lingonberries and then doused with *Kirschwasser* and set ablaze, he turned to his daughter and said, "Sandy, you're a hot-shot assistant district attorney; maybe you'll have some ideas about this damned case."

"Hey, I thought this was a social occasion," protested Lyman. "You're the one who said to hell with the case for a couple of hours."

"I've changed my mind," smirked Hargreave as he slid back his chair and loosened his belt a notch. Then, so succinctly and brilliantly that Lyman could only grin, shake his head in amazement at his boss' virtuosity, and nod in agreement, he described the case in minute detail, concluding by turning to Sandra and asking, "Whatcha think, babe?"

"I'm putting my money on it being one of the leather boys," she said, glancing at Lyman. "I don't envy your assignment, having to hang out in those places. It's pretty gruesome."

"Gruesome or not, you'll be dying to prosecute the case," said her father teasingly but admiringly.

"And how," she laughed.

"I'm not so sure about the gay thing being tied into it, either," said Hargreave.

Startled, Lyman blurted, "Then what the hell am I doing?"

"Well, it's an angle that's got to be explored, doesn't it?"

Sensing an impending eruption, Sandra cut in, lifting her beer stein and declaring, "A toast! Here's to crime!"

Clinking his stein against hers, Lyman chuckled, "Crime."

Hargreave said, "To crime . . . solved."

Then it was time for Lyman to go to work and for Sandra to wend her way home with her bulging briefcase of work—tomorrow's court cases, primarily.

And time for her father and Lyman's boss to go home, too.

The quiet of his apartment reached out to him and made him suddenly aware of how tired he was. The heavy Luchow's food was part of the reason, he decided as he went into the bathroom. His age was another; gone were the days when he could pack away food and beer as readily and without regret as Lyman had done. And Sandy. A pair of youngsters made for one another, it seemed to him.

Studying himself in the mirror above the sink, he made a face and muttered, "You're becoming a meddling old fart."

The previous day's memorial service for Helder was still on his mind and making him vaguely aware of his own fragile mortality in the unforgiving glare of the white lights and the cruel reality of the mirror that helped to drive home the inevitability of his own dying.

He had always anticipated that the event would occur with Nancy at his side. Even if he were abruptly killed in the line of duty, he'd always thought that somehow she would be there for his last gasp. Now that she was gone, he expected his death would mean an inconvenience to someone. Probably he would collapse in a street and tie up the traffic. Or someone at Manhattan North would worry about him being late for work and send a patrol car around and then be told by the uniformed cops that Lieutenant Hargreave had been found dead in bed, an apparent coronary.

That he would be shot to death opening his apartment door had never been on his list of likely ways to die. But that's what happened early the next morning as he was leaving for work. Opening the door. Closing it. Double-locking it. Turning. Catching a glimpse of a sudden movement in the stairway. A figure lunging toward him. A muzzle flash. The sting of the bullets.

Chapter Twenty-Three

Postmortems

Mrs. Schneidau from upstairs saw the man but he'd been just a fleeting glimpse. She'd been on her way down with a small bag of trash to put into the garbage cans out front and heard the shots below. Then she'd smelled the gunsmoke. Leaning over the bannister and peering down, she'd seen Mr. Hargreave face down on the floor and someone kneeling beside him and going through Mr. Hargreave's pockets. "A young man," she said. "A mugger, I'm sure. I yelled, 'What are you doing?' I suppose that was a terribly foolish thing to do, what with him having a gun and all. But it scared him off."

The building superintendent, Mr. Raphael, thought he'd heard the shots and a car speeding away on Seventy-fifth Street toward First Avenue but couldn't swear to it.

That there'd been just the one assailant had been certified with the unspoken proviso of the crime-scene investigator that nothing could be judged off-the-cuff absolutely, but all the immediate evidence pointed to a lone assailant who had stood in the stairwell for about an hour on a landing with a direct view of Hargreave's apartment door. Waiting, he'd smoked four cigarettes, tramping them out on the black-and-white tiles; Lucky Strikes, they were; lighted with paper matches torn from a book. He was probably left-handed, judging by the ripped ends of the matches. A scrutiny of one of the crushed cigarette butts led to the conclusion that he'd worn sneakers. Getting into the apartment house had been no problem for him apparently, even though the vestibule door was locked. There were no finger-prints left by the perpetrator.

The Deputy Medical Examiner, Dr. Turner, reported that his postmortem showed two .22 caliber bullet wounds fired behind the left ear at point-blank range. "One would have been enough," he said to Detective Lyman.

The news media reported the murder as being a "gangland-style" execution and cited Detective Hargreave's record as a member of various racket-busting squads that had cracked down on the Mafia families whose existence had been brought to the public's angry attention in the 1950s when gangster Joseph Valachi had lifted the veil on what he called "La Cosa Nostra" in testimony before a Senate investigating committee. "At that time," a story about Hargreave's murder noted, "the gutsy young detective had been singled out by an angry Frank Costello, the boss of bosses of the Mob in the fifties, as 'our number one pain in the ass.'" The Mob, the article suggested, had a long memory. But the Organized Crime Unit of the New York Police Department could find no intelligence data to indicate any involvement in Hargreave's death by the city's five Mafia families. Nor did the widespread system of police informants that was intensively trawled over the days following the homicide point investigators toward a suspect.

Lyman insisted on being put in charge of the investigation, but his Captain vetoed the idea with excellent reasoning. "You'd be too damned personal about it," he said. "Besides, you've already got the Helder homicide."

"They're connected, you know," Lyman blurted.

"That's nonsense," frowned the Captain, an able and clever but visionless and uncreative man.

Chapter Twenty-Four

Footprints

Alone, Amnon Dorot drew the red scrambler phone from the wall safe in the windowless office of the Deputy Ambassador for Cultural and Educational Affairs at the Israeli Mission to the United Nations, a holder of degrees in music and drama from four universities on three continents in the name of Chaim Yoffe. Since graduating at the top of the Class of 1958 at Kfar Sirkin he'd been known to Amnon by the Mossad workname Mogen, chosen for him by Amnon and the General because it meant "star" in Hebrew. Though surprised to see Colonel Dorot in New York, Mogen did not inquire as to the reason. Nor did he hesitate to vacate the office.

"I have paid a call on the firm in hopes of discussing business with Mr. Judah," said Amnon when the General came on the line. "Unfortunately he was not in at the time."

"Is the firm defunct?"

"The office itself appeared to be still a going concern. Mr. Judah's personal effects were in place. The distinct impression of the premises was that he had been called away on an urgent matter in every expectation of returning. And there was no sign whatsoever that he had abandoned our mutual enterprise in favor of a personal venture, as you had feared."

"Will you be remaining there?"

"That's my intention, yes, sir. Of course, if you prefer not . . . ."

"No. Stay."

"I have something else for your attention, sir, but I am taking the liberty of sending you the details by way of flash courier."

"Very well."

"The party whose phone I'm using will have my local address should you interpret the package I'm sending you differently from me and wish to reach me."

"Very well."

The package which Amnon handed to Mogen was a bulky portfolio within an envelope placed inside a second envelope and then into a locked briefcase. Its contents were his report on his search for Daniel Ben Avram and clippings from three newspapers concerning the murder of the detective who had been in charge of investigating the death of Helder. Doro included a lengthy explanation as to why he believed that the killing of Hargreave had been a result of that investigation and not, as the papers speculated, the result of a Mafia vendetta or a simple bungled robbery attempt. Also, he wrote, he had found nothing to indicate that the two murders had been committed at Daniel's hands. In the hope of contacting Daniel, he informed the General, he was checking into the Hotel Lexington and would be following up on information he'd discovered in Daniel's room. "This is to go by special courier and then by hand to the General, his eyes only," he explained to Mogen. "Not, repeat not, with the daily diplomatic pouch. You are to be Tel Aviv's contact with me. I'll be at the Lexington. But under no circumstances are you to attempt to reach me there unless the General orders you. Or unless you receive any communication from an agent working with the name Judah. Or if there is anything related to Judah that comes to the attention of our people here or in Washington. Got it?"

"Got it," said Mogen with a confiding wink.

Smiling, Amnon said, "How's trade, old friend? Are the American newspaper columnists right? Are the Arabs looking for another war? Is Nasser beating drums in the Sinai?"

Teasing, Mogen said, "Out of the loop, old boy?"

"Have a nice day, Mr. Ambassador," Amnon grinned, shaking hands with Mogen.

Leaving him, Amnon found Second Avenue awash in sunshine.

New York City! The Big Apple, whatever that meant. Home to more Jews than Jerusalem, Tel Aviv, and Haifa combined. One of New York's United States Senators, Jacob Javits, was a Jew. In businesses Jews were prominent. In publishing, entertainment, the arts. And among them for almost all the years since American soldiers had thrown open the gates of the death camps and revealed Nazidom's Final Solution for what they called the Jewish problem had lived the beast August Grenier with the respectable face of Peter Helder. Now that the beast was dead did it really matter if he'd been slain by a young Jew from Haifa by way of Kfar Sirkin? Had Danny taken the fate of Grenier/Helder into his own hands and strangled him, wouldn't it have been an understandable act? By ordinary measure, of course.

But Daniel Ben Avram was not ordinary. He was a trained agent, a skilled operative with a specific assignment—he'd taken an oath concerning that mission—and the son of a hero of the Israeli War of Independence who would never bring discredit to his father's name by taking the law into his own hands.

If all that were true, Amnon asked himself as he walked basking in New York City's May sunlight, where was Daniel Ben Avram, known to worried comrades as Judah?

Registering for a room at the Hotel Lexington, he peered past the desk clerk to the mail slot for room 1416 where he found that the note he'd left for Danny remained uncollected.

In his own room he sat at a desk identical to the one in Danny's three floors below and studied the entries in Danny's notebook where in effect he'd left footprints on the trail of his quarry.

172

The first concerned a visit to the New York Public Library, Amnon noted with a smile, remembering his lecture at Kfar Sirkin on the value to agents of freely available information. "Our capable adversaries, the Russians, know this," he'd taught. "In America, for instance, the KGB has a staff of agents working full time in the periodicals department of the libraries in New York and Washington."

In the theatrical pages of the *Times*, Daniel had noted in his book, he had come across what he had not dared to hope to find—a photo of a group of men and women in evening attire smiling for the camera around a pert and obviously pleased woman wearing a tiara and holding one end of a check. At the other end was a balding elderly gentleman. The caption noted, "Mrs. Elaine R. Ruderman, Director, Combined Jewish Women's Charitable Organizations and organizer of last night's gala benefit performance at the Brooks Atkinson Theater of *Sing, Israel, Sing*, receives $500,000 donation from Mr. Peter Helder, financier and renowned art benefactor. Check is on behalf of the Helder Galleries which held an auction of art works and matched the funds collected." Beneath this entry Daniel had written, "Beginner's luck!" and then, "Resemblance to Grenier is amazing. Too amazing to be merely a coincidence, I believe. But will check further."

He'd begun at the Helder Galleries, Amnon learned on the next page of Daniel's book. "'Best chance of catching him, and it's only a chance, is late afternoon,' the woman at the gallery told me," he'd written. "She says Helder lives above his galleries.

173

Waited four hours. At six o'clock the woman in the gallery came out, locked the door and left. At 6:30, Helder appeared. Accompanied by a young man. At 11:00 they emerged wearing black leather jackets and trousers and black boots. They took taxi. I couldn't follow. Tomorrow I must rent a car."

The next day, his book recorded, he'd used a credit card provided by the documents section of Mossad to purchase a camera and a telephoto lens along with ten rolls of 36-exposure black-and-white film at Willoughby's on West Thirty-second Street and to rent a Valiant sedan for the weekly rate of $33, plus eight cents a mile, from the Alexander's rent-a-car. Receipts for these were folded into the notebook.

At four o'clock he staked out Helder's address.

At six o'clock, the woman he'd spoken to yesterday in the Helder Galleries closed up and left.

Half an hour later, a cab arrived with Helder and the same young man.

"Photographed," Daniel noted in his book.

It was almost eleven o'clock when they came out.

"Photographed coming down the steps and waiting for a taxi."

He'd trailed Helder in the rental car. "Nearly lost them! Waited two hours across street from a private club in Greenwich Village called the Pit. Photos but poor lighting. Followed Helder and boy back to Helder mansion. Broke off surveillance."

The next day at a shop on Eighth Street in Greenwich Village he'd used a credit card to buy a black leather motorcycle jacket, pants, and boots for $200 that now were not to be found among his possessions.

That night when Helder and the boy returned to The Pit, he'd followed them and managed to meet Helder, he wrote, adding, "While I was his *pick-up*, I was not invited to his home as I had expected—and hoped—to be. I do not know if this was simply because Helder had gone to the bar with a boy named Greg, to whom I was introduced and had seen on two occasions earlier while I had the Helder Galleries under surveillance, or if Helder does not make it his habit to take a young man he'd just met to a home that must be filled with valuables. Perhaps it is because he was afraid I would rob him. Or perhaps he is cautious with all strangers until he can get to know them and trust them, given his past. I am convinced Helder is Grenier. Now, more than ever. But I know that I have to observe him further. I know I must gather as much data about him as I can in order to make an airtight case. I have a date with him tomorrow night. He says he is going to take me out on the town. 'No leather,' Helder told me. Must wear my best suit and tie. It will be an elegant evening. He intends to show me off."

The next pages recounting the conversation of that night were written like a play:

"Where'd you come from, Mr. Helder?"

"Holland."

"Why'd you come to the United States?"

"For the same reason everyone else comes."

"Did you come here right after the war?"

175

"Shortly after. I was fortunate in having helpful friends."

Then Daniel wrote, "Toured the bars. Not invited home. Date for tomorrow night at the Pit. Helder said, 'Wear your leather.'"

Amnon could imagine Daniel Ben Avram clearly, seething with frustration, storming into his hotel room and spilling his thoughts into his Operation Judah notebook. "To get this close to Grenier is why I have come to New York but I have yet to be with him except in public. If there is conclusive evidence that Peter Helder is Grenier it will not be found unless I am admitted to Helder's home."

"I must get him alone," wrote Daniel with "alone" underlined. "Tonight, if he doesn't invite me to his place, I'll suggest it."

It was the last entry in the book.

While Amnon Dorot wondered about the abrupt ending of Daniel Ben Avram's notes like a trail of footprints across the white sand beach at Ashkelon that suddenly vanishes, wiped out by the onrush of Mediterranean surf, a sea of navy blue uniforms was flooding into a quiet street in front of an Episcopal church in Queens for the funeral of a cop.

The tradition of the New York Police Department was to afford one of their own slain in the line of duty an Inspector's funeral, no matter his rank. Customary, too, was attendance at these elaborate ceremonies by representatives of police departments from across the country because every cop everywhere

176

understood that the uniforms they wore, however they differed in design and insignia, were the outward sign of a unique fraternity in which the death of one—especially a violent death at the hands of a sworn enemy—was a blow against all lawmen.

Carrying his detective's shield in a wallet made especially for that purpose and with his Smith & Wesson .38 caliber Police Special holstered on his belt, Lieutenant David Hargreave had been killed in cold blood leaving his apartment on his way to work for a reason which a small army of investigators working around the clock had not determined in the four days leading up to his burial next to his wife in a crowded cemetery in Queens.

In many respects like a military funeral, the interment of a police officer ended with the presentation of the American flag which had draped the coffin to the dead cop's next of kin. At the burial of her father, Sandra Hargreave received the tightly folded pillowlike triangle showing only the blue field and white stars from Sergeant Sheldon Lyman, who was wearing white gloves with the uniform that on this cloudy May day was a drop of blue in a sea of it as hundreds of New York City police and their multihued brethren from near and far saluted the fallen one, each of them appreciating that one of them could be the next to die.

At the wake the night before at a funeral home only a few blocks downtown on Madison Avenue from the Helder Galleries where Hargreave's last murder case had begun the mourners who would march in a solid blue phalanx the next day had paused to express their

177

condolences to Hargreave's daughter, then stopped to console Lyman. They appreciated that a cop's partner was as close as a brother or if the partnership consisted of an older cop and a younger one, as in the teaming of Hargreave and Lyman, that the bond was often like a father and son.

All of these knowing mourners who lingered to speak to him in the muted clipped cadences of grief spoke with an awareness of the Helder case and wondered aloud if the strangled art dealer and the assassinated detective might have been victims of the same killer. "I believe so," Lyman had answered, though there was not a shred of evidence to back him up.

From the wake he'd escorted Sandra to her apartment and sat talking with her about her father—and his, too, in many ways, he'd told her—for more than an hour in her tidy feminine apartment until she'd thrown him out at last, gently reminding him that it would be an early rising for both of them.

Not wanting to return to his bleak bachelor's studio, he drove to her father's apartment and found the white tiles of the hallway outside the door were stained with a faint pinkish shadow where the pool of blood had been. Keys to the apartment had been given to him the day he'd become Hargreave's partner. "In case you ever have to get into my place," Hargreave had said with no further explanation.

Lyman had been invited to Hargreave's place on three occasions, each for a dinner Hargreave had prepared—twice with just the two of them having

178

hamburgers and beers at the kitchen table, once in the dining room when the fare was spaghetti and the third person at the table was Sandra. A fledgling effort in Hargreave's sporadic campaign to light the fires of romance between his daughter and his partner, the evening had consisted mainly of a Hargreave discourse on the literature of crime. "You ought to read detective stories," he'd implored them. "Very stimulating, very intructive, very helpful. The sleuths in those books are terrific thinkers! Never mind all the scientific crime lab stuff that we all know is the real basis of modern crime solving. The detectives in the books *think* about their cases. They use what Hercule Poirot calls 'the little gray cells.'"

A detective novel, *The Fuhrer of 86th Street* by an author named Somerfield, lay facedown and closed on the table beside the bed as Lyman entered the room looking for . . . what? He asked himself the same question in the kitchen, the dining room, the living room, and finally ended up in the study, Hargreave's private world of crime texts and tales, a quiet thought-filled place.

Sitting in the reclining chair, he looked around at the disheveled and dusty room, still wondering what he was looking for, until his eyes fell on a pile of oversized envelopes bulging with what appeared to be documents. As he gathered them up, he saw that they were a thick computer printout of Peter Helder's stock market transactions, his banking records, and a lengthy list of members of the Atlantis Club. "What the hell did he expect to find in these?" Lyman wondered.

Leaving them, he'd driven to his own apartment, gotten a few hours of sleep, then showered, shaved, and put on the heavy blues and crisp white gloves to join hundreds like him for the funereal bagpipes and muffled drums of the street in front of the church, the flag-draped coffin being carried inside on the beefy shoulders of cop pallbearers, Christian hymns brimming with the certainty of glorious and joyful resurrection, and the long cortege to the plot where a rifle squad would fire a volley to send Hargreave honorably to rest beside his beloved Nancy.

When all this was done and Sandra was in a car with an aunt and two cousins who would see her through the rest of the day, Lyman walked almost a half-mile to the unmarked police car whose flashing lights and siren Hargreave had been so reluctant to use.

Leaning against the car, waiting, was Dick Lomax in a misshapen hat and rumpled trenchcoat that turned him into a living caricature of a sleazy private eye that might be found in one of the mystery novels in Hargreave's unvarnished bookcases. "Whaddaya say, Sarge," said Lomax, straightening. "It's a hell of a sad day."

"If it's a comment you want, Lomax, forget it," said Lyman, opening the car.

Wounded, Lomax grabbed the door. "Look, Sergeant, I didn't come to the funeral looking for a comment. I came because Hargreave was a cop I respected and liked and because I'm gonna miss him. Since you're his partner, I wanted to tell you how sorry I am."

Lyman cracked a begrudging smile. "I guess you're not the total pain in the ass you seem to be."

"Oh, I'm a pain in the ass all right. And I will continue to be. That's what I get paid to be. That reporters should be an ache in the keister is right there in the First Amendment. Not in so many words but between the lines. But where's it written that a guy with a microphone and a tape recorder can't be a human being?"

Lyman shrugged, as close as he was willing to come to conceding the point. "Can I give you a lift back to the city?"

"My mobile unit's over there," said Lomax, jerking his head to the left.

"So you *are* working today!"

"Well, since I'm here I might as well file a story for my station."

"My answer is still 'No comment.'"

"Look, Sergeant Lyman, I really would like to talk to you about what's been going on. I mean, a person would have to be deaf, dumb, and blind not to wonder how come it is that the detective who's been in charge of the Helder homicide suddenly ends up dead in a gangland-style rubout. You have to wonder if maybe this art dealer had mob connections."

"Lomax, I can see that you're on a fishing expedition. Well, I'm not biting."

"I'm gonna be straight with you, Lyman. There's a hell of a story in this. This newsman's nose of mine has picked up the scent. These two murders are definitely linked. I know and I'm certain you

181

know it."

"So what are you saying Lomax?"

"I'm telling you that I'm sticking with this story as long as it takes to get it."

"Shooting for a Pulitzer Prize?"

"Only newspaper guys get that. And screw the prizes. I didn't go into the news business to collect a lot of plaques and certificates of appreciation to stick in a drawer or hang on my wall. So what I'm saying is that when a big-shot art dealer gets strung up with a black hood over his head and a few days later the cop who was investigating the case is himself murdered à la the boys from Murder Incorporated the taxpayers of New York have a right to know why. You see, I'm what you might call a practitioner of the people's right to know."

"Admirable, Lomax. All very admirable. Only I still have no comment."

"Did it ever occur to you that I could be of help to you? I know a lot of people in this town. I've got contacts. Been at the news business longer than you've been a cop, longer even than you've been old enough to shave. I could be of help to you, Lyman, if you'd open up to me a little. Strictly off the record! Nothing on the air until you make an arrest. Whatcha say?"

"No dice."

"Okay, but I'm not giving up on this story, Lyman."

"It's a free country, Lomax, but if you get in the way I'll come down on you like the proverbial ton of bricks."

Driving away, he muttered, "That's the last thing I need: a goddamned newsman playing detective."

Briefly, before the General recruited him, Amnon Dorot had been a detective of the Israel National Police posted in the seafront hotel district of Tel Aviv where a tourist trade was burgeoning immediately after independence. It had been boring work consisting mainly of apprehending the swindlers and thieves who saw easy pickings amongst the baffled visitors and the General had been a rescuing archangel. But now, standing before a dubious young woman at the automobile rental counter where Daniel had obtained his Valiant, he found the skills of his old trade coming back to him. He was, he'd declared to the woman, a friend of a young man who had rented a car from her firm on the date in question. "He was to have driven to Brooklyn to meet me, but he didn't arrive. I do know for sure that he rented a car here." To show this, he produced the credit card receipt. "I was wondering if you could tell me if he returned it and when."

"Yes, I can check that for you, sir." From a file she drew a folder. Frowning, she said, "Oh dear, there was a problem with that car. It was not returned by the renter, your Mr. Goldstein. The police found it abandoned."

"Abandoned? My God! Do you know when and where?"

"It was on May fifth on the West Side Highway near the Seventy-sixth Street ramp."

"And what about the driver?"

"I presume the police are looking for him," she said as she studied the file intently. "I know we are. His account is outstanding, you see," she said, looking up.

But by then, Amnon was gone.

Chapter Twenty-Five

The Prophet

The body was stuffed into an old smokehouse that dated back to the Revolutionary War but had been abandoned long ago to the eroding weather and the weeds until the collapsed stones had come to appear like a cave on the north side of Buckberg Mountain which four teenage boys out on a hike had decided was worthy of a little spelunking.

A corpse in the rugged woodland hillside of rustic Stony Point in Rockland County west of the Hudson an hour's drive north of Manhattan seemed to Lomax to be a little far out in the boondocks for a city boy to travel for a story. But it was early Sunday morning, always a drought in the news business, and Freddie the editor had pleaded on the phone, "I know it's your weekend but I am climbing the walls in my desperation for the sort of colorful coverage only you can provide, Dick *bay-BEE!*"

So Lomax had coaxed his cranky mobile unit to

life and sped to the scene, swarming now with reporters and TV film crews eager for shots of the body being manhandled by cops laboring up the steep slope because it was impossible to get a stretcher down there. A close-up "eyewitness" picture of a corpse was the highest priority of the editors and producers who worked in the video medium which Lomax called "flash and trash" and sometimes the "pretty boy parade" or worse. Once he said from the stage during an Inner Circle Show that had been written by Alex Somerfield, "Television journalism is a contradiction in terms. It is to news what a military band is to music. To paraphrase Oscar Wilde, 'Television news justifies its own existence by the great Darwinian principle of the survival of the vulgarest.'"

This was just sour grapes from a radio guy, retorted the insulted TV news people, pointing out that a pretty boy Lomax was not, being bald, short, paunchy, thick-waisted and with the flat nose and pugnacious jowly chin of a plug-ugly bulldog.

Chain smoking and waiting for the body to be hauled up for the benefit of the TV crews and for a Stony Point police spokesman to brief the milling reporters, Lomax sat in his battered mobile unit watching all the brothers of his peculiar trade as they meandered in their "Police Line—Do Not Cross" roped-off confinement, bumping into one another, muttering impatiently, cursing all those who had sent them into this wilderness and the hayseed cops who were keeping them at bay in their hungering for

186

the meat of this rare Sunday story like sharks attracted by the scent of blood in the water.

"The victim was shot in the back of the head at least twice," briefed the portly representative of the Stony Point Police Department presently. "Because of the decomposition of the body, it's not possible to affix a precise date as to how long it's been there. The best guess of the Medical Examiner at this time is that it's been at least a week. As the body was nude when found, it has not been possible at this time to identify him. He appears to be a white male in his twenties with light brown hair and blue eyes. There are no immediately noticeable scars or tattoos or anything like that except what looks like an ink stain on his right wrist like the mark that's made at a swimming pool or maybe a dance so a person could go in and out without having to pay again for admission. The mark is hard to make out on account of the body being there so long."

"Do you have any suspects?" asked a TV reporter.

Lomax almost laughed. Even he could have answered that one. A suspect? You gotta be kidding. They'll be lucky if they ever identify the body. The question ought to be the one he was now going to ask. "Have there been any reports of anybody matching this description being missing?"

The cop replied, "None that we know of in Rockland County."

Meaning that the kid had been killed elsewhere and the body dumped in Rockland, thought Lomax. Probably a mob killing. Two shots to the back of the head were a gangland hallmark. Like the pair of .22s pumped into Detective David Hargreave's brain.

His fascination for stories about gangsters was a fault in Lomax, said his colleagues openly to him, but always as a well-meaning criticism. Even his best friend, Alex Somerfield, had voiced the view. "You ought to show some selectivity in the stories you go after, Dick," Alex had suggested with a look of grave concern, "or the big shots in the mob are going to do something about it." This had been said after Frank Costello had encountered Lomax in a Little Italy restaurant, had come over to Lomax's table to wag a finger under Lomax's nose and bellow, "Behave yourself, Richard."

Blithely, to the man who had succeeded Lucky Luciano as the boss of organized crime in America, Lomax said, "I am behaving myself, Frank."

Stone-faced, Costello grumbled, "No, you ain't."

The following year when a gunman waylaid Costello in the lobby of his swank apartment building on Central Park West and with the words "This is for you, Frank" fired one bullet which wounded but did not kill, Lomax said on the air, "It was a shot that means Uncle Frank is washed up in this town."

The prophecy was accurate but many of Lomax's inner circle of journalists wondered whether P for prophecy belonged amongst the five W's and the H.

Ten years after he'd predicted the eclipse of Costello, Lomax's forecast that the Stony Point Police would never identify the dead youth whose nude body had been found on Buckberg Mountain also proved true despite widespread publication and

188

use on TV newscasts of a police artist's sketch interpreting how the young man might have looked in life.

Seeing the picture, Lomax's wife, Patricia, said to him, "To me he looks Italian."

"Nah," asserted Lomax. "That guy's Jewish."

Chapter Twenty-Six

Hot Line

TRANSCRIPT OF TELEPHONE INTERCEPT
889-6497
New York City to Tel Aviv
1000 Hours, 15 May 1967

VOICE 1:   Shalom.
DOROT: Scramble please.
VOICE 1:   Moment. Go ahead please.
DOROT: General?
GENERAL: Are we scrambled?
DOROT: Yes, sir.
GENERAL: Report.
DOROT: Judah is dead.
GENERAL: This is confirmed?
DOROT: I did not see the body personally.
GENERAL: But you are certain?
DOROT: There is no doubt, sir.
GENERAL: Tell me all.

DOROT: The body was found in a wooded region north of the city. Local police report that he was shot twice in the head. There were no identity papers. Nothing to connect him with us. There has been speculation in the press that this was related somehow to the American Mafia.

GENERAL: And what do you believe?

DOROT: It must have been Grenier.

GENERAL: But Grenier is dead, is he not?

DOROT: So it would seem, sir.

GENERAL: What do you mean by that?

DOROT: Maybe it wasn't Grenier who was hanged.

GENERAL: By God, that'd be some trick.

DOROT: Grenier was a clever man, sir.

GENERAL: Yes, I do see your point. Grenier somehow picked up on Judah's purpose, killed him, staged a fake death. That would be one for the books.

DOROT: There is another possible scenario. Another party could have killed them both.

GENERAL: Another party? Who?

DOROT: I don't know, sir, but with your permission I'd like to remain here and see what I can find out. Of course, if you need me more urgently at home, given the growing crisis with our neighboring enemies.

GENERAL: We have a multitude of enemies. By all means, remain on your post for now.

	What about Judah?
DOROT:	Sir?
GENERAL:	At some point we will have to claim his body.
DOROT:	In time, sir, of course.
	END OF INTERCEPT: 10:03.

Chapter Twenty-Seven

Advancing the Story

Lomax woke up at four o'clock to be on the radio at 5:30, which was the beginning of the peak listening period known as morning drive-time because the biggest audience of the day was in automobiles going to work. Over the years he had become expert at not waking his wife and his teenage son and daughter, using the downstairs bathroom and keeping the radio low as he listened to his station to catch up on whatever may have happened between last night's dinner and his breakfast of orange juice, black coffee, and a bagel with cream cheese.

This morning the main story was the crisis in the Middle East told in the somber tones of a network correspondent in Tel Aviv who painted a gloomy picture for another war between the Arabs and Israel. In New York, with its big population of Jews, this was considered a local item.

If things were that slow, Lomax said to himself,

there might be time to do a little work on the Helder murder, maybe come up with something to advance the story a bit.

Before getting into his car, he went through a ritual of walking around it, looking in front and in back of the wheels, lifting the hood and studying the wiring and getting down on the ground and looking under the chassis for signs of a bomb; his mob-rubout fetish, his colleagues called it.

Rising and brushing himself off, he decided it was safe to get into the heap—no bomb, no gifts from the boys in the double-breasted suits. When he turned the ignition key the police radios came on, chattering and winking routinely. A moment later in answer to his call, Freddie the editor came over the two-way. "Nothin' happenin', babe. Dig me up somethin'."

Find the news, then find more—my life in a nutshell, thought Lomax as he backed from his driveway in the predawn quiet of the middle-class neighborhood in Queens that had been his home as long as he'd been married and as much time as he'd been a newsman on the radio. None of that TV stuff! News on the tube was bullshit. No pictures, no story! What the hell kind of journalism was that? There were zillions of good stories without pictures to go with them. Great stories that could be *told*.

This was his rationalization because he had never made it in TV news, he'd been told. But the truth was, even if he'd had the looks to qualify for television he would have stayed with radio. TV was too complex, a team effort, crew work. TV could never be so elemental as prowling the streets and then going on the air from the scene of the story and telling it in his clear, deep, beautiful voice—Dick Lomax working alone.

On the road at 4:15 a.m. he was a full hour in advance of the flood of Manhattan-bound vehicles that would clog the Cross Island and Southern parkways and the Van Wyck, Grand Central, and Brooklyn-Queens expressways cutting swaths toward Manhattan and what the people of the other four boroughs of New York called "the city."

But even that early he was not alone.

The first car, a blue Ford with two men in it, had appeared in his rearview mirror a block from his home and had stayed behind him, tailgating.

The second, a yellow Chevy with only the driver inside that had been at the side of the road, shot ahead of him as he accelerated out of an on-ramp of the BQE.

The third, a brown Dodge with two men in the front and two in the back seat, zoomed from far behind him as if to pass but fell in alongside on the left. Drifting rightward, it forced him to veer close to the steel roadside barriers.

With no one in front of him, he sped up and reached for the handset of his two-way radio. Urgently he called, "Freddie, this is Lomax. I'm in big trouble on the BQE! I got bad guys all around me. I need the cops."

The Dodge had sped up, edging far enough ahead to keep him from moving into the center between it and the Chevy while the Ford kept close behind, boxing him in on the rail as they raced up an incline where there was a sharp leftward curve known in the shorthand of his radio station's traffic-reporting

195

helicopter as Dead Man's Bend.

On the two-way Freddie's voice was barking: "Lomax, say it again. Repeat please. What's the trouble, Dick?"

He was doing 50 in a zone with signs warning "25 MPH" and "Dangerous Curve Ahead" and "No Passing" and "No Parking on Shoulder."

Blocked, he was on the shoulder. No going right. No going left. No stopping. Nothing to do but speed ahead and up the hill and around the curve and wait for the men in these cars to try whatever they had in mind. Would they force him to stop? Did they have guns? Were they trying to force him out of the car? Setting him up to be gunned down?

There was nothing to do but keep trying to outrun them.

Flooring the gas pedal, he hoped the striving old mobile unit had the guts for taking the hill. God willing, he'd break loose going around Dead Man's Bend.

The cars to his left held their positions.

In his mirror he saw the following Ford slowing, falling back, and swerving left.

Then as he crested the hill at the start of Dead Man's Bend he saw the dumptruck straight ahead of him. Parked.

Hitting the brake, he wheeled sharply right and sidelong into the barrier. He was acutely aware of everything that happened. A long screeching, scratching, and scraping of rending metal. A rooster tail of brilliant fireworks sparks. The smell of burning paint. The smashing of glass. The right-side door being gouged open. The whole front end of the car slamming and shuddering, then convulsing, then collapsing toward him. Hood and dashboard and steering wheel rushing backward. Steel engulfing him like the petals of a flesh-eating flower. A crushing like the embracing arms of a strong woman. The salty taste of blood in his mouth. Nostrils stuffed as if by cotton wads, stifling breathing. Everywhere, the worst pain he'd ever known. Then a tingling from head to foot. A floating and at the same time falling sensation that a person sometimes feels when drifting to sleep. Blackness. Nothing.

"That Mr. Lomax survived this crash," said a surgeon on all the TV newscasts that night, "was a miracle."

Said a police spokesman, "Why that truck had been abandoned on Dead Man's Bend is being investigated."

Part Two: Deerstalker

Chapter Twenty-Eight

Railroad Buff

Alexander Somerfield watched the approach of a train that was a mockery of railroading as he liked to remember it from the unspoiled days of halcyon youth before discovering he had a duty to slay dragons.

The slowly approaching stubby silver-colored self-propelled commuter lacked the mystery and romance of the legendary trains of the golden age of railways—the Broadway Limited which had taken him to Chicago and then the Rock Island Rocket transporting him to college in Iowa so long ago it seemed like an event from another incarnation; the Twentieth Century Ltd.; the Super Chief. Later, there were other trains with rattletrap coaches—cattle cars snaking through mountains in Southeast Asia. The Blue Train in South Africa. And the storied glitter of the Orient Express from the Balkans to Paris when he was worldly enough to appreciate its opulence and his duplicitous reason for riding it, a story worthy of all the espionage yarns of the Cold War. So many trains, so many memories, so many dragons grappled with.

Now, this toy 'was coming for him at Paoli, Pennsylvania, crossing three sets of tracks from a marshaling yard and easing onto Track One eastbound to stop at the center of the platform, an electrically powered arrival with nothing to recommend it but simple efficient transportation. No huffing. No puffing. No hissing. No gusts of steam. No blood-curdling but satisfying squeal of brakes. Still, despite the silence, like the poet Edna St. Vincent Millay, there was not a train he wouldn't take no matter where it was going. And no call from Dick Lomax he couldn't accept even if it meant descending into Hell.

He'd received it in a room in his remote woodland house where he did his writing. The telephone he'd used was from the 1930s. The desk was of even earlier vintage. A massive mahogany chair upholstered in a blue velvety fabric was Victorian. Lamps were heavy brass with Tiffany-style shades. A museum, his friends called the room, especially when they wandered around gaping in amazement at walls festooned with the memorabilia of Alexander Somerfield's checkered lifetime. Plenty of eight-by-ten photos of himself here and there doing this and that with this famous person and that one were sprinkled amongst the brazenly displayed memorabilia of the public man a journalist and author becomes. But nowhere could be found any sign of the other side of him, no trophies of a secret life he had chosen to follow and had followed for more than a decade until he'd quit in disgust, storming into Russ Branson's office and launching a tirade against the utter insanity of guilt and self-recrimination that had seized the national mood after the Bay of Pigs, the assassination of President John F. Kennedy, and then Vietnam, much of his spleen directed at the Agency.

He'd rarely seen Russ Branson since that memorable afternoon and Dick Lomax even less.

"Local to Philadelphia," said the conductor bounding to the platform.

The last time Somerfield had taken this train had been in January to attend the annual dinner of the Baker Street Irregulars in New York when he'd been decked out in full Sherlock Holmes regalia—Victorian-era evening wear, a navy blue Inverness cape, a gray deerstalker cap, a walking stick with a silver dog's head for a handle, a bent pipe clenched between his teeth. "Smoking in the rear, Mr. Holmes," the conductor had chuckled. Now, taking no special notice of the portly gentleman in a blue pinstriped suit boarding his train, as if he were just another businessman on his way to an office in Philadelphia and not an old warrior being fetched from blissful retirement for a reason only God and Dick Lomax knew, this conductor shouted, "First stop is Daylesford."

Somerfield knew the litany of the route by heart: Daylesford, Berwyn, Devon, Strafford, Wayne, St. David's, where Somerfield's old boss Richard Helms of the CIA hailed from, Radnor, Villanova, Rosemont, Bryn Mawr—the elegant Welsh-named suburbs of Philadelphia strung out like pearls along the

203

westward trunk of the late and lamented Pennsylvania Railroad with quaint stations done in a variety of picturesque motifs from rococo to Arabian mushrabia, remnants of a lifestyle as out of date as the stories Somerfield had read in college by F. Scott Fitzgerald and John O'Hara about an era when all boys were handsome and all girls beautiful and when America's future was brimming with promise, well before the jet engine made long-distance trains obsolete and many thousands of computer-programmed nuclear-tipped intercontinental missiles in Soviet silos placed Doomsday only half an hour distant, about the amount of time required for the Paoli Local to make the run to the 30th Street Station.

In the vast echoing grandeur of one of the country's last remaining railway palaces Somerfield would board a Penn Central coach to New York, tingling with the thrill of changing trains as only an old railwayist will. The observation of the other passengers being as much a joy of railroading as the journey itself, in waiting rooms he always stood or sat a little apart from the others. Being the slightly aloof observer was the habit of a lifetime but had he not had the innate desire of the journalist to watch people he would have had to acquire the skill in order to function in both a profession that had appealed to him from the earliest years of his youth and in the unexpected secretive world of intelligence and espionage to which Russ Branson had introduced him fifteen years ago, both bizarre callings lasting until he decided out of the sheer schizophrenia of being both a newsman and a spy to retire quietly into a wilderness of his own choosing, as everyone in the journalism and the espionage business vowed to do but rarely did, "to write."

What he wrote was mystery novels and while they sold in reasonably good numbers and while for a few years in the recent past his had been a fairly familiar face on television news broadcasts reporting from foreign datelines, he was confident that no one in the concourse of 30th Street Station would spot him. Less confident about not being recognized by someone from the shadows of his secret past, he bought a newspaper to hide behind, a wary old dog turning to performing old tricks one more time. His stealthy scrutiny of the hustle and bustle around him consisted of a series of quick glimpses. Snapshots. Eyes lifted momentarily from the paper, an idle scanning of the crowd for a quick shifting of someone else's eyes. A turn of a head. A rapid reversal of direction. A retreat from being spotted, caught. Watching out for watchers. Looking for anyone looking at him. Spying a spy.

Immediately he spotted a red-haired youth whose glance at him had been a trifle lingering, but instantly he felt foolish and embarrassed. After all, there was no reason to suppose that his phone was tapped after all these years.

Had he been younger, at the sound of the phone ringing he would have sprinted up the long driveway from his mailbox to his house but although he was in his mid-thirties, he was a trifle too fat and given to fleeting pangs of angina pectoris. His fixed opinion was that if a call were important but unanswered the caller would replace it, so, expecting the ringing to stop long before he got to the phone, he'd taken his time, but this caller had not hung up. "Alex, it's Dick Lomax!"

Seated in the smoker, Somerfield watched the familiar Philadelphia skyline slide past the train as it skirted the Schulykill River, then he settled back to doze, one of the attractions of rail travel being the ease with which one could sleep rocked and lulled in the sway of the coach and serenaded by the music of steel wheels on steel rails, but instead, his mind dwelt on how fragile his peculiar life was when it could be so easily disrupted by a call. "I can't give you the details on the phone," Lomax had said mysteriously. "You must come to New York right away."

Chapter Twenty-Nine

The Ex-Man

While a taxi rocketed through the Queens Mid-town Tunnel on the last leg of his journey to find out what Dick Lomax had been so cryptic about on the telephone, Somerfield's mind hopscotched between flashes of memory of other cabs. The roomy black London hacks and their courteous drivers. Snippity Parisian cabbies. The obsequious Japanese. Italian kamikaze pilots at the wheels of Vespas. Gondola taxis in Venice. Flat-bottomed boats in traffic jams on canals the color of coffee with too much cream in Bangkok. The hush of hired cars in Russia because the driver was assumed to be an NKVD agent.

As this rattling New York taxi emerged from the tunnel into Queens on a warm June afternoon, Moscow came back to him fresh and freezing. A cold city in the depths of the Cold War: 1956. Stone steps of a dark staircase led upward in the belfry of Ivan the Great and a gust of wind as he came out on the platform nearly took his fur hat away. Spread out below was Moscow, a giant wheel whose spokes centered on the hub of the Kremlin, as if all the world's roads led to the ground at his feet. Meandering through the wheel was the narrow ribbon of the Moscow river with many bridges, a steel gray still-frozen stream contrasting against snow reluctant to melt and stolid buildings with rippling roofs, factory chimneys, and obsolete domed churches.

Misha Shilovsky had handed him binoculars and directed him to the broad prospect of Gorky Street, Kalinin, Pushkin, Ordynka, and the sweep of snowy Gorky Park to the southwest, Sokolniki, where the czars went falconing and thus gave the name to the woods, Stalin Park to the east with its pine trees, and Ostankino of the northern edge of the city, site of agricultural exhibitions. "This is my favorite place in all of Russia," Misha said, his eyes glistening with tears.

Down from the tower, they left the Kremlin through the eastern wall and came onto Red Square. Stone blocks that paved it glistened like a coat of mail armor. The only snow was in traces beneath a long row of fir trees by the wall, which had been planted in memory of heroes of wars and other revolutionary struggles entombed in the wall itself, including the early American apologist for the Communists, John Reed, whose *Ten Days That Shook the World* had been required reading for all of the recruits at the farm in Virginia where America trained its secret agents. But the most imposing of the memorials was a terraced building of red and black marble in which Nikolai Lenin lay looking as if he were made of wax in his khaki tunic below his name inlaid in the wall in red and black and before whom Mikhail Shilovsky paused with the same awed reverence with which Alexander Somerfield stood in the Lincoln Memorial. "Now," whispered the Russian presently, taking the American's arm, "permit me to treat you at my favorite café, Russkaya Tchaynaya, at the Metropole Hotel. We shall stuff ourselves with blinshiki."

The crepes with cherry preserves dusted with powdered sugar were as sweet as Misha's conversation. Enchanted, Somerfield ate and listened and drank in stories of the war, gossip about Stalin and Khrushchev, glowing descriptions of Misha's gala evenings at the Bolshoi with his wife Natalya, afternoons with his infant son at the Puppet Theater, starlit concerts in summertime parks featuring the music of Tschaikovsky or wild gypsy dances, of hunting trips gunning for deer and boar in the Northern Caucasus, of summer interludes at spas on the Black Sea, and for the benefit of the railwayist in Somerfield, a vivid account of taking the Trans-Siberian train from Moscow to Irkutsk.

Misha had been a Soviet agent, of course, trying to compromise the green American already known to the NKVD by his Agency workname, Deerstalker, a whimsical concession to Somerfield's passion for anything having to do with Sherlock Holmes.

That night at the embassy he'd filed his first report as an agent. At that moment he was committed. Before then it all had been an elaborate game—army basic training, learning Russian at the language school at Monterey, transfer to the Agency, the lectures and exercises at the Farm. But at that moment, as he wrote a report on Shilovsky's attempts to suborn him, he knew there was no turning back. The Agency had baptized him. Shilovsky was his Confirmation. In the name of the Father, the Son, the Holy Ghost, the CIA, the NKVD, and the Cold War, thou art Alexander Somerfield . . ."

"Agent of influence," blurted Somerfield aloud a dozen years later.

"What's that? You say somethin'?" asked the cab driver.

"No," said Somerfield. "Just clearing my throat." A lie in a lifetime of them. "Agent of influence." The phrase had been coined by the Russians. Maybe it was American. Whoever invented it, he'd heard it first when he was a college sophomore.

Like the oncoming traffic, memories of Iowa came hurtling back. The Rock Island Rocket gliding to a stop at Iowa City and there was Russ on the platform grinning. "Alex! Welcome to Indian Territory! This is great. What a terrific time you and I are going to have! No girl in town is going to be safe."

Getting a degree in Journalism had not been the plan. The Navy was. He'd taken all the tests, gone through all the screenings, passed the physical, been accepted. Then came Russ's letter. For the taking if Alex Somerfield applied, there was a scholarship available at the University of Iowa. They'd be together again—the old pals from high school, the daring duo.

Russ had introduced him to Warren Davis Agency head hunter *extraordinaire!*

"I want to offer you a job after you graduate

Alex," Davis had said. "Part-time. Decent pay."

Later, Somerfield would hear the name of Warren Davis resounding through the Agency. The legendary Warren Davis! The archangel Warren! Chief comber of the college campuses in the 1950s, gleaner amongst the so-called Silent Generation's crop of neatly trimmed, button-down strivers unflinchingly ready to shoulder the duties required of them by their country.

"I'm not looking for gun-toting heroes," Davis had said. "Do I look like a hero?" he asked, mocking his dumpy physique and houndlike face. "I want smart guys." He tapped a pudgy finger against a gray temple. "I want people who will win the Cold War by using their brains. Forget about there ever being a shooting war between us and the Russians. That's not how the struggle is going to be carried out. It's going to be a long wrestling match on television. Words will be the deciding factor. So I'm not looking for gunslingers. I'm looking for word-slingers. I don't want secret agents. I want agents of influence."

"I'm going to be a newsman, Mr. Davis. I'm not interested in lying."

"I'm not asking you to lie. I'm asking you to help guard the truth."

"A newsman can't get involved in the story he's covering."

"If you were a reporter covering a murder and you found out who the murderer was, would you not tell the cops? If you got a tip that some nut was planning to assassinate President Eisenhower, wouldn't you let the Secret Service know? If you were covering the United Nations and uncovered a Russian spy ring, would you really not let the FBI know about it? You've got to make up your mind, Alex. Are you a newsman above everything else or are you a patriotic American?"

They were in the coffee shop of the student union building on the Iowa campus. "I'm like the girl in the backseat of a Chevy with a guy who's got a hand on her tit and two fingers in her twat," Alex said. "I want to but I keep asking myself if I'll respect myself in the morning."

"You say you want to have a career in journalism —in TV and radio—and so I assume you're familiar with the work of Edward R. Murrow?"

"Certainly."

"Murrow's an ideal for broadcasting students, I hear."

"That's right."

"I knew Murrow! During the war. I was in London when he did those broadcasts. Did you hear them?"

"I was a kid but my folks tuned in."

"Pretty good reporting, hunh?"

"The best."

"Bullshit. Those broadcasts were unadulterated propaganda aimed at getting the American people into the war with Germany. Murrow was a dyed-in-the-wool anglophile who didn't let so-called journalistic objectivity get in the way of his opinion that the time had come for the United States to rush to the aid of Britain. There's no way to measure the value of those Murrow broadcasts in capturing the hearts and minds of the American people. Hearts and minds. That's what the Cold War is all about, my friend." He paused, thinking, then went on, "I was with

Murrow when he did his broadcasts from the Buchenwald death camp. That *was* great reporting. And I believe he got it right when he went to Korea. He tried to get the American people to understand. You see, we don't understand the Cold War in this country. But I assure you the Communists do. The Russians have an army of people all over the world posing as journalists, soldiers in the war for hearts and minds. We are way behind, believe me. But this is America and you are free to make up your mind about what you want to do with your life. If you want to be selfish and leave the battle to others . . . ."

"I don't believe it's that easy. Things aren't that clear-cut. It's not as simple as black-and-white. It's—"

He stopped talking while a waitress brought their check. When she was gone, Davis asked, "Why did you quit speaking when that girl came to the table?"

"Well, I assumed you wouldn't want her to overhear us."

Davis smiled. "Afraid she might be a spy?"

"Your word, not mine."

"No one's asking you to be a spy. You'd be what we in the trade call an 'agent of influence.' You'd be a man who listens, observes, and reports the interesting stuff to someone else. Say! That's a fair description of a newsman, isn't it?"

Agent of Influence.

There'd been hundreds of reports since the first one from Moscow. Observations noted. Faces noticed. Names taken down. Suspicions recorded. The talent for handling the two-edged sword, for dealing with the professional schizophrenia which Warren Davis had discerned in Alexander Somerfield coming to fruition. Straight news accounts for his network and Top Secret messages to the Agency from the capitals and crisis centers of the world through the fifties and sixties. A face familiar among the fraternity of journalists. Being everywhere with a notebook in his pocket, a microphone in his hand, and his face to the camera. Observer. Reporter. But everything in duplicate. One copy for the air, the other for the Company.

Dick Lomax suspected. No proof, of course. Just a newsman's intuition. Adding up the checkered past. Filling in the gaps.

Then came the Kennedy assassination and widespread rumors that the Agency had done it. And now the Vietnam war. On college campuses true believers like Warren Davis were unwelcome. The President was taunted with "Hey, hey, LBJ, how many kids did you kill today?" Draft cards were burned. And the flag.

He'd had his fill of it.

Now he was a man with an "ex-" before the descriptions of what he used to do for a living. The ex-foreign correspondent. Ex-radio newsman. Ex-crime reporter. Ex-agent of influence.

Now he was a writer of books.

So what in blazes did Dick Lomax want to see him about?

What was so secret he couldn't mention it on the phone?

Why so hush-hush?

How come all the cloak-and-dagger stuff?

Chapter Thirty

The Old Warhorse

The wheelchair was a shocker but Lomax was game about it. "Don't say it, Alex. I know! I look like an overloaded shopping cart with a canteloupe on top," he laughed, rubbing his bald pate with his good hand. His crushed legs had been reconstructed with stainless steel pins and rods, his right arm was in a cast, and he'd lost a lot of weight, he explained, deciding to get all that behind them. "But I'll settle for the inconvenience, considering what the alternative could have been. I've been sentenced to six months in this thing." The living room had been converted into a combination bedroom and office complete with a microphone and a direct line to his radio station for a daily commentary that had been created to keep him on the air. "As you know, Alex, the audience is fickle and has a short memory," he said. "If they don't hear you, they forget about you."

"They'd never forget you, Richard," smiled Somerfield, sinking into an overstuffed armchair.

"Maybe," said Lomax.

"How'd this accident happen?"

"Oh, it wasn't an accident. It was attempted murder."

The police had determined that the truck had been stolen the night before from a New Jersey construction company, he explained as Somerfield slumped slack-jawed and stunned. In perfect running condition, the truck had been deliberately parked on Dead Man's Bend, not abandoned as first thought. The three cars had been stolen, also, and left on Manhattan streets. In none of the vehicles had there been any clues as to the men who'd used them nor to their reason for wanting to make the death of Dick Lomax look like an accident. "Whoever they were," he concluded, "they knew what they were doing and had had me staked out. They knew routines. It was a nifty set-up."

Leaning forward incredulously, Somerfield asked, "By whom? You must have some suspicion."

"Naturally, I've been thinking about little else since it happened three weeks ago."

Somerfield was almost out of the chair now. "And?"

"At first I assumed it had to be the mobsters. You know I've been a pain in the ass to them since Costello's regime. But the more I thought about it being a mob hit the more it didn't add up. This was not the mob's style. Hell, if they'd wanted to bump me off they'd've done it in the usual manner. A thug appearing out of the dark and pumping a couple of slugs in my head. Or gunning me down in a barber's chair the way they'd iced Albert Anastasia. They'd've left nothing to chance. Parking a truck on a roadside and forcing their target to run into it? Nah. It couldn't have been the mob. In addition to which, I haven't done a story on the underworld in a long time."

"What were you working on?"

Lomax's face lit up, the old journalistic warhorse hearing the bugle call to charge. "Ah, that's the really interesting thing about all this!" Exultantly, he cried, "The Helder case!"

Somerfield shook his head. "Never heard of it."

"You must have, Alex! It was on all the networks and in the news magazines. Late in April, Peter Helder, the famous art dealer was found hanged in a little torture chamber he'd rigged up in the basement. The body was nude save for a black leather hood. Is it coming back to you?"

Somerfield shrugged. "Vaguely."

"It was a hell of a story, believe me. First the cops said it was suicide. They tried to keep the mask part a secret. I broke that angle on the air. Then they admitted it was a homicide. It's had them stymied ever since. But there's more! The detective in charge of the case was also murdered. Then came the attempt on my life. That's a hell of a lot of coincidence. Just the kind of thing you'd've loved to have covered before you rushed off to become a big hot-shot foreign correspondent . . . and whatever else it was you did traipsing the world in a Humphrey Bogart trench coat. That's why I called you."

Drifting back in the comfortable chair, Somerfield

217

could not contain a bemused grin. "What idea have you been cooking up in that blessedly undented but devilishly cockamamie head of yours?"

Bubbling with excitement, Lomax rolled his wheelchair close. "Since I'm obviously anchored to this room for weeks, maybe months, to come, I was thinking that maybe you'd find all this intriguing enough to want to work with me on the story. You do the legwork and when you've got the goods I do the story for my station and maybe there'd be enough in it for you to write a book about it!"

"The mask thing is interesting," said Somerfield guardedly as he rose to pace the crowded room, gazing nostalgically at the microphone on Lomax's table. "The killing of the cop's a bizarre twist. And, of course, what happened to you. But even with all that I'm not sure that it's not too local. It's the kind of story that an editor is likely to see more as a magazine piece than a full-length book on sale around the country."

Lomax snorted. "What are they, blind?"

"Book editors are cautious creatures," said Somerfield, returning to the chair.

"'Stupid' sounds more like it," grumbled Lomax, wheeling away. "So does that mean it's a no from you?" Spinning about, he glared. "Has Alex Somerfield lost the old inquisitive spark? Stopped being a buttinski? Given up the chase? Have you gotten too fat and comfortable on royalty checks, Alex? Satisfied to make up crime stories rather than go after the real ones like you used to?"

"I didn't say no."

"You didn't say yes, either."

"Tell you what," sighed Somerfield. "Let me borrow your files. I'll look 'em over and decide."

Jubilant, Lomax slapped his good left hand on the arm of his wheelchair and shouted, "Great!"

"No promises," said Somerfield.

"There's one more thing," exclaimed Lomax. "The detective on the case, the partner of the one that was murdered? His name's Sheldon Lyman. A nice Jewish boy and a damned good cop!"

"What about him?"

"He's been transferred. Yanked off the Helder case."

Chapter Thirty-One

The Ex-Insider

"I know you're about to insist that I stay here at your house but I don't want you nipping at my heels while I go over this stuff," declared Somerfield, bundling Lomax's files under his arm, "so I'll get myself a hotel room in the city where I'll have some peace and quiet!"

Confident that once his old friend had familiarized himself with the Helder case he'd be hooked, Lomax grinned, "No problem."

Whenever he came back to New York, Somerfield embraced it, but New York, of course, never embraced back. Its attitude to anyone who'd strayed and then returned was, Oh, were you gone? Blasé New York. The Manhattan merry-go-round. Walt Whitman's City of Spires and Masts. Hellinger's Naked City. Damon Runyon's Baghdad on the

Hudson. Evan Hunter's Asphalt Jungle. Mayor John Lindsay's Fun City. Somebody's Ragged Purple Dream. "A sucked orange," someone else had said. With its lofty buildings and streets like logjams, it was center stage for the celebrated. Top of the heap. The only place in the world where it really meant something to be somebody.

On a network television newscast connected with some event in the city that he could not now recall, Somerfield had stood in the heart of Times Square when all the garish advertising signs were ablaze and the news was alight in a white strip ribboning its way around the *Times* building and said, "We've come here, all of us, to conquer what you see behind me. We've come here on a colossal ego trip. We come to subdue the glorious dragon and claim the Holy Grail of Being Somebody. It's not that we really care if head waiters know us by our first names. Or if a producer can get us the best seats for a sold-out Broadway show. Or if we're recognized by cab drivers. Or that the newspapers put our names in their columns. Or that we're on radio or TV. We care about these things only because they proclaim that we've conquered this town. We could vanquish other cities, of course. But so what? Who wants to triumph in Rome or London or Hong Kong? This is the place where the parade matters! But it's also a terrific spot to disappear!"

That was it! He'd made that flowery speech about the lure of fame drawing people to New York because he'd been assigned to cover a story about the arrest of a notorious fugitive. Someone who had been on the FBI's Ten Most Wanted Fugitives list a decade earlier had been nabbed trying to pilfer a hot dog and orange drink at a Nedick's on Broadway. Ten years a wanted man yet he had been living openly in New York all that time, unnoticed and anonymous. It was a city that left you alone if that's what you wished. Here you could be known by everybody on your block, move two streets over and remain a stranger the rest of your life if you chose to. Or you could be Dick Lomax on the radio for a decade, go off for a week and be forgotten about. Or you could be Alexander Somerfield, who'd had all the fame that went along with the glitz of what Lomax called "flash and trash TV," then quit, gone to Pennsylvania to write crime novels and, judging by the lack of recognition of his once-famous face by the desk clerk at the Dorset Hotel, hadn't been missed.

He'd chosen the Dorset on West Fifty-fourth Street because it was around the corner from the new CBS and ABC headquarters buildings and five blocks up from the elegant seventy-story reach of the RCA Building and NBC's offices, studios, and newsroom. Along this "broadcast row" on Sixth Avenue, the networks were known as the rocks. Because NBC's official address was 30 Rockefeller Plaza, it was called Thirty Rock. Because CBS's building was made of black marble it was Black Rock. ABC, because it was in third place in the program ratings, had been labeled Little Rock.

In these broadcasting citadels were employed people who were old friends of his, all the brethren of the Fourth Estate, electronics division, and a few who went back to Alex Somerfield's days belonging to the Inner Circle and his own invented Sacred Order and College of Cardinals of the First Amendment. One o two may have been consecrated into that even higher *sanctum sanctorum*, the Misfits and Malcontents.

At intervals—some long, some short—he'd worked at all of the Rocks and loved every minute of it, especially the headiness of being one of the first people to know when something important had happened. On several occasions he'd even relished the knowledge that an event across the world of monumental significance had been revealed to him before the news of it reached the President of the United States. And far too numerous to recall were the times when what he knew—and all newsmen knew—had not been given to the public: President John F. Kennedy's zest for women, his chronic health problems as a result of a wartime back injury and the drugs that were needed to keep him functioning; Lyndon Johnson's roaming eye; the drunkards in the Senate and the House; the adulterers among elected officials; the closet homosexuals on the government payrolls; who the spies were at the United Nations; and who in Congress, on the Congressional staffs, in the antiwar movement and even in the news media took their marching orders, directly or sympathetically, from the Kremlin. As long as these things were known by the vigilant and watchful insiders of the press, that was sufficient. No need for the public to know and fret so long as the news media were on the alert!

Now Alex Somerfield was an "ex-" in a hotel room close to the places where he used to be an insider.

Another reason he'd decided to stay at the Dorset was a small cocktail room at the front off the lobby where the decor was the shiny black plastic and chrome of the Art Deco of the 1930s when Somerfield's fictional detective sleuthed among speakeasies and clubs decorated similarly. Into this holdover from that era of illicit hooch, jazz, and mobsters he ventured for a scotch and water and to read Dick Lomax's files containing his notes and scripts and the newspaper clippings on the Helder murder and the killing of the detective.

Drinking and smoking a cigar as he read, he found himself liking Lieutenant David Hargreave, even admiring him despite his decidedly unadmirable effort to keep the black hood out of the news. While he fully appreciated Hargreave's reasoning and his desire to hold the hood as a secret shared only by the police and the killer, as a newsman—ex-newsman!—he found it deplorable, a flagrant violation of the spirit of the First Amendment.

What Lomax's file did not convey about Hargreave was a plausible explanation for his unsolved murder. Signaling his waiter to bring him another scotch, he thought, "Assassination is more like it." Or, in the parlance of secret agentry, a wet job. What the Russians called *mokrie dela*.

A flurry of questions arose concerning the detective and his approach to the case that could be answered only by either having access to Hargreave's case file or interviewing his partner, Sergeant Lyman. What lines of investigation had Hargreave been pursuing? Who were the suspects? Were there suspects? What about the classic test for zeroing in on a suspect? Who had motive, means, and opportunity? What had they found out about the leather hood? Was it a message of some kind from the killer? The body was found in what the news media described as a dungeon or torture chamber; what about that? Had Helder been a sadomasochist? Had the denizens of the world of S and M been questioned? What about Helder's—for want of a better word—"normal" life? Enemies? Money problems? Was there any evidence that he was being blackmailed? Might there have been, as Dick Lomax once suspected, a mob connection? Who was Helder, really?

In the file, Helder had come across as an enigma as black and impenetrable as his death mask.

Finished with his scotch and the reading, Somerfield beckoned for a check, smiled slyly, and thought, *"Death Mask.* Catchy title for a book."

Chapter Thirty-Two

Cooling It

While Alexander Somerfield basked in the 1930s grandeur of the Dorset Hotel cocktail lounge mulling over Dick Lomax's files with a scotch in one hand and a cigar in the other, Detective Sergeant Sheldon Lyman was at his desk across town in the Manhattan North detectives' squad room. It was change of shift time. Phones were ringing, typewriters were chattering, and the business of police work was experiencing a sea change as pairs of partners assigned to night duty came on and the day-side couplings went off, all voicing pleasantries or supplying the appropriate friendly and understanding gestures to him who was temporarily without a patner . . . and a case.

"I'm sorry to have to do it, Lyman, but I'm going to close down the Helder investigation," the Captain had told him more than a week ago. It was getting nowhere, he'd pointed out. What were the chances of a break? he'd asked. "Somewhere between unlikely and nil," he'd answered himself. Of course a murder case is never closed until there's an arrest and conviction, he went on, creating a fantasy for both of them that one day the case might be reopened. But they both knew the truth: many homicides lie in the "dormant" files, as dead as the victims themselves. "So what I want you to do, Shelly," the Captain concluded, "is cool it. Take a little time to catch up on your backlog of paperwork until I can hook you up with a new partner and a fresh case. Okay?"

"Put me on the Hargreave investigation," Lyman had pleaded. "The two are tied together!"

"We've been over that ground already," the Captain groaned. "You're not getting involved. I told you! There are plenty of men working on it."

"And getting nowhere fast," Lyman said in disgust.

"They'll break it," grunted the Captain. "So you just let me worry about it, okay? Clean up your desk and your files and be ready for a new assignment when the time comes. Okay?"

It wasn't okay, thought Lyman. Cooling it was not acceptable. But what could he do about it? There was no point in arguing. All he had to say about the Helder case and the murder of Hargreave being connected had already been listened to by the Captain and rejected. What could be done? Go over the Captain's head? Take his reasoning about both murders to someone higher up? Dare he risk his future career on what amounted to nothing more than a hunch?

Sandra Hargreave had had a one-word answer for

him to all those questions. "No." He'd telephoned her and arranged to see her during a hasty lunch in a coffee shop near the Criminal Courts Building. There in the uproar caused by hurried patrons who were a mixture of lawyers and their clients, the worried families and friends of those being weighed in the balances of justice, the DAs who were prosecuting them, witnesses, cops, and jurors, Sandra spoke with cool, calm, and measured wisdom. "By pressing this theory of yours with nothing more than a gut feeling you'd only be hurting yourself, Sheldon. What's your evidence to link the two cases, after all?"

"It's too much of a coincidence," he'd blurted, his anger rising momentarily above the din of the place.

"Evidence is needed," she insisted quietly.

She was right, of course, he admitted to himself as he walked her to the courthouse where the pavements and the steps were awash in people with business pending inside the bleak building bathed in summery sunlight.

When she left him he gazed up at an enclosed passageway that spanned the narrow gap between the daunting and towering courthouse and the high, forbidding, slate gray walls of New York City's men's jail known as the Tombs. Halfway up the clifflike sides of the buildings, the bridge provided an easy access between the cells and holding pens of the Tombs and courtrooms and so had been named after a similar span between a grim medieval prison and the Palace of the Doges in Venice, Italy—The Bridge of Sighs.

In an endless stream from their cells to the

228

courtrooms, across this modern bridge flowed the losers, the luckless, the lawless, and the hapless while waiting for them in the crowded courthouse corridors were their worried and bewildered friends and relatives, huddled in hurried conferences with lawyers, babbling their fears and hopes in a multilingual mayhem in the courthouse's cavernous and echoing lobby.

Turning away, he wondered how many hundreds of his cases had been through the mills of justice represented by the two structures. What number of civil-rights, antiwar and political protesters who had turned "civil disobedience" into the high art and street theater of the tumultuous 1960s? How many of those who'd been arrested for blocking Times Square and trapping him in his car along with all the rest of the traffic had had their day in court? How many muggers, thieves, extortionists, con artists, rapists, hookers and Forty-second Street male hustlers were awaiting the judgment of the law? Would the killer of Peter Helder and David Hargreave be in there one day?

Walking north on Centre Street he passed the domed Police Headquarters building and felt the tug of temptation as a rebellious voice within him screamed at him to barge in and demand to see the Commissioner in order to inform him that the Hargreave killing and the Helder murder were somehow linked and that it was wrong of the Captain to take him off the investigation. "The hell with cooling it," this voice cried. In answer came an inner voice of reason that sounded remarkably like Sandra's. "Go in there and you'll promptly get your head handed to you!"

Presently he reached Greenwich Village and found in the hard daylight a far different place than the one he'd been prowling in the night looking for a shadow named Danny. What he found in the daylight of the Village was a weak echo of the legendary intellectual, artistic, and politically radical enclave of the twenties and thirties that was the closest America ever had come to claiming its own Bohemia.

That Greenwich Village had already vanished by the 1950s when a teenage Sheldon Lyman had roamed its narrow streets and alleys hungering for forbidden fun. Its great crusade for personal and sexual freedom against an older and more puritanical America had been swept aside by the Second World War and the subsequent scramble of its veterans to build their lives in their own way, leaving the Village in the fifties to become domesticated and bourgeois and dull. Around Washington Square in the classrooms of New York University and on campuses all across the country the generation coming of age with Sheldon Lyman in the first decade of the Nuclear Era had been as cool as cool could be . . . so cool they became known as "the silent generation."

Now in the latter years of the sixties the Village belonged to the Dannys of the day and to the pervasive permissiveness of drugs, sex, and rebelling against "the establishment."

Though he'd never met the mysterious Danny—if he existed at all—Lyman believed he knew him well. Were he to find him, he expected to encounter a youth bred on television, weaned on the drug culture, and drowning in the honey of the Sexual Revolution all to the accompaniment of the music of the Beatles, the Rolling Stones, Simon and Garfunkel, and Bob Dylan warning that "the times they are a-changin'."

Danny was the key to the mystery of the Helder homicide.

And Peter Helder's murder contained the solution to the murder of Hargreave.

This belief had not faltered.

And would not falter, pledged Lyman as he went about "cooling it" and working on his paperwork.

Chapter Thirty-Three

The Game's Afoot

"I'll need to go back to Pennsylvania and collect my things," said Somerfield on the telephone from his hotel room the next morning. "And there are a few loose ends to tie up in my personal life."

Excitedly, Lomax said, "How long will you be gone?"

"Couple of days. Meantime—"

Lomax cut him off. "Meantime, you want me to set up a meeting between you and Lyman!"

"In the meantime, I want no such thing," snapped Somerfield. "I want you to sit tight until you hear from me again. Before I have any meeting with this police detective—if he agrees to meet with us!—I want to do a little poking around on my own. Check out the geography. Sniff the air. Get the feel of the texture of all this that you can't get reading the files."

Saying this, he recalled a snippet of a long-ago lecture at Warren Davis's school for agents. "Files are great but there's nothing as good as an agent on the ground seeing for himself."

Hanging up, he recalled that Davis also had taught the uses of a lie like the one he'd just told Lomax.

Picking up the phone again, he dialed a number that would connect him with another old journalistic friend, Ray Taylor, and arranged a meeting.

Strolling from the Dorset to Rockefeller Plaza, he paced himself against the flow of the crowds heading for their homes in the onset of dusk and arrived at the plaza ten minutes early so he could bask in the glories of the singular spot in Manhattan that never failed to stir his love for the most improbable city in the world which for the greater part of his working years had been his home base.

Leaning against the wall behind and above the gleaming golden statue of Prometheus bringing fire to mankind that overlooked the sunken plaza, he observed a mixture of tourists and New Yorkers already having dinner al fresco under gaily striped canopies that come autumn would be stripped of tables and flowers to make room for the ice skating rink and, before anyone realized it, a towering Christmas tree.

Turning his back to the colorful plaza, he craned his neck to peer up the long slim facade of the RCA Building, a cathedral of Art Deco style that was the same age as himself. When the building and he had turned forty he'd thrown himself a birthday party in the splendid Rainbow Room atop the skyscraper, as tall buildings used to be called before someone invented the utterly mundane and unromantic term "high-rise." It had been a glittery black-tie event to which he'd invited sixty of his family and friends to celebrate his four decades of living and the coincidental publication of a new thriller that unfolded at Rockefeller Center in the 1930s.

Sixty floors down from the Rainbow Room and five years before the party, he had worked for Ray Taylor who had been foreign news manager at the network long before Alexander Somerfield put on a foreign correspondent's trenchcoat and set out to cover the world. And to spy on it, he thought, his eyes lowering to the congregated flags of the nations of the world rippling on a gentle breeze around the plaza and coming to rest on the red banner of Soviet Russia with its yellow hammer and sickle, symbol of all that he was against then, now, and forever.

A few paces away on the fifth floor of the Associated Press Building were the offices of the Soviet Union's news agency, TASS, where from time to time over the years had worked Mikhail Shilovsky, the incarnation of all that the Russians stood for. There were two Russias, Warren Davis had taught and Somerfield had discovered by himself. One was that which the West knew and which Somerfield believed was the true Russia—a grim, prisonlike, half-frozen, and totally paranoid country which had thrown off the Czar and gotten Stalin in his place and had erected an iron curtain and whose goal was nothing less than the remaking of the world on Soviet terms. The other one was Mother Russia spilling as poetry from the cupid's bow lips of Misha Shilovsky—vigorous and optimistic, land of dedicated patriots who had been brutally treated by the

West but remained undaunted and fervently dedicated to the principles of Marx and Lenin. The Russia of the outsiders—Somerfield's Russia—and the Russia of the Russians—Shilovsky's.

Somerfield and Shilovsky. They had been a mirror image—but the mirror was the distorting kind found in an amusement park fun house—and their story would be grist for a dozen spy thrillers if only the author could open the files and take out the folders with their childlike codewords of spies and their masters: APPROBATION, APEX, ARCHANGEL, DEADEYE, QUICKSILVER, VIXEN, ZULU; tales about double agents, double crosses, turns, burns, nets, and cells; actions blown or just plain botched; stuff that deserved medals and stuff that cried out for the firing squad; information sought, bought, stolen, or given; truth and lies; information worth its weight in gold and disinformation worth its weight in lives. A deadly game with plenty of guilt to go around, Somerfield said to himself as he spotted an innocent named Raymond Taylor.

"Alex, you old fart," Ray exclaimed with a bearhug, "what a surprise!" Although he was second-generation Irish-American, he had a trace of Irish lilt in his voice, more than a trace of Ireland in his ruddy face, sparkling green eyes, and auburn hair going rapidly to silver, and far too much of the auld sod in his thirst for whiskey, a penchant which he had managed to stop through Alcoholics Anonymous and gallons of diet colas swilled down while dealing with the crises and calamities of the world flowing across his desk.

"How's the news business, Ray?"

"Not the same without you, Alex."

"Still ladling out the blarney, I see."

"Blarney, hell. I'd give my right nut to have you back in harness. Today I've got correspondents who think they're in show business and that the only questions worth asking are what color necktie to wear, is my hair combed, and what shade of Max Factor pancake makeup to use. They are ignorant of tradition, have no sense of history, and think the world began on their birthday. God, do you realize that I have been in the news business longer than most of my correspondents have been alive?"

"Don't tell me. Let me guess. You've had a hard day at the office."

They had dinner at an old haunt, Jimmy's Irish Pub on Fifty-seventh Street where the food was superb and comfortably priced and Irish rebel music from a jukebox set the proper background for the bragging bar talk and the darts that were reminiscent of countless nights in joints whose name Alex had long forgotten.

There'd been saloons on the waterfront below the Presidio of Monterey in California reeking with the atmosphere of John Steinbeck novels and offering respite from the grueling study of Russian in Army Language School classes thirty hours a week; tight-lipped hangouts where Warren Davis's spies-in-training took a breather from schooling at Camp Peary, the Agency's "Farm" near Williamsburg, Virginia; dark gossipy journalistic watering holes on Capitol Hill where the booze was costly and the leaks of inside information from "informed sources" came cheap; bars nearest to the site of whatever disaster had become a media circus attracting droves of newsmen like vultures to a carcass; hospitality suites at political conventions set up by canny men of smoke-filled rooms whom pundits called king-makers and who despite autocratic and even venal ways had picked pretty good candidates for President; and swank clubs and cocktail lounges in the press hotels at summit meetings between this American President or that one and the Bolshevik thug dressed up in Italian-designer silk suits who happened to be boss of the Red Empire at the moment.

Over the years the summits became one more battlefield of the Cold War and the Russians grew more sophisticated and adroit when it came to dishing out disinformation to a Western Press that appeared to be increasingly naive, ignorant of history, and more interested in the marvels of their emerging technology which resulted in them becoming appallingly gullible and ripe for seductions.

Ray Taylor had been a newsman through most of it—straight and honest and fair and innocent and with no knowledge of the other side of his friend Alex, although hardly an innocent in all matters.

"You used to have an apartment," said Somerfield. "Your little hideaway? That dreaded den from which no woman ever left a virgin?"

"Still have it," leered Ray.

"Might it be, uh, available for a couple of days? Maybe even a week?"

Ray's smile stretched to a grin as he fished a key

ring from his pocket. "It's all yours for as long as you like," he said, unhooking the key and slapping it into Alex's hand; no questions asked.

After dinner there was still time before the department stores closed, allowing Somerfield in a span of eighteen minutes at Alexander's to buy clothing straight off the rack, premeasured and pretailored and not bad for the price—a gray suit, brown sports jacket and navy blue slacks that would go with either the gray coat or the brown one, two ties with blue and brown stripes, three packages of white cotton briefs three-to-a-package and a half-dozen pairs of knee-length black socks.

The apartment was a few blocks away on Sixty-fifth Street, but before he turned into the block he paused to scan it, checking, looking for anything amiss. Going by rote. The caution drummed into him years ago by Warren Davis having become instinctual—once learned, never forgotten, like riding a bike, driving a car, tying a shoelace. All the rules for going safely coming back in a flood. The clutter of Fibber McGee's closet tumbling forth at the opening of the door. The art of leaving the back way. Never sit with your back to a door. Looking for the exit signs. Noticing without being noticed who occupied the next table. Who was seated in a hotel lobby as you entered? Who was in the phone booth? What cars were parked outside? The coats worn by men and women on the street. Where their hands were, in pockets or out. Might a rolled-up newspaper conceal a weapon? Is the basket of fruit in the hotel room when you check in bugged? Could an umbrella have a poisoned tip? Was the agent you were working

238

with a plant? All the intricacies of the spy fiction of John LeCarré's realistic spies and none of the bogus razzle-dazzle of Ian Fleming.

As to the book he'd been working on and which the call from Dick Lomax had interrupted, he had at least fifty more pages to write and had misgivings about the plausibility of the suspect he had decided would turn out to be the murderer in the story which was due at his publisher's office in September.

Sleepless at three o'clock in the morning and prompted by the clock and his dinner with Ray to think of time and Irishmen, he recalled a line from F. Scott Fitzgerald. "'In a real dark night of the soul,'" he said, turning on a light, "'it is always three o'clock in the morning.'"

Then, as always, other Fitzgerald aphorisms flooded his head. "Show me a hero and I'll write you a tragedy," from his *Notebooks*.

"'Draw your chair up close to the edge of the precipice and I'll tell you a story,'" he muttered in the pale grayish yellow light of Ray's hideaway bedroom. *Ibid*.

How he had admired Fitzgerald in those days of youth when he longed to be a writer and thought the way to get there was studying journalism, leading him to recall the first day of his first creative writing class at Iowa and the professor leafing through registration cards turned in by the students and coming upon his, reading his name aloud and sniffing the air as if he'd smelled something awful. "Well, Mr. Somerfield, I see that you are from the Journalism Department. I hope you make tons of money."

He'd done some good writing for that class but never got more than a C.

"All good writing is swimming under water and holding your breath," Fitzgerald had put in a letter to someone.

Three o'clock in the morning!

How many three o'clocks had he known in his checkered existence? Staking out a story as a journalist. Staking out an enemy as an agent. And finding no contradiction.

"The test of a first-rate intelligence is the ability to hold two opposed ideas in the mind at the same time, and still retain the ability to function," wrote Fitzgerald in *The Crack-up*, a line worthy of a burnt-out spy in a LeCarré yarn.

Abandoning all hope of sleeping, and sitting up on the edge of his borrowed bed of sin, he became keenly aware of the New-York-at-three-in-the-morning quiet no one except a New Yorker would ever believe possible. When he'd lived in the city and went down to Pennsylvania to visit his family for holidays such as Christmas and family reunions they'd scoffed when he claimed that the only place he could ever get a good night's rest was New York and that the supposed tranquility of the countryside was a damned lie because each and every night when he was at home all he ever heard was dogs barking, babies wailing, crickets, and birds yelling their heads off at the first crack of dawn, making sleep impossible.

How he had managed to grow up in such a noisy place was a puzzle but, miraculously, since he'd moved back to Pennsylvania all the noise seemed like music.

This morning, however, it wasn't noise that had him awake but loosened memory and the stirring demands of a weary body.

For thirty years he had tried to defend America in his own way and remain true to himself while balanced on the cusp of truth and duplicity, Fitzgerald's man holding two opposed ideas at the same time and hoping he'd still be able to function—a dilemma he had sought to escape, at last, by retiring from both the news business and spying.

"Silly boy," he said with a flashed grin at himself reflected in the bathroom mirror as he awaited the functioning of his kidneys. Lately, the need to urinate and not an ideological crisis was more likely to be the reason for his being awake at three in the morning and quoting the dead Irish-American hero-novelist of his possibly squandered youth while wondering how the hell he got to feel so middle-aged so soon.

Looking for the answer in a face that didn't appear half as haggard and old as he felt at that moment, he found in his reflection a person who had managed rather well through the years to live up to Fitzgerald's admirable but unwitting description of what was required of one of Warren Davis's agents of influence.

"'So we beat on,'" he said, muttering the last line in *The Great Gatsby*, "'boats against the current borne back ceaselessly into the past.'"

Another line came. "'The world is small when our enemy is loose on the other side.'"

Was that Fitzgerald, too? he asked himself as he went back to bed. "No, some other Irishman," he murmured. Then, smiling and thinking about the puzzle and the challenge which Dick Lomax had presented to him, he remembered a phrase written by another Irish writer with an Irish name—Sir Arthur Conan Doyle—and spoken rousingly at ungodly hours of the morning to the indomitable Dr. Watson by Sherlock Holmes: "The game's afoot!"

Chapter Thirty-Four

Legends

When Somerfield awoke with the murder of Peter Helder on his mind it was with the not unpleasant realization that no one in the world, save the reliable secret-keeper Ray Taylor, knew his whereabouts. The feeling was not new. As a freshman in college, he and Russ Branson had taken off for two weeks, telling none of their friends they were going to hitchhike to California just for the hell of it. Four years later he'd effectively vanished from the face of the earth going the other way—west to east—immediately after finishing language school training. In 1963 he'd cashed in airline tickets supplied by his British literary agent for a return from a conference in London on foreign rights to his latest novel and without telling anyone sailed to New York on the Queen Elizabeth's last crossing before she was turned into a Caribbean cruise liner. In those five days he came to appreciate the beauties of purposely losing himself, of decompressing, of being free to mull over things such as plots for new books and the purpose of his life.

Today's purpose was clearer. To turn Dick Lomax's files into reality by seeing as many as possible of the places and people which figured in the entwined mysteries of the murders of an art dealer and a homicide detective. In the army he'd learned that the outcome of a battle depends upon two factors: the situation and the terrain. "This statement is true," said Warren Davis at the Farm, "but how does a general come to know and understand the situation and the terrain? His Intelligence Officer explains it to him! And how does the Intelligence Officer get his information? The same way Joshua found out the weaknesses in the walls of Jericho. SPIES! Oh, yes, gentlemen, it's a holy and blessed endeavor, spying!"

And Warren Davis had been its prophet.

"Invent an index of legends for yourself," he'd advised his students. "Don't just pick a name. Work out an entire life story. Create a character. Carry an entire roster of these legends in your head, ready for you to assume as your own identity in the twinkling of an eye!"

Sitting on the edge of Ray Taylor's bed, Somerfield wondered if that's what had gotten him started in the fiction business; his knack for making up legends. If so, he thought while he shaved, Warren Davis might be justified in asking for a ten percent royalty on his books, all written under his true name, by the way, no literary legends. If ever one of his books landed on a best seller list it wasn't going to be with a fake author's name!

Were he to decide to do so, he ruminated as he dressed in one of his new suits, he could leave Ray's hideaway apartment with any identity he cared to choose from the phony biographies he'd created for himself following Davis's advice, although in all his years as an agent he'd never actually used a workname. He'd been given the one for the record that had amounted to nothing more serious than an office joke—Deerstalker—but had never affixed it to a report nor used it in a crash call as he'd been instructed should he ever find himself in jeopardy.

He'd never even come close to being in a tight spot! After all, he wasn't one of those glamour boy agents to whom Walther PPK pistols were issued. No codebooks. No James Bond stuff. No L-for-lethal cyanide pills for taking one's own life if trapped by the enemy and facing torture. His only torture had been some of his coworkers and stupid assignments handed out by the dolts on the newsdesk when Ray Taylor was off-duty or on vacation. Through it all as newsman, agent of influence, and author he'd always been Alexander Somerfield and happy to heed the advice Sherlock Holmes had dealt out in *The Blue Carbuncle* to the bungling thief, James Ryder: *"It is always awkward doing business with an alias."*

When he addressed the handsome woman wearing black dress and pearls at the Helder Galleries whom he assumed to be the Eleanora Swaim mentioned in Lomax's file, he announced, "Somerfield is my name."

Then he became a legend speaking lies. "I'm in the market for a painting. I wonder if I might speak to

Mr. Helder?"

With a mild look of surprise, the woman said, "I'm sorry, sir, but Mr. Helder is deceased."

"Oh, I am so sorry," said the legend, noting that this woman who'd found the body hanging from the rafters was remarkably controlled. "What a tragedy for the world of fine art and those who knew him."

Looking quizzical now, she asked, "Were you acquainted with Mr. Helder?"

Somerfield hesitated. Did she see right through his legend? "Only casually, I'm sorry to say," he said, barging forward in his deception as absorbing eyes that had been trained to both report and spy roamed the gallery to the rear and what he assumed was the door leading to the cellar where Helder's body had been discovered by this steel-nerved inquisitive woman. "I would see him at various exhibitions and so forth," he continued casually. "I've been abroad. I'd no idea he was ill."

"He died . . . suddenly," she said, sounding as if "suddenly" were the cause of death. She did not say "as a suicide" nor "murdered."

"What a blow that has to have been for his family," he said sympathetically as he returned his eyes to her. "I should like to . . . ." What? Hear the truth from you? Get a confession? Know everything you know about Helder? ". . . express my condolences in some way to his . . ." His what? To her? Who was she? His lover? ". . . survivors."

"There was no family, Mr. Somerfield."

"How sad. Might there be someone in charge of creating an appropriate memorial? A charity to which I might contribute?"

"You'd have to speak to the executor of the estate," she said, betraying a hint of bitterness by a slight pursing of lips.

Give me the name please, he thought as he asked, "Would you happen to know who that is?"

"The president of Mr. Helder's club, the Atlantis Club," she said with an air of distaste. "His name is von Bork."

Now there's a sinister-sounding name! "What a responsibility has devolved upon him," he said, raising his arms as if to encompass the galleries. "All this and, I expect, quite a private collection. Mr. Helder had such exquisite and discriminating taste," he went on, appearing to be admiring the displayed art but actually memorizing the layout and registering the fact that from her desk Eleanora Swaim commanded a view of the entrance to Helder's apartment above. "My taste in art was always in accord with his. That is why I've come now that I'm in the mood to buy something."

"As to that, I'm afraid there would be a delay," she said crisply. "You see, until the estate is settled the assets are frozen. It would be quite impossible to close a sale at this time, although you may place a request to buy. I expect there will be an auction eventually."

"Yes, I do see. In that case I suppose it's best that I wait until it's all sorted out."

Were this fiction and not real life, he asked himself as he left the galleries, what role would he ascribe to Eleanora Swaim? What did she know about Helder? What might she be keeping secret? Might she turn out to be the villain of the piece? Make that villainess! Might she be as dissembling and conniving with the sleuth in the piece as Brigid O'Shaughnessey was with Sam Spade in Dashiell Hammett's *The Maltese Falcon*? As clever as Irene Adler in outwitting Holmes in *A Scandal in Bohemia*? If he were to write a novel about a murdered art dealer and fictionalize Eleanora Swaim might he characterize her as Dr. Watson had described Irene Adler—"of dubious and questionable memory"—and whom Holmes would seldom mention under any other name but *"the woman?"* Should Eleanora Swaim be included in Holmes's caveat? *"A woman is not to be trusted. Not the best of them."* Or was there nothing there at all except the incarnation of his fertile imagination?

The stolid facade of the Atlantis Club he observed from across Park Avenue, deciding that here were walls like those of Jericho requiring considerably more intelligence data before any attempt could be made to breech them and thus approach the executor of the Helder estate, Mr. von Bork, who seemed to be held by Eleanora Swaim in the same esteem as Dr. John H. Watson held Irene Adler—a person of dubious and questionable memory.

For that kind of data, to find out anything about the private clubs and otherwise secretive institutions of New York, Somerfield knew the only person to turn to—B. Alexander Wiggins, the proprietor of a singular Manhattan establishment where no legend would be required: the Usual Suspects Bookshop.

Chapter Thirty-Five

The Usual Suspects

With the skill of a manufacturer of instant antiquities who might be found haggling over prices in a shop near the Pyramids of Giza, or grabbing tourists in the suk to sell them a sliver of the True Cross near the Damascus Gate in Jerusalem, Wiggins had deftly created the impression of having been in the book business for decades rather than four years.

Located in the heart of Fourth Avenue's cluster of stores selling used books, it was scented with the familiar and hospitable fragrance of an old library crammed with cherished volumes, of mellowed paper, of leather bindings, of dust, of furniture oils and of the pungent bouquet of tobacco. The premises had been laid out scrupulously by Wiggins for his architect and interior designer according to the description of his favorite bookstore, "Parnassus at Home," which had never been a real bookstore but was the literary invention of Christopher Morley, who had also invented The Baker Street Irregulars, of which Wiggins was a member—insisting to Somerfield that he was a descendent of the street urchin named Wiggins who was the leader of the original Irregulars in the Sherlock Holmes adventures. "This is the store I want," he'd announced, flipping open Morley's *The Haunted Bookshop* and pointing with a stubby finger to the pertinent passages that described how two stories of an old house had been thrown into one with the lower space divided into little alcoves while above a gallery ran around the wall and carried books to the ceiling and in Wiggins's plan could be ascended to by way of a spiral staircase that extended to the floors farther above where Wiggins resided.

Like Morley's mythical emporium, the shop had a warm and comfortable obscurity, a kind of drowsy dusk stabbed here and there by bright cones of yellow light from green-shaded library lamps with a pervasive drift of tobacco smoke eddying and fuming under the shades, foglike, but while "Parnassus at Home" was stuffed with the ghosts of all great literature, The Usual Suspects was crowded with murderers, thieves, kidnappers, blackmailers, thugs, muggers, and all the rest of the sinister creatures, malign presences, and lurking villains, real and imagined, who had leapt off the pages to thrill readers from the father of the mystery yarn, Edgar Allen Poe, to the latest best-selling hardcover chillers and mystery yarns including, Somerfield was happy to note, his own.

There were also books of dark tone—the occult, black magic, and secret societies and their rituals.

Certainly no human being played the role of a man of mystery better than Wiggins. Nor looked the part, going about the streets in the winter in a Sherlockian deerstalker cap and Inverness cloak, although until he opened his store he had rarely stirred from a Greenwich Village apartment cluttered with books, newspapers, magazines, and artifacts of every description having to do with Sherlock Holmes, the flat having become world famous as an address where a researcher on any aspect of the world's first consulting detective could find answers, either directly from a vast library on the subject or from the expert's memory trove on almost any subject.

Weighing at least three hundred pounds and bald as a pumpkin, as he sat in a spacious armchair at the center of this archive, an oriental robe draping his immensity, his amazingly tiny feet in ornate Persian slippers, a collection of pipes at hand, he resembled a Buddha, but those who knew parts of the Alexander Wiggins biography appreciated that he was not what he seemed to be. It had been confirmed that he had been one of the youngest European operatives in the Office of Strategic Services during the Second World War. Suspected but not proved was his connection to the Central Intelligence Agency's activities in pre- and post-Castro Cuba including the Bay of Pigs and the 1962 missile crisis when the store became a safe house where crash meetings were held between CIA and KGB agents frantically trying to avert a thermonuclear exchange.

"In its earliest days, the house had achieved notoriety as the site of the murder of Cleopatra Ducoyne by Robertus Flynn, a remarkably adept deceiver of rich women," Wiggins was fond of relating. "Less than a year after the house had been commissioned by the fabulously wealthy Cleopatra, a leader of High Society in her Victorian day, Robertus did her in with a meat cleaver which also served the purpose of chopping the corpse into chunks small enough for Robertus to tuck under his arm in the form of neatly wrapped brown paper bundles and carry uptown to a slaughter house where he was employed, one of many assorted abattoirs then located on ground now occupied by the United Nations. There Robertus discreetly discarded the remains of Cleo amongst the offal of the legitimate butcheries, all in all a fancy scheme. But, of course, there was left the problem of Cleo's head, which would have stood out in the scraps, so Robertus decided to place the *objet* in a stone and brick weighted burlap bag and dump it in the East River. Unhappily for Robertus, a nosy neighbor with a suspicious nature observed Robertus flinging the sack into the water and promptly fished it out and just as promptly ran to the cops. It's been said that the abbreviated ghostly form of Cleo roams the rooms to pester occupants by inquiring whether they have seen her head lying around anywhere. I only hope the painters haven't driven the old girl away."

Tainted by the murder, the house seemed doomed to infamy. In the Speakeasy age a saloon at the address was owned by Owney Madden, the Irish hoodlum who also bankrolled the Cotton Club in Harlem and was a rival to Lucky Luciano. In the 1940s it was turned into a whorehouse featuring very young women and run by a pimp by the name of Jake

Elmore. "In the fifties it had been a meeting place for a cell of artistic and literary Communist sympathizers driven underground during the McCarthy period who thought they'd escaped the probing eyes of the FBI," laughed Wiggins in the telling, "only to discover at their trials that the wild-eyed and depraved-looking young men on the top floor whom they had believed to be a couple of poetry-writing fairies were actually G-men from the Red Squad."

Somerfield had never heard him talk about the use of the address as an Agency safe house in 1962.

The following year Wiggins had thrown open the door to purvey that highest of intoxicants—the mystery story.

Arriving at eleven o'clock, he found the door locked and the green shade drawn.

In the window were two signs:

THANK YOU
FOR NOT ASKING ME
NOT TO SMOKE

CLOSED
BUT IF YOU ABSOLUTELY
MUST HAVE A BOOK
KNOCK LOUDLY

Somerfield banged the door hard.

A shadow that could not have been anyone's but Wiggins's fell upon the shade and his unmistakable basso voice boomed: "Who is it?"

"Deerstalker!"

Lifting the shade a crack and peering out, Wiggins said, "Are you alone?"

"Certainly I'm alone."

"Are you sure you weren't followed?"

"Why should I be followed? And by whom?"

"By *them*."

"Them?"

"They are everywhere."

"They?"

"The Communists, of course," Wiggins laughed, throwing open the door and spreading his arms in what Somerfield knew was prelude to a breathtaking bear hug. Then tea would be required. And catching up on old times and recent gossip.

"I encountered your old school chum Branson the other day," said Wiggins as he poured his latest favorite herbal brew into delicate cups. "Though he wouldn't utter a word about it, I understand by way of the grapevine of that special old-boy network we must both deny we belong to that Russell has again been elevated in the hierarchy. Now he is in charge of the Arab Desk in Middle East Operations. This strikes me as being as appealing as being put in charge of a harem, a job which, as you know, traditionally demands immediate conversion into a eunuch."

"I can't picture Russ letting anybody emasculate him."

A giggle shook the fat folds of Wiggins's enormous body like an earthquake. "'Iron balls!' Wasn't that what everybody used to call him back in the good old days?"

"Besides, the Arab Desk is probably pretty hot right now. There's a new war in the making, isn't there?"

"How would I know, dear boy? I've been out of the loop lo these many years."

"And your chat with Russ was just a happy coincidence!"

"Yes, it was! But I'll never persuade you, I see. You have not lost an iota of your notorious skepticism as you pursue your muse in that leafy glade where you've pitched your tent."

"How is Russ?"

"As inscrutable as ever," said Wiggins, setting aside his tea and settling back in a giant chair with his pudgy hands folded upon the swell of his belly. "Now tell me what's brought you out of the Pennsylvania wilderness to come tap-tap-tapping like the Raven at my door."

"What do you know about the Atlantis Club?"

"Ah, Somerfield, that is a long story."

"I'm in no hurry."

"Do you know your Plato?"

"Philosophy was not my strong point in college, mostly because the lectures always seemed to be always scheduled at eight in the morning!"

"Plato in *Timaeus* and *Critias* spoke of the Athenian jurist Solon describing Atlantis as a powerful nation larger than Libya and Asia Minor combined and peopled with sages and scientists, the greatest minds that ever existed, all of whom were destroyed when Atlantis was engulfed by the sea. Since that time it has been the spiritual magnet of many occultists, dreamers, utopians, end-of-the-world visionaries, racial supremacists, declarers of Doomsday and downright demented troublemakers. In Europe these loonies sprouted like mushrooms and, of course, some of their spores floated across the Atlantic to the New World. The Atlantis Club here was founded around the turn of the century on Macdougal Street in a cafe that was avante-garde even for the Village. It's quartered now in a grand old mansion on Park Avenue, proving once again that there's money in madness. Or vice versa. The person you really ought to see if you need to go deeper into all this is a professor at New York University, Norman Levitan."

Chapter Thirty-Six

Of Gods and Beasts

He was not able to arrange to see Professor Levitan until the next afternoon.

"So you wish to know about the Atlantis Club, Mr. Somerfield," said the Professor, a small gray figure who appeared to be in his mid-60s as he sat behind a paper-littered desk in a bookish third-floor office in a former carriage house on quaint Washington Mews. "May I ask why?"

"It may figure into a novel I'm thinking of writing," said Somerfield, mixing legend with truth. "I write mysteries."

"I have little time for fiction," said Levitan with a shrug as he directed Somerfield to a chair. "No offense intended!"

"None taken," smiled Somerfield.

"To understand the Atlantis Club you must begin with Atlantis itself. What is not generally appreciated about that mythical place, sir, is the profound—no, devastating!—effect it has had on history. I don't know the thrust of the book you are writing but if going back that far strikes you as being rather afield . . ."

"Not at all, professor. My mind's wide open!"

The professor smiled wanly. "A rarity these days, Mr. Somerfield."

"Alas!"

"My specialty here is an oddball mixture of ancient and modern history, religion and philosophy, political science and sociology. I suppose you could say that I put history on the psychoanalyst's couch, paying special attention to the various ideological tides that have swept men along. I have a keen interest in secret societies and cults. Atlantis has always been a favorite of those who are drawn to the occult and a wellspring of inspiration for individuals and groups who believe in their natural racial superiority over others. Ripe for this sort of myth-making was Germany, especially in the hard times after the end of the first war. I know this because I was there and saw the rise of a German *volkisch* cult patterned after the Atlantean myth and known as the Thule Society. In their cant, the Thulists asserted that Atlantis—which they called Thule—was in the far north and the original home of the Aryan master race. The Grand Master of the Thule Society called himself Baron Rudolf von Sebottendorf. He published a recruiting pamphlet titled *Runen*. One of the first to read it and join Thule was Helmut von Graubatz, a friend of another disgruntled misfit named Heinrich Himmler. You perhaps detect where this narrative is heading?"

"The Thule Society was a precursor of the Nazis?"

"I hope you do not think that because I am a Jew I'm giving all this a slant. Because there is nothing that needs to be made up or imagined about the link between the Atlantis myth and what the Nazis did to the Jews."

"I'm here to learn, professor, so please continue."

"By late 1918 the Thule Society had less than two thousand members, all in Bavaria, where I came from, with about 250 in Munich. Among members of the Thule Society were Ernst Rohm, who became leader of the brown-shirted Storm Troopers; Julius Streicher, the Nazi party leader of Franconia; Friedrich Krohn, a dentist who designed the Nazi swastika insignia; Rudolph Hess, Hitler's secretary and first adjutant; and, apparently, Hitler himself. Are you still with me, Mr. Somerfield?"

"Indeed I am!"

"Now at the same time in Germany there were many groups being organized, not all of them as far-fetched as the Thulists. I don't want you to think that all the Germans at the time were chasing these ridiculous theories. It was a period of great hardship and panic. One must bear in mind that while all this was going on in Germany, the Ku Klux Klan was having a stupendous rebirth here in America. There was in Germany, however, a rather unique connection made between the hardships of the everyday life and the influence of a supernaturally inspired evil. Therefore, groups which offered mystical explanations for problems and a supernatural resolution of them easily found root in the desperate times of Germany after the Great War. It was easy to persuade them that their mutual enemies at the time were the Communists and the Jews, who often were one and the same. Have you heard of *The Protocols of the Elders of Zion*, Mr. Somerfield?"

"Heard of 'em; never read them."

"You are not alone in that," said the professor as he rose from his desk to search the shelves of his haphazard library. "Of that piece of racial filth, many had heard and few had read. Yet the *Protocols* became one of the foundation stones of anti-Semitism. These *Protocols* were believed to be the blueprint for Jewish domination of the world. Yet they were a fake! Fiction."

He found what he was looking for and passed it to Somerfield—a pamphlet printed in German.

"What you have in your hands," said the professor, returning to his desk, "is the imaginings of a German journalist, Hermann Goedsche, writing under the pseudonym Sir John Retcliffe. His novel *Biarritz* published in 1868 had a chapter in it titled 'In the Jewish Cemetery in Prague' in which the Devil appears to twelve Jews. Together they plot a Jewish takeover of the entire earth. This concoction was taken out of context and peddled as truth. And it was right down the alley of groups like the Thule Society. And others that flourished then. Hitler believed in the *Protocols*."

Somerfield laid the pamphlet on the desk.

The professor stared at it. "Hitler believed in the *Protocols* and in the Atlantis myth. He is quoted somewhere as saying, 'In the depths of his subconscious every German has one foot in Atlantis.' It's no wonder that he would declare, 'Gods and beasts, that is what our world is made of.' I know this for a fact, for I was there when he said it!"

Somerfield lurched forward, exclaiming, "You actually heard Hitler speak in person?"

"It was that very speech that finally persuaded me that the Nazis weren't jesting and that the time had come for me to get the hell out of Germany," smiled the professor. "That was in 1932. I was barely thirty years old and thought to be quite brilliant. My job when I managed to reach America was as a janitor in a tenement on the Lower East Side. But America is a place of opportunity and now you see me exalted!"

"You did very well, sir."

"So you can see how it was," the professor said, shrugging off thoughts of himself and returning to his subject. "With Hitler and many of his top men imbued with these harebrained ideas of lost civilizations, of demigods and gods, and that a superrace of Aryans was destined to inherit the earth, is it any wonder, then, that the instrumentalities of the Nazi regime would be patterned on those myths? And that their sworn enemies would be the Jews? It was a small step, sir, from swearing an oath as a Thulist to the crematoria of the death camps."

"But what's the connection to the Atlantis Club?"

"Besides the Thule Society," the professor replied, "there was the Vril Society, a secret community of occultists also known as the Luminous Lodge. Their belief was also based on the Atlantis myth and the idea of supermen who thrived on a magic fluid called Vril. This group was in close contact with the Golden Dawn Society in England and a small band of like-minded occultists and fantasists here in New

York known as the Atlantis Club."

"The one which still exists?"

"Quite so, although it now has a reputation as a club for geographers, explorers, conservationists, and oceanographers, indicating that the organization is quite different today from its beginnings. One thing about it has not changed, however. No Jews need apply!" He paused, thinking, then with a sly smile said, "Did you know that one of its members was recently murdered under rather mysterious circumstances? A very interesting case, worthy of a book."

With a chuckle, Somerfield said, "Am I that transparent?"

"In that club are some of this city's wealthiest and most powerful men, Mr. Somerfield. They cherish their secrets and guard them ruthlessly."

"In the murder which you referred to, the executor of the estate of the dead man, Peter Helder, is the president of the Atlantis Club. His name is . . . ."

"Helmut von Bork. A most unpleasant and, I think, a very dangerous and unscrupulous man! He has been at the head of the Atlantis Club since before the war. During it, he and the club were kept under surveillance by the FBI because of suspicions that it was a front for Nazi espionage. There were no arrests, however; no proof. As to von Bork, he is an expert Egyptologist and wrote a brilliant paper several years ago based on his research into the influence of Atlantis on Egyptian monotheism and the impact of those Egyptian ideas on Judaism and especially on the Essene cult—famous as the creators of the Dead Sea Scrolls—and thereby on Christianity."

"That is quite a breathtaking intellectual odyssey," exclaimed Somerfield.

"Mr. von Bork has spent a great deal of time and money seeking proofs for his theories. It would be quite a thing, wouldn't it, if he could show that Christianity grew out of Egyptian religious thought and not Hebrew? What impact might it have on the relationship between the United States and Israel, for instance?"

"With all due respect, professor, the Israeli-American equation is based on keeping the Russians out of the Middle East, not because of any notions of Judeo-Christian brotherhood."

"That is true, but showing that Christianity was as much Arab-based as Jewish might lead to a more balanced policy in the Middle East. Why hasn't the United States tried to build an anti-Soviet bulwark with the Arab nations? The answer von Bork suggests is that Jews have cleverly made the connection between the survival of Israel and the sentimentality of American Christians towards the Holy Land, meaning Israel. If it could be shown that the Arabs have as much a claim to the edification of Jesus Christ as the Jews, why then should the United States be so adamantly pro-Israel and anti-Arab? It's a tantalizing postulation with profound implications!"

"Very interesting, of course," said Somerfield, "but how could von Bork possibly make such a case?"

"A man who can believe in Atlantis and supermen can be expected to believe almost anything is possible. One of von Bork's beliefs is that there exists written evidence of the years Jesus spent in Egypt. A so-called 'Lost Gospel' that fills in the gaps in Christ's biblical biography and has him in Egypt receiving his inspiration from God, much as Moses received his in the land of the pharaohs! He alleges that the existence of this gospel has been suppressed by the Jews. But he contends that a copy of it is located somewhere in Egypt. He's spent millions looking for it."

"And being swindled, of course," suggested Somerfield with a wry grin.

"He's not the only Atlantis Club member chasing a will-o'-the-wisp," said the professor. "This fellow who was murdered, this man Helder, was also seeking a relic of Christ. This object is known among the Atlanteans of the world as the Spear of Destiny or the Heliga Lance. It's said to be the weapon that pierced Christ's side on the cross. Whoever possesses it, the legend goes, rules the world, for good or evil. How does one recognize the Heliga Lance, according to the myth? Its shaft is entwined by interlocking golden swastikas! In the current vernacular, Mr. Somerfield, 'How does that grab you?'"

"Do you suspect any link between Helder's murder and his friends in the Atlantis Club?"

"I'm not a detective. I'm a professor. I do not have to answer questions. I only have to ask them. You are a writer of mystery yarns! You untangle puzzles!"

"That's true, professor, but the puzzles which I untangle through my fictional detectives are puzzles which I created in the first place. That is quite different from solving a real murder."

"If that is the direction in which you are heading by probing the Atlantis Club," said the professor gravely, "I have some advice for you, if you'd care to hear it."

"Of course I would!"

"In the *Suttapitaka* of Pali canon, the sacred scriptures of Theravada Buddhists, believers were admonished to go for refuge to the Doctrine, to the Order. But with this warning: 'Think not lightly of evil.' My translation for your benefit would be, 'Watch yourself! Proceed carefully!'"

Chapter Thirty-Seven

The Buddha in the Sun

Sunshine, warmth, and memories of pleasant afternoons on the campus of the University of Iowa drew Somerfield from the professor's office into the refuge of Washington Square Park where New York University students basked in their youth as he had in his. But as he found a sun-drenched bench, his mind was shadowed by his subsequent past, directing his wary eyes to scrub the seemingly innocent loungers and their springtime surroundings as he had searched the travelers of train station concourses all over the world.

Confident that he was not being watched and feeling foolish for thinking that he might be, he sat Buddha-like in the sun and played with how he might have described himself if he were a watcher assigned to surveilling himself. He was posing professorial, perhaps, because of the proximity to the university and wearing a suit while youngsters cavorted in tee-shirts, jeans, and sneakers, the uniform attire of the supposedly rebellious and individualistic 1960s. Was he in the process of meeting someone? In the next few minutes would someone come and sit beside him for a moment of whispers? Perhaps leaving something on the bench? Instructions? A codebook? The secret plans of Russia's latest breakthrough in missile technology? Or might the watcher conclude that the pause in the park was for the purpose of seeing if he were being watched? The watched watching out for a watcher?

What might the kids be thinking of him? Did they see him as a professor? In their way of looking at things, because he was over the age of thirty he was not to be trusted, of course. The aroma from his pipe marked him, too; Balkan Sobranie tobacco mixing with the burnt-rope smell of the marijuana smoke that drifted from their pipes and cigarettes across the immutable square. Did he look very uncool? Was he possibly an undercover policeman, the dreaded and scorned narc? An FBI agent spying on NYU campus radicals? A CIA spook? Would any of them see in him an author?

What the hell am I doing here when I have a book to finish? he thought. What was it to him if an art dealer and a cop had been murdered? Did he really care about Atlantis and the society named for it? How could he have let himself be seduced from completing a book by Dick Lomax's wild imaginings? How much truth was there in that far-fetched story of attempted murder on the Brooklyn-Queens Expressway? Why on earth should he pick up a case that the New York Police Department thought so little of that the detective in charge of it had been pulled off it? What could he come up with that a trained investigator didn't find? Why had he just spent all that time listening to bizarre conjectures from an academic about Atlantis, Nazis, Egyptian mono-theism, Jesus Christ, and the effects of Jews on American foreign policy in the Middle East? What on earth did any of it have to do with Alexander Somerfield?

Rising from the bench, he muttered, "Go home!"

Instead of walking eastward to the Astor Place subway station he wandered west, deeper into Greenwich Village and in so doing unknowingly retraced much of the path Sheldon Lyman had paced following his conversation with Sandra Hargreave about his being directly ordered off the Helder murder and, indirectly, off the murder of David Hargreave. Like Lyman's on that bitter day, his thoughts were immovable, dwelling on the two homicides and rejecting any notion that they were not linked but merely a fluke of coincidence.

In his wanderings and ruminations he paused from time to time to study antiques in shop windows, a display of lewd greeting cards in a stationery store, modern-style clothing in boutiques, the menus posted outside several restaurants in order to check his back for followers and watchers, strictly out of habit.

After an hour he found that he had doubled back on his route to the north side of Washington Square a few blocks from the Fifth Avenue Hotel, a scene in one of his private-eye novels, although he could not remember at that moment which one. In the book it was wintertime, he remembered as he approached the hotel which now was decked out for springtime with a sidewalk café under striped awnings vainly imitating Paris. Inside off the lobby was a vast 19th-century lounge decorated with swagged curtains, Oriental rugs, and library tables. Seated with a scotch and soda, he might have been a Wall Street businessman meeting someone for dinner or one of the long-term tenants who had been the hallmark of the historic old hotel since the glory days of lower Fifth Avenue as a gathering place for New York's most powerful men in their exclusive clubs built around solid cores of interests: the Union Club and the Union League Club, strongholds of stalwart Republicans; the Manhattan Club, bastion of Democrats; the intellectuals' Atheneum; the Lotos, for the literary and the artistic; and the Knickerbocker, for New York's old families. All eventually moved uptown with the inexorable flow of the city northward and the list of private clubs had grown as the city grew, each becoming a sanctuary for members drawn together by singularity of purpose, among them the Atlantis.

Leaving the hotel, he turned uptown intending to walk as far as Fourteenth Street and then taking a taxi to Ray Taylor's apartment. But the evening was fresh and inviting and walking in it was a pleasure. From the hotel to a spot opposite the Atlantis Club took him three-quarters of an hour.

At no time during this promenade did he detect the follower who had been shadowing him from the moment he left Professor Levitan's office.

Chapter Thirty-Eight

The Man Who Knew Kipling

The apartment contained all that a man might need for whatever purpose he'd come, whether for the pleasures of womanly flesh fueled with abundant liquor, romantic records, a stereo, and an ample bed; just to sleep when there was no other place; to be alone to think and to add up what life was all about; or to be safe where no one could ever find him. Over the years Alex had visited for all of these reasons with never a question from Ray as to why.

In the apartment and slightly winded by the walk from the Village, he fondly recalled other hospitable places he'd shared with Ray. A flat in London. Bistros in Paris. The bar in Shephard's Hotel in Cairo. Harry's Bar next to the Grand Canal in the heart of the *serenissima* splendors of Venice. Hurley's wedged into the corner of the RCA Building at 49th and Sixth.

"We were something," he muttered with a shake of

the head as he approached Ray's bar. Back when it was really fun to be a newsman, when Ray and he and a couple of other journalistic galoots were inventing television news. Somerfield the dashing foreign correspondent. Ray, his field producer and sometime-cameraman when the crew they were supposed to have never showed up and they couldn't scrape one up from the locals. Covering every world crisis as if it were the last one and praying to God that when the last one did come some asshole newcomer at a desk in New York would recognize it for what it was and wouldn't assign someone else. Now, all that was finished.

Ray once asked him, "Don't you miss it, Alex?"

"I get a pang once in a while but, as Churchill said about getting the urge to exercise, 'when it comes over me, I lie down till it passes.' I'm content to leave the news to you and the younger generation. What's the current term for that? 'Burned-out?' I do miss some of the people."

"We miss you, Alex," Ray had said. "We miss those wisecracks of yours. I always intended to write them down and collect them. Like Bartlett's. *Somerfield's Quotations*."

"I never knew I was quotable."

"Oh yeah. You were always coming up with some quip or pun or otherwise outrageous comment. Usually about the nature of the gang in the Kremlin. We always got a big kick out of your fixation about how the Russkies were behind everything bad going on. *The Somerfield One Big Commie Bogey Man Theory of History*. You had a button you wore sometimes. A big blue one that said, 'I'd rather be killing Communists.' Remember?"

He remembered. The pin was on a wall in Pennsylvania with a lot of other buttons he'd collected. And the press passes. The ID badges. The credentials. "Relics of my disreputable past," he mumbled as he picked out a bottle of scotch from Ray's plentiful assortment of liquors.

Seated on a commodious couch and sipping the whiskey in the glorious aloneness of the place, he recalled being with Ray in a noisy dive on Tu Do Street in Saigon in 1965—just two years ago, he said to himself in wonderment—with sandbags in front and heavy metal screens on the windows to keep the Viet Cong from lobbing grenades in when the life he'd shared with Ray unexpectedly crossed paths with the one he'd sworn to Warren Davis as Davis pushed himself between them at the bar, introducing himself as Paul Smith, a correspondent for the Wallace Network, his legend at a time when the war in Vietnam was fresh enough to seem winnable.

Had there been no war, Alex recalled, Saigon would have been a lovely city to be in. But there was a war and it had left the city dirty and strewn with garbage, its gracious French-style buildings pock-marked by bullets or artillery rounds, and guarded by bunkers. Many streets were closed to traffic by wood, cement, or barbed wire barricades. Yet beneath this ugly veneer he'd detected the loveliness of the Oriental city with its European flavor of tree-lined boulevards and elegant hotels.

The Caravelle overlooking the old opera house had been the headquarters for the journalists covering the war and there, in its rooftop restaurant,

Warren Davis had come as close to revealing himself to Alexander Somerfield as he ever would. Peering through windows that were taped in a crisscross pattern like the glass in a Tudor house so a bomb would not shower the room with splintered glass, he pointed to yellow dots of light floating in the distant darkness like fireflies. "Flares," he said matter-of-factly. "They mean there's patrolling going on in the boonies. When the wind is right you can even hear the shooting. I confess that I've never gotten used to sitting up here dining on French cuisine while killing is going on out there." His eyes came in from the night. "Of course, the war won't be won out there until we can win it at home. Out there isn't the main battlefield at the moment. The combat is being waged on American television screens! And I am not optimistic about how it will turn out. If we don't win the hearts and minds—to use an unfortunate term in common usage at the moment—the hearts and minds of the American people, this war will be lost. Maybe it's already over and we who are out here don't know it yet. Perhaps we are already at that point in the old poem:

And the end of the fight is a tombstone white
     with the name of the late deceased,
And the epitaph drear: 'A Fool lies here
     who tried to hustle the East.'"

"Rudyard Kipling," said Somerfield in amazement.
"Indeed so," smiled Davis.
"Since you quoted him, may I?"
"Of course!"

"It's a newsman's poem, I think:

I keep six honest serving men
(They taught me all I knew);
Their names are What and Why and When
And How and Where and Who."

"Those serving men suit your other job, too," said
Davis with a wink. Turning his head toward the
flares again he was grim-faced as he recited:

"We're poor little lambs who've lost our way,
    Baa! Baa! Baa!
We're little black sheep who've gone astray
    Baa! Baa! Baa!
Gentlemen rankers out on a spree,
Damned from here to Eternity,
God ha' mercy on such as we!"

"Are you a Yale man?"
"As it happens, I am," Davis said, jerking his head
back into the room. "But that's also Kipling." He
flashed a nervous smile, realizing that he had gone too
far concerning himself. "And what was *the* song," he
said, looking to recover, "at good old Iowa?"
"The football song or the Alma Mater?"
"Oh, please! Both!"
"The Alma Mater was called 'Old Gold' and was
sung to the tune of 'Believe Me If All Those
Endearing Young Charms.' 'Oh Iowa, calm and
secure on thy hill, looking down on thy river
below . . . .' And so forth. There was a pretty good
football song written by Meredith Wilson, 'The Iowa

Fight Song.' It's probably the most famous:

> C'mon and fight, fight, fight for Iowa,
> Let every loyal Iowan sing;
> The word is fight, fight, fight for Iowa,
> Something, something, something,
> Until the game is won!"

"Winning is all," said Davis, grinning as his eyebrows arched appreciatively. "In football . . . and all else . . . including any war you get into! Were you a real rah-rah team booster?"

"Fight, fight, fight for Iowa! That was me!"

"A curious phenomenon, American football songs! They ought to be studied for their psycho-sociological impact. The truth is, if you really compare the football songs of American colleges to the marches and songs of the Nazis, there's very little difference. You could take the Horst Wessel anthem *Die Fahne Hoch*, which means 'Raise the Banner,' put some football pep rally words to it and there'd be no difference!"

"The difference *is* the words," said Somerfield as he turned to watch the falling flares. Looking away, he said, "At this moment, those Iowa football songs seem pretty remote and silly. And I guess you could say that in those days I was pretty silly. Just a crazy college kid."

"Everyone is more or less mad on one point," declared Davis solemnly. Then with a sunburst smile, he said, "That's also a Kipling quote."

It was the last thing of any consequence that Warren Davis said to him. And the next to the last time he'd seen Davis, the last being two days later when Davis waved at him from the back of a jeep on his way out of Saigon ostensibly as the war correspondent Paul Smith but really to fight a personal war against Communism that to many who knew him seemed madness.

Everyone is more or less mad on one point.

Such as Ray Taylor being more or less mad to lend this apartment, thought Alex as he poured another scotch.

The men of the Atlantis Club and their peculiar fixations on a place that probably never existed; were they mad?

Professor Levitan and his fascination with the study of the more bizarre aspects of mankind's history. Mad?

Himself and the members of the Baker Street Irregulars and thousands of Sherlockians all over the world who dressed up in outlandish fore-and-aft hats and cloaks and insisted that Sherlock Holmes was a real person who was still alive and keeping bees in Sussex?

Dick Lomax being more or less mad about the mob being out to get him, he thought as he took the drink into the bedroom.

Detective Lyman wanting to solve his partner's murder and that of the art dealer, he thought as he drew back the drapes and peered through the window to scan the street for anyone who might be a threat.

Surely this is madness, he thought as he let go of the drapes, thinking that anyone could be watching me.

Chapter Thirty-Nine

Messages

This date again observed Subject first noticed and reported on 2 June in vicinity of Helder Galleries and subsequently opposite the Atlantis Club and entering apartment building, possibly a safe house.

Subject today proceeded to offices of the New York University for a conference with a Professor Norman Levitan, a noted scholar on Jewish subjects. Subject then traveled circuitously to the Fifth Avenue Hotel but was not seen to contact anyone.

Subject returned to apartment building by walking unaccompanied. Subject appears to have been trained in agentcraft, as he often makes observations of his surroundings and whether he is being followed. Will attempt photograph of him. Am certain Subject is unaware of my surveillance.

"Who the hell is this guy?" Amnon Dorot asked himself as he encoded the message in the office of the Deputy Ambassador for Cultural and Educational Affairs of the Israeli Mission to the U.N. just before 1:00 A.M., realizing that in Israel it was already dawn of June 5.

Entering the cipher room, he was astonished to find it busy. At one in the morning in New York, he had expected to find a skeleton night staff to mind the teleprinters, like there would have been in Israel. Of the nearest cryptoanalyst, a delightfully witty woman known to him only as Elaine, he asked, "What's going on?"

His answer came from behind him in the form of Mogen's breathless voice as he barged into the room. "It seems we're at war again." He was dressed in a tuxedo, summoned from a roaring party at the British U.N. Mission. Peering over Elaine's shoulder and scanning the blocks of digits coming in on the printer, he said, "Right, Elaine?"

With cobalt blue eyes scanning the numbers as fast as they cleared, she said, "As of oh-seven-forty-five Tel Aviv."

"Damn," growled Amnon, "what in blazes am I doing here?"

Ignoring him, Mogen deciphered aloud. "Israel Air Force under command Major-General Mordecha

278

Hod launching preemptive strike against . . . all wings Egyptian Air Force . . . ."

"Brilliant!" cried Amnon. This is the payoff of perfect intelligence work, he thought. Perfect timing. At this hour in and around Cairo and at airbases in the Sinai, in the Nile Delta and along the Nile Valley most Egyptian Air Force Command personnel would be in their cars on their way to work after breakfast at their homes. And if the intelligence reports were correct—and when had they ever been wrong?—the attacking Israelis would find the enemy force sitting ducks: all 30 of the long-range Soviet-built TU-16 bombers, 27 medium-range Illyushin 28s, a dozen Sukhoi Su-7 fighter bombers, more than 130 MiG fighters, three-dozen transports and helicopters.

Mogen was still reading. "Operations are under way at Ismalia . . . Bilbeis . . . Heliopolis . . . Embaba . . El-Fayum. . . ."

Amnon exclaimed, "We'll have complete air superiority!"

"Don't count your chickens before they're hatched," said Mogen sternly as he turned his attention to the diplomatic printer operating in the clear. "All Foreign Ministry stations hereby alerted and ordered to prepare for adverse and hostile reaction in all Western capitals and cities with consular or mission offices," the message said. "Worldwide propaganda campaign is expected in which Israel will be blamed for hostilities despite overwhelming evidence that Arab States led by Egypt were prepared to attack Israel. All statements must emphasize that today's actions were preemptive in nature and that Israel will

279

never hesitate to employ all means to defend the right of the Jewish People to exist in their own state, which is Israel."

"Some chickens," laughed Amnon as he pocketed the message he'd brought for sending, insignificant now, it seemed.

Chapter Forty

Drive Time

Feeble dawn light seeping through the drapes of the apartment woke Somerfield at 5:30. Although he had stayed up late reading a biography of President Franklin D. Roosevelt from Ray's expansive library of the complimentary copies of books given out by publishers' publicists in the hope of receiving favorable—free!—comments, he was quite tired and determined to sleep a few more hours. But habit and his nature prompted him to turn on the radio and dial up Dick Lomax's station—"All-news! All day! Always!" being its frequently trumpeted slogan—just to find out what had happened in the world while he'd slept.

Apparently a war had happened, he deduced as he came in at the end of a correspondent's report. ". . . thus, in three hours, the Israelis have swept the skies clean of Arab aircraft. . . ."

"Swept the skies *clear*," Alex muttered, judging

the word *clean* to be pejorative and probably prejudicial in this instance, as if Arab planes and their crews were dirty and unkempt and had soiled the skies.

The next report was by Lomax, an excerpt of an interview with a spokesman for the Israeli Mission to the U.N., one Chaim Yoffe, identified by Lomax as the Deputy Ambassador for Cultural and Educational Affairs, which seemed to be an odd choice for questioning about a shooting war in the Middle East. But, Alex recalled from his own days on the air, at five in the morning you take whomever you can get. "Our government has and presently will share with the world abundant evidence that a concerted attack was being planned by Egypt, Jordan, Syria, and others against my country," said the Israeli.

"Ah, Mr. Yoffe," chuckled Alex, "I know who you are! Cultural and Educational Affairs? My ass! *A-G-E-N-T!* That's you! 'Agent of Influence!' Warren Davis would love you!"

"That evidence will persuade all fair-minded people who are familiar with the history of Israel's troubles with her neighbors," Yoffe was continuing, "that a preemptive strike was our only recourse."

"That preemptive strike," reported Lomax immediately, "has left the Egyptian Air Force totally destroyed and a shambles."

"Dick, please," Alex begged of the radio. "How can anything be *partly* destroyed?"

Inwardly, he said, "Carping criticism aside, Richard, a fine report! Leave it to you, crippled and in a wheelchair at home with a phone and a tape deck, to get in on the reporting of a war a third of the world away!"

There could be no going back to sleep now, Alex knew as he rolled out of bed and padded barefoot into the living room to turn on Ray Taylor's TV set for whatever coverage the networks might have of the hostilities. What he found was reports phoned to New York by correspondents in Tel Aviv speaking while maps were displayed on the screen. It would be hours before film would be available. Meantime, TV had become illustrated radio.

Alternating between it and Lomax's station, he soon understood what had happened and formed an opinion as to what would occur in the hours and days ahead—a rout of Arab ground forces left naked and vulnerable by the destruction of all air cover. An Israeli victory was in the making. The only question was, how long would it take?

Not long, he supposed.

Then, suddenly—an amazing coincidence—on the radio with Lomax was heard Professor Levitan saying, "Anyone who is surprised by this action by Israel has not paid attention either to recent history . . . or that in the Bible! 'So David prevailed over the Philistine with a sling and with a stone.' Today, there are many hundreds of Davids. Their slings are jet planes. Their stones are rockets and cannons. The weapons have changed but the determination of the Jewish people to survive has not! Nor will it ever! The powers of destruction in all their forms, whether they be cloaked in the black uniforms of the Nazi SS, in the flowing white robes of Arabia, or in the business suits of men with power, they cannot prevail against us. As it is written in *Psalms*, 'This is the day which the Lord hath made. I will lift up mine eyes unto the hills from whence cometh my help. My help cometh from the Lord, which made heaven and earth. Behold, he that keepeth Israel shall neither slumber nor sleep.'"

"Nor shall I," retorted Alex as he dressed.

An hour later, in a taxi going against the flow of morning drive-time traffic toward the city, he felt the pangs of envy for Lomax doing his best to grab a piece of the big story of the day—and perhaps ever, if the war escalated to involve the United States and, inevitably, the Soviet Union.

He thought back to the last war Alexander Somerfield had covered, however briefly—Vietnam. And to that greater war of which Vietnam was a part, according to the Gospel of Warren Davis—the Cold War, of which Alex Somerfield had a dual role: Alex, the reporter; Deerstalker, the agent.

In the cab careening into Queens, the heart strings of both his roles were quivering with nostalgia—the agent feeling left out of the loop and the reporter longing to be working again. With a possibly historically decisive war raging, he thought glumly, all he had on this bright June morning was a pair of murders. "Hardly something for the history books," he muttered.

Over a shoulder, the cabbie said, "You say somethin', pal?"

"Just thinking out loud!"

"I do that a lot," laughed the driver. "Keeps me sane!"

"They say everyone is more or less mad on one point."

Chapter Forty-One

The Briefing

Personally and professionally, Detective Sheldon Lyman's feelings toward reporters had always been ambivalent. In many aspects they were like cops. Proud. Aggressively competitive. Driven. Individualistic. Yet part of a tribe. A warrior tribe, of course. Learners and keepers of rituals. Bonded one to another. Man-to-man, for no matter how many women managed to break into the ranks, being a cop or reporter was always a man's job and if a woman were to flourish in either she would have to become like the men. Like cops, reporters were forced to deal with the harsh realities and brutalities of life and so they veneered themselves with cynicism. Yet he'd often seen them moved by deeply human tragedies and calamities that were part and parcel of their daily routines. He'd seen bravery in their ranks. And cowardice. Genius and stupidity. And more of the latter than the former. But most of the time he thought reporters were nothing less than a pain in the ass and obstructions to be avoided or overcome by a cop if he were to get his own job done. In those moments when what a cop had to do clashed with a reporter's job he'd found them to be brazen, cocky, arrogant, and caustic. Self-appointed overseers of the public conscience, they flaunted the First Amendment like a sword, becoming hostile, defiant, self-righteous, thin-skinned, and clannishly protective if thwarted or forced to confront their own shortcomings. All of this experience with them had taught him that while there might be times when the members of the press could be useful, mostly they were to be avoided. Therefore, when Dick Lomax phoned, he went immediately on guard.

"I'd like to talk to you about the Helder and Hargreave homicides," Lomax whispered.

"I'm listening."

"Not on the phone. Face-to-face. How soon could you come out to my house? Today, I mean."

What an arrogant bastard you are, Lyman thought, expecting me to drop everything and jump just because of your call. But what was there to prevent him from going? On his desk was a pile of useless paperwork destined for the files! He had notes to go over in advance of a meeting tomorrow with a fledgling assistant D.A. in a case that had taken him and Hargreave three weeks to nail down almost a year ago and which would end up being plea-bargained without ever going to trial. He'd not been assigned to a new homicide since he'd been waved off Hargreave's murder and ordered to shove the Helder murder to the back burner. Glancing at the clock on the wall and at the wrist watch his father had given him, he said, "An hour."

Putting down the phone, he loudly announced to the uninterested squad room that he had a date with a confidential informant and minutes later signed out one of the cars from a motor pool created from a variety of sources—illegally parked vehicles that had been abandoned, ones that had been confiscated as evidence and defaulted after trials, and city fleet vehicles that were still serviceable but too shabby and unsuitable for agency executives to be seen in any longer but were fine for undercover police work.

Under the takeoff and landing paths of LaGuardia Airport in a middle class Queens neighborhood where streets bore numbers rather than names, the Lomax address was the last in a row of attached brown brick houses built above two-car garages whose driveways were no longer than the vehicles in them. Next to Lomax's new but unlovable green mobile unit, Lyman parked his pick of the motor pool. Let into the house by Lomax's wife and directed to the living room, he was surprised to find Lomax was not alone.

Not since Warren Davis's headhunting interviews at Iowa had Somerfield felt so scrutinized as in the moments it took Lomax to introduce him to Lyman and to explain his presence. But in that interval he also took Lyman's measure and by the time Lomax was through had made up his mind that the way to begin was to get straight to the point. "Dick tells me that you've been taken off the investigation of the murder of the art dealer Peter Helder."

"In departmental lingo," said Lyman more bitterly than he'd intended, "the investigation is *pending.*"

"I also understand that you believe the Helder homicide and the killing of your partner are connected. So do I. It's a gut feeling for me. I'm not one who buys easily into things happening by coincidence. But I'd like to hear your reasoning."

Lyman looked hard at Lomax. "Off the record?" Somerfield answered. "Of course."

The telling was plain and precise—a cop's chronology in cop and legalistic language, as if testifying in court. The call concerning a possible homicide at the Helder Galleries. The body in the cellar. First impression: suicide. How that notion quickly dissipated. No note had been found. All the evidence pointing to Helder being a man with his eye on the future and his heart set on living. The leather bondage mask pointing to the likelihood that what they had on their hands was a homosexual murder. Their hope of keeping that aspect of the case secret. "Until Lomax got the story and broadcast it," he said factually, glancing at Lomax without a flicker of recrimination. Hargreave's two-pronged strategy for tackling the case in which Lyman investigated Helder's secret existence among the gay bars and S and M clubs, looking for a kid named Danny, while Hargreave probed Helder's public life, past and present. The curiosity Hargreave had shown toward Helder's interests as demonstrated by his peculiar library and his membership in the Atlantis Club.

Here occurred Somerfield's only interruption. "What was so fascinating to him about that?"

Lyman cracked a tenuous smile. "'*Si monumen-*

288

tum requiris circumspice,' David said. It's Latin and means—"

"If you seek his monument, look around," interjected Somerfield. "Please go on."

"I had the feeling we were dealing with a combination of *Dr. Jekyll and Mr. Hyde* and *The Picture of Dorian Gray*," continued Lyman. The murder of Hargreave, he said, was totally inexplicable save for the theory that it had been the settling of an old score by an old enemy unrelated to the Helder case. "Which I didn't buy then," he said, "and I don't buy now."

Somerfield asked, "What theory do you buy, Detective?"

"I guess you could say I've come around to my partner's view of the case. At first I was sure Helder's killer would be found among his gay buddies, but after David was killed I had to ask myself why would they want to kill him? That's when I came around to his point of view, that it was someone from Helder's circle of peculiar friends who killed Helder and then had to kill my partner because they were afraid he was getting close to the truth."

Somerfield rose from his chair. "Would it be possible to have a look at your files?"

"That would be highly irregular," said Lyman with a faint smile. "Illegal, in fact."

"I know a little about cops," said Somerfield, "and one of the things I know is that there are the official files and there are the unofficial, the ones a cop keeps with him. Notebooks. That sort of thing. Judging from what I've heard about Lieutenant David Hargreave in the past few minutes, I'd venture to say

289

that he was that kind of cop."

Lyman nodded slowly.

"Might I take a look at Hargreave's file?"

"That's not my decision to make, Mr. Somerfield."

"Call me Alex! Whose decision is it?"

"His daughter's."

Chapter Forty-Two

The Casebook

They met Sandra Hargreave for lunch at her favorite spot in Chinatown only a short walk from the courthouse where she was pressing a weak case of criminal trespass and destruction of government property against three student radicals who'd trashed an attempt at U.S. Army recruiting on the campus of Columbia University, pouring red ink that was supposed to symbolize blood onto stacks of brochures and pamphlets as their protest against the war in Vietnam.

"I'm as frustrated as Shelly about the lack of progress in both the murder of my father and Helder," she said. "I also feel that the two cases are connected. But I appreciate the difficulties facing the police. They're at a dead end. Both investigations have run their course. What's needed now is the sudden break. That, I take it, is what you hope to find. You think you can do unofficially what the authorities have not been able to do. As an officer of the court I can't say that I approve."

"I'm not asking an officer of the court," declared Somerfield. "I'm seeking Hargreave's daughter for permission to have a look at his personal files. A *literary* enterprise!"

"My father was murdered, Mr. Somerfield. Who's to say the people who killed him wouldn't do the same to you if they got wind of you nosing around? Your friend Lomax says they already tried with him!"

"I believe they did. Whoever 'they' are."

"And you're willing to run that risk?"

"If I weren't I wouldn't be taking up your time."

"Why are you so sure my father kept a file?"

"Some of my best friends are cops. I know how they work. I know that the best of them keep meticulous records, aside from the official ones."

When she first turned upon Alexander Somerfield her discerning prosecutor's eye, she'd instantly judged him favorably, this assessment having nothing to do with the fact that he was brought to her by Lyman nor that she had read all his books, as had her father, and that she was acquainted with his previous occupation as a reporter, if reporting and authoring could rightly be deemed occupations. To her, one's work pedigree conveyed little, if anything, about character. That, she adamantly believed, was etched into the face and in Somerfield's lived-in but open Irish looks she found righteousness aged by reality, chivalry, and loyalty, a gentle man of steely purpose who'd been around and who would go all out against all odds for a just cause. A Celtic knight plopped into the wrong century.

"Dad did keep files," she said. "Meticulous, of course. They're still in his apartment."

"Does that mean I may see them?"

"I'll be in court this afternoon. I could meet you at Dad's place at, say, seven this evening? Shel can bring you. We'll both be there when you go over them. I must insist on that."

"Fair enough," he said, jutting out a hand to seal the bargain.

At seven she was waiting outside the apartment house.

Three keys were required. One for the lobby door and two for the apartment, not opened since Sheldon had been there on the day of the wake. "I've kept putting off deciding what to do with all of this," she said sadly as she opened the door to the warm, stale-smelling apartment that had the look of the den of a scholar. "I was thinking of putting everything in storage and selling," she continued as Somerfield drifted around the room that was the heart of the place. "Dad owned it, you see. A co-op. I'm glad now that I procrastinated. Perhaps I had an intuition that you were going to appear, Mr. Somerfield."

"Never discount intuition," he said jocularly, settling into her father's favorite chair—her gift—as she handed him the Helder notebooks and file folders crammed with papers.

"I must make up my mind about it eventually," she said wistfully.

"Yes, I suppose so," he said, already distracted as he opened the first notebook to begin an extraordinary journey that to him as a writer of mystery stories seemed to be akin to that of Dr. John H. Watson's in recording the adventures of Mr. Sherlock Holmes of 221B Baker Street. In the pages of the notebooks, Somerfield was following in the footsteps of a man who demonstrated on every page that he had been an exceptionally astute, sensitive, intuitive, deductive, and creative detective worthy of comparison to the fictional one of Watson's chronicles.

As he read, there was, too, a resemblance to moments from Alexander Somerfield's other existence, the secret agent pouring over someone else's documents.

The facts of the Helder murder filling several pages were much as Lyman had sketched them and as he found them in Lomax's files. But facts were not what he was looking for. Insights were. He was seeking clues to what Hargreave had been thinking. Needed were pointers to Hargreave's reasoning.

The first appeared early in the notes, a listing of titles of books housed in Helder's library in the apartment above his artistic enterprise on Madison Avenue.

Below these, printed and encircled, was the title of another, *The True Believer*, and the comment, "Beware of fanatics!" On the next page he found a notation of Hargreave's routine inquiries about Helder among official records and the entry: No FBI file. Next to it he'd written: ???

And below it:

Immig. and Nat. has no N file. ???

And then:

294

1946 ???

Followed by:

PH entered US sponsored by von Bork of Atlantis Club.
Atl. Cl. also beneficiary H's will. ???

Scrawled below with an arrow drawn up to the words "Atlantis Club" was:

Crackpots and idealists!

At the bottom of the page was written:

Dutch govt advises no records re: PH

Sandwiched between the third and fourth notebooks were looseleaf papers. Helder's banking records and stock market transactions, they were difficult to read because they were poor photocopies of the lightly printed computer printouts and would have been of no interest except for Hargreave's circling of investments Helder had made going back several years in stocks in petroleum firms doing business primarily in the Middle East.

Only the first page of the fourth—and last—of the books was written on. But of all the others, this page was, to Somerfield, the best because it was Hargreave speaking to him as loudly and clearly as if he had been alive and in the musty book-cluttered room:

Questions to be resolved:

Where did Helder really come from?
How did he get here so easily?
When?
Who bankrolled him?
Why?
What is the purpose of the Atlantis Club, really?

Kipling's honest serving men! Who? What? Where?
Why? When? How? Good questions from a good cop.

Like a grenade, Lyman's voice exploded from a
corner where he'd been standing like a schoolboy
awaiting a teacher's judgment of his homework.
"Well, Alex, what do you think?"

"I think . . . I'd like to have a look around Helder's
digs. Can you arrange that, Shel?" His eyes slid
toward Sandra's mischievously. "Or must I resort to
breaking-and-entering?"

Chapter Forty-Three

Shop Talk

"Miss Hargreave seems to be a very capable young woman," said Somerfield. "Loyal to her dad." An odd trait to apply to her, he thought, as if a daughter being loyal to her father were all that rare. As if loyalty to anyone or anything had become a peculiarity to him in a lifetime in which its presence must always be suspect. The legacy of Warren Davis! And a journalistic maxim.

Cheerily, Lyman said, "Sandy's a pip, all right."

Pip? God, thought Somerfield with an astonished look, how long's it been since he'd heard anyone say someone was a pip, especially a person of Lyman's generation? The Now Generation! The Under-30 Set who seemed to have already taken charge of the world and imposed upon it a wholly new vernacular and a definition of loyalty in which the burning of a draft card or the flag became an act of patriotism.

Sandra had left them—'I've got a pile of cases to go

over and you'll want to talk," she'd said as they'd left her father's apartment—and now they were in the Cadillac all-night coffee shop at the corner of York and Seventy-eighth where the lights were bright enough to dispel all shadows and the long menu's numerous plastic-laminated pages were freighted with Greek entrées but proffered breakfast at any hour in the city where not everyone's day began in the morning. Somerfield had gone directly to a booth at the rear with no one seated nearby and sat facing the door in unconscious acknowledgement of what could only be called a fear that out of his past might materialize an enemy from the ranks of either of his bizarre callings thirsting for a reckoning for some real or imagined sin. "Fill me in about your line of investigation," he said to Lyman, noting the slightest hint of a crease made by the strap of a shoulder holster in the lie of Lyman's blue jacket. "You were checking out the gay angle?"

Before Lyman's discourse began they awaited the departure of their waiter with their orders for black coffees and Lyman paused when the cups were brought, then proceeded unimpeded to an inconclusive finish. "I never turned up a clue regarding this kid Danny and maybe the whole thing was a wild goose chase, 'cause the only reference to him was that notation in Helder's calendar. Maybe Helder never kept the appointment. Maybe the kid didn't show. Perhaps the kid heard about the murder and skipped town. Danny prob'ly wasn't his name anyway. They all use aliases. It was a waste of time." He reared back and drew apart his jacket so that Somerfield caught a glimpse of the strap of his holster. "Of course, it had

298

to be checked out."

"What piece do you carry?" asked Somerfield.

"Pardon?"

"Your gun," muttered Somerfield with a nod at the crease in Lyman's coat.

"Oh! A Dan Wesson .357 Magnum six-shot with a four inch barrel."

"Heavy stuff."

"Hargreave gave it to me last Christmas."

What did I give my friends? Somerfield asked himself. My latest book? Lomax had coined a joke for them, his friends. "You always know what Somerfield's giving for Christmas if he's got a new book out!" Did they ever read them? he wondered. Were they cherished? Put on a special "Somerfield shelf" and pointed out proudly to their friends with a boastful "I know the author" and taken down to show the autograph inside? A few, perhaps, he thought as Lyman sipped the steaming strong Cadillac coffee.

Were any of his friends jealous and resentful of his success as an author? Did they think that somehow he was rebuking them because he had turned his back on their trade? Did they believe he had betrayed them and their calling? Found them and what they did for a living wanting? Had he turned disloyal by writing about them, as he sometimes did, however obliquely and disguised? Had he broken their code? Drawn back the veil of their trade secrets and rituals?

Of the world he'd shared with Warren Davis he had never written. At the very beginning there'd been a paper to be signed regarding that! A solemn oath bearing his signature was notarized and duly filed in a Company dossier attesting that at no time would he reveal anything about his work without written permission and clearance. Otherwise, severe criminal penalties applied.

Did someone in the Company read his books? Somewhere, was there a person whose job it was to go through his novels line by line looking for a violation of his solemn oath? Was there a Company library somewhere with a shelf of Somerfield titles well-thumbed in a search for a breech of loyalty to the oath he'd taken as a fresh-faced and idealistic recruit at the Farm, one of Warren Davis's Cold Warriors—a 1950's-America Samurai?

As clearly as he saw Detective Lyman opposite him, a Samurai with a .357 Magnum under his jacket, he recalled Warren Davis on a podium at the Farm on the first day delivering his legendary orientation speech to the newcomers and quoting the 17th Century Samurai Yamaga Soko. "The business of the Samurai consists in reflecting on his own station in life, in discharging loyal service to his master if he has one, in deepening his fidelity in associations with friends, and, with due consideration of his own position, in devoting himself to duty above all." It was Davis's *tour de force* on the meaning of loyalty. "Looking at you," he boomed to his rapt and scared audience, "I know what Shakespeare meant when he wrote, 'In thy face I see the map of honor, truth, and loyalty.' It will be my task to strengthen you in your purpose, to stir in you those fires of morale that will be required as you embark on your perilous journey. In this I shall be guided by the words of one of our greatest patriots, General George

C. Marshall. 'Morale,' he said, 'is the state of mind. It is steadfastness and courage and hope. It is confidence and zeal and loyalty.'"

Davis would not ask them to pledge their loyalty to something as amorphous as America, Democracy, or the Free World! Nor to mankind and the planet earth! No! "I'll require of you only loyalty to this outfit," he thundered. "To the Company. The Firm. Whatever you may choose to call the organization which you join today. What about . . . 'the Club?' That's what we are, you see. A club."

Then to this pepper he added the salt of the humorist E.B. White. "'It is easier for a man to be loyal to his club than to his planet,'" he declared. "'The bylaws are shorter, and he is personally acquainted with the other members.'"

It got a howl of bonding laughter. Initiation by joke.

Now, years later, across a coffee shop table sat a mirthless young man who also belonged to a club. "Hargreave didn't truly believe it was a fag murder," Lyman was saying. "He saw it as something deeper and darker than that. More complex. Some mumbo jumbo motive. You do, too. Right?"

"Well, I don't get what you mean by mumbo jumbo."

"Right from the start my partner was fascinated by the things he found in Helder's library. He was far more interested in the guy's books than in that torture chamber where he was killed. I'm sure you noticed it in reading his notebooks. That's why you want to have a look at Helder's inner sanctum."

"The scene of the crime," said Somerfield, wagging

301

a finger at the waiter to bring the check. "When do I see it?"

"Why not first thing tomorrow morning?"

The waiter came and Somerfield waited before saying, "Tomorrow it is."

Grabbing the check, Lyman said, "Shall I pick you up?"

"That'd be fine."

"Where?"

"Sixty-fifth and First. Southwest corner. You tell me when."

"Ten o'clock?"

Ridiculous of me not to give him the address, thought Somerfield chidingly as Lyman paid the check at the counter by the door, but when Lyman offered to drive him there, he said, "It's a short walk and God knows I can use the exercise."

In every legend there is a kernel of truth, he thought as he turned north on York Avenue. He did not take care of himself physically. The long vigorous treks at the sides of the beautiful, hilly, wooded roads that had been part of his reason for moving to Pennsylvania had never become a part of his daily ritual. "You ought to take up jogging," his doctor had suggested, a ludicrous prospect that brought back a memory of news pictures of President Kennedy's press secretary, the debonair and rotund Pierre Salinger, running in the craze of fitness that for a time had captured the fancy of the knights of Kennedy's Camelot on the Potomac before darkness overcame them and the country in the form of a rifle shot in Dallas.

He'd been in Moscow that day attending a

reception for foreign correspondents given by the Soviet Foreign Ministry in a graciously charming old house on Vorovsky Street—the headquarters of the Board of the Union of Soviet Writers, said to have been the model for the home of the Rostov family in Tolstoy's *War and Peace* and with an appropriate memorial statue to the author in the garden. Admiring it, he'd been startled by someone behind him speaking Russian. "*War and Peace* is so much better a novel than *Dr. Zhivago*, wouldn't you agree, Mr. Somerfield? It's not that Boris Pasternak has no style. I don't agree with the reviewer in *Pravda* who wrote that *Zhivago* was merely noisy reactionary propaganda about a literary weed. I take offense at any poet, even a fictional one such as Zhivago, being called a weed. I just found Pasternak's work tiresome. What did you think of it, Mr. Somerfield?"

"I'm afraid I haven't gotten around to it," Somerfield said, embarrassed at admitting to not having read the controversial bestseller. "Thick books put me off, I'm afraid."

"I can appreciate that. Given the choice, you'd pass up a weighty Russian novel in favor of *The Hound of the Baskervilles.*"

Translation: "I have read your file, Mr. Somerfield, and I know who you are! Your legend as a news correspondent may fool others but it doesn't fool me!"

Moments later a Ministry official announced the assassination.

"I am so sorry," Shilovsky had said in English with a conviction that laid to rest then and there for Somerfield any suspicion that the Russians had done it, although he learned later that it was Shilovsky

303

who created and ran a KGB disinformation campaign through various American peace groups to lay the plot on the doorstep of the Company.

A light rain began as he pressed on toward Ray Taylor's apartment but he kept a leisurely pace, lost in silence and remembrance, tracing a zigzag course of sudden turns, jaywalked crossings, and abrupt pauses to light his pipe or kneel ostensibly to tie a shoelace but really to look around for anyone who might be following or watching from the side or in front.

"Mikhail Stepanovich Shilovsky was more than just your average happy-go-lucky Russian Communist and reporter, wasn't he?" Warren Davis was lecturing in awakened memory as he walked in the mist. "By the time you received Shilovsky's condolences regarding Kennedy in 1963 he was already a colonel in the KGB and their ace agent of influence. Chief spokesman and apologist for the Kremlin in the Khrushchev years. Ardent seducer of western journalists. And a hard-boiled Moscow Centre hood and boss of hoods for at least a decade. Close friend and confidant of Yuri Andropov when Yuri was ambassador to Hungary and the Butcher of Budapest during the revolution in 1956."

This conversation had been in a coffee shop, too, he remembered. In London? Paris? Memory failed on the geography. Russ Branson had been present, silent as a Buddha, his brilliant mind a sponge.

"Boy wonder of the Kremlin," said Davis, slyly suspicious eyes watching a waitress. "He was already a major in the Red Army in 1945 during the linkup at the Elbe back when you and Russ were in grammar

304

school. Shilovsky was eighteen or nineteen years old then. A fucking teenager and he was already a major in the Red Army, for crissakes. Talk about your prodigies!"

Since that conversation, Somerfield recalled as the rain increased, forcing him to hurry, Shilovsky had become the main contact between the top echelon of the Kremlin ruling circle and a worldwide network of terrorists that the Russians were beginning to organize and support with their rubles and their expertise. "The Soviet Union's Pied Piper of Terrorism," Davis had called him. "He runs the First Directorate of the KGB. It is listed as Department 8 and it is where he perfects the finer arts of sabotage, abduction, and assassination. He's got a camp near Moscow called Balashika to which come students from all over the Third World to learn the techniques that will be required to free the so-called oppressed peoples of the world. The emphasis now is on training Palestinians."

"I can't believe Shilovsky would be doing that," Somerfield recalled saying. "He's never been a muscle man."

"I am surprised at how forgiving you seem to be," scoffed Davis. "Suddenly you're feeling *sympathetic* to your old nemesis Shilovsky?"

"I'm not sympathetic."

"Good! For a moment—only a moment—I was afraid you'd—"

"Gone soft on Communism, Warren? You needn't fear that. I have never embraced even a shred of the so-called revisionist history of the Cold War. I never thought the crap some people dole out about

305

American culpability. How we are as much to blame for the Cold War as the Russians. The music and the lyrics for that unhappy tune originated in Moscow Centre, a good deal of it written by Misha Shilovsky himself."

"It's a ditty that still ranks high on the Western Liberal Hit Parade. It's on the charts . . . with a bullet."

"I'm not a devotee of any of the modern music. I'm not much anymore for anything modern, I'm afraid. I've become an anachronism."

And I still am, he thought as he turned into Sixty-fifth Street, all wet shadows and reflections in the puddles.

Unlocking the door of the house and holding it open, he paused, wondering. Assaying his senses. Checking his memory.

Had he seen something?

A movement? A flicker of a fleshy shadow in a doorway across the street?

"Ridiculous," taunted his reason as it dragged him in from the rain.

"Have another look," coaxed his training and experience when he reached the dry apartment. But through the cloudy and rain-streaked window he saw only sheets of obscuring water.

The Roosevelt biography tempted him but he fell asleep almost immediately and rested peacefully dreaming happily of untainted boyhood and secure from the intrusions of dragons from his past. When he woke up in the middle of the night he was momentarily confused and groggily disoriented wondering where he was, but then he heard the hum of the city and remembered he was once again in New York, snug and secure in Ray Taylor's convenient safe house.

Then he remembered the figure in the doorway.

Cautiously parting the curtains, he peered out into rainless dark.

Nothing now; probably nothing before, he thought. "Except my overheated imagination," he said, finding his way through the three o'clock dark to the bathroom.

Chapter Forty-Four

Significant Events

While Somerfield returned to bed to sleep in the early morning of June 7, Amnon Dorot stripped off his clothes, wet from being out in the rain, and listened to thrilling historic news on the radio in his room in the Lexington Hotel. "At ten o'clock this morning, Jerusalem time," a correspondent reported from Tel Aviv, "Israeli paratroopers fought their way to the Wailing Wall and restored the most sacred site of Judaism to Jewish sovereignty for the first time since the destruction of the Temple by the Romans in 70 AD."

"It shall be ours forever," said Amnon fiercely. And one day soon, he vowed as he threw himself naked and weary onto his bed, he would go there to pray and to mourn for Daniel Ben Avram, the hero of Israel who had expressed grave misgivings concerning himself as a Jew, an Israeli, and a man but had given his life and now lay unclaimed and his death unavenged. "I shall come for you, Daniel," Amnon whispered in the dark stillness of his hotel room. "And then you will be buried in Jerusalem with a stone to mark your sacrifice."

By the time Somerfield was awake again and hearing the news from Lomax's radio station all of the city had been surrendered by the Arabs, and expert military analysts in Washington were already declaring that a regional Israeli victory of monumental significance was imminent. In the long term, one of these knowing men was saying, the swift crushing of the Arab forces would foster an even more influential role in the affairs of the Middle East by the Soviet Union as Arab nations angry at American support for Israel would turn evermore toward Moscow, thus heightening the dangers of a confrontation between the Russians and the United States. Grimly, he continued, "We are much closer today to World War Three—and perhaps Armageddon—than we were at this time yesterday."

"There's a pretty prospect," grumbled Somerfield as he filled a small saucepan with water to boil for the making of instant coffee to accompany his toast. "Doomsday. The Big Showdown," he muttered, waiting impatiently by the stove and remembering the views of Warren Davis on the subject of where the final cataclysm would occur. Expressed as they waited for Somerfield's flight to be called at the Athens airport in the autumn of 1961—Somerfield had been in Berlin; the Wall had just gone up—the Somerfield opinion was that Berlin would be the locale if a shooting war were to start between the Russians and the U.S.

Davis had been in Amman, Jordan, on secret orders. "It won't be Germany," he'd declared with the brash confidence that was a major part of his legend. "It will be in the crucible of the Holy Land, for it is written, 'Multitudes, multitudes in the valley of decision; for the day of the Lord is near in the valley of decision. The sun and the moon shall be darkened, and the stars shall withdraw their shining. The Lord also shall roar out of Zion, and utter his voice from Jerusalem; and the heavens and earth shall shake.'"

It was a discussion Somerfield had longed to continue but the flight was announced, separating them until their paths crossed again in the Caravelle in Saigon five years later.

"Where might you be this morning, Warren, old boy?" Somerfield wondered as the water boiled. "Are you perhaps in Jerusalem keeping an eye on things," he speculated as he ate his toast, dipping it in the coffee, the habit of a lifetime, "so that Uncle Sam's interests will be looked after should this morning turn out to be the beginning of the end as mankind plummets into the valley of decision?"

Right on time, Lyman pulled his motor-pool car to the curb at the southwest corner of Sixty-fifth and First. At the Helder Galleries, Eleanora Swaim greeted them with icy disdain and Somerfield prayed she would not remember him.

She did not challenge their entry, although, Lyman admitted as they climbed the stairs to the residence, "She has every right to object. A proper lawyer could kick us out on our asses and maybe even have a case for locking us up."

"That would hardly do," chuckled Somerfield. "You being a policeman."

"What about you, Alex? Ever been in the slammer?"

"Once."

"Interesting! You were doing some research for a book?"

"Oh no," chuckled Somerfield as they reached the oak doors of Helder's library. "I was under arrest at the time."

Lyman gasped. "What was the charge?"

Opium trading had been suspected. The border town of Chieng-rai, Thailand, was the place. He'd had a meeting with a Chinese double agent who'd sneaked across the low and sluggish Mekong River from Burma. The jail was makeshift, a locked room in the basement of an historic Buddhist temple. He'd been kept there until the American Embassy in Bangkok could straighten everything out—five hours in all.

He told none of this to Lyman, however.

"It was just a case of mistaken identity," he said, blithely continuing the legend that had persuaded the Thais to release him. Pausing on the threshold of Peter Helder's remarkable library, he said, "Well, well, well, isn't this something?"

"The man was a reader," sighed Lyman.

To Alexander Somerfield, Alexander Pope seemed appropriate. "'All books he reads, and all he reads assails.'"

Not to mention Pope's admonition, *Fools rush in where angels fear to tread,* he thought as he silently crossed the thick-carpeted room with the rising excitement that always gripped him in the presence of books. Once more he was a boy in his hometown of Robinsville, Pennsylvania, searching rows upon rows of dusty volumes for the slimmest one he could find for an overdue report for Miss McKeon's English class. From the line whose authors' names began with the letter D he drew one that was encouragingly thin. *The Hound of the Baskervilles* by Sir Arthur Conan Doyle. When he opened it somewhere near the front his eye fell on the captivating last sentence of a chapter. "Mr. Holmes, they were the footprints of a gigantic hound!"

Often since, he'd wondered what course his life might have followed had he wandered into library stacks whose authors' names started with F or R or T—as he'd often wondered what might have been had he simply said to Warren Davis, "Thanks, but I'm really not interested!"

Quickly scanning the shelves, he recalled someone had said that all books are divisible into two classes: the books of the hour, and the books of all time. Clearly, Helder's choices of titles had never been guided by the *Times* bestseller lists. Those he remembered from Hargreave's notebooks he pulled from the shelves, leafing through some, merely studying the covers of others.

Presently, Lyman joined him, but listlessly, weighing each thick volume in his hands as if applying what one of Somerfield's favorite writers of bestsellers, John O'Hara, called the heft test. With a smile, Somerfield said, "Back in 1871 when Edward Gibbon published his enormous *Decline and Fall o the Roman Empire* he presented a copy of it to his friend William Henry, Duke of Gloucester. Know what the Duke said, Sheldon? 'Another damned, thick, square book! Always scribble, scribble, scribble! Eh! Mr. Gibbon?'"

"I don't see how all this adds up to anything significant," complained Lyman, thrusting the book onto the shelf.

"'Give me a condor's quill. Give me Vesuvius' crater for an inkstand,' said Herman Melville. 'To produce a mighty book, you must choose a mighty theme.' On these shelves, my friend, are some mighty books; some mighty themes. Look at the topics of so many of these books. Evil! These works are the microscope into Peter Helder's mind. Evil themes. An evil mind. 'Great book, great evil,' to quote Callimachus. Ben Jonson said it of Shakespeare. 'Reader, look not at his picture but his book.' Different context, of course. There was nothing evil about the Bard, was there? The picture that comes through of Helder from this library is that of a dark and evil man. I need more time! But I know you have other things to do."

"Yeah, that's true."

"It would be wrong of me to stay, of course," teased Somerfield. "I'm not a policeman, after all."

With a sly, insinuating smile, Lyman replied, "Of course, the woman downstairs doesn't know that!"

"She never even asked!"

Cautiously, Lyman ventured, "And what if she does?"

Somerfield winked. "I'll . . . lie."

"If it comes to that," whispered Lyman conspiratorially as he edged toward the door, "I don't know you."

Where have I heard that before? thought Somerfield as he turned again to examine Helder's books. The agent Somerfield? There is no one engaged in work for the Company by that name! Workname: Deerstalker? Ridiculous! Spy novel stuff. "Agreed."

"We should rendezvous some place, some time," said Lyman from the doorway.

"Seven o'clock? The bar at my hotel. The Dorset."

Then a hush. A bookish quiet. Like dusty autumn afternoons of his innocence when classes were done and he was studying in the Robinsville Junior High School library while his classmates were practicing football or rehearsing with the RJHS marching band or sipping Coca-Cola at the soda fountain across the road before any of them understood that once the Nazis and the Japs had been defeated there would not be the peace that the wartime bond-drive slogans and patriotic songs promised but a long deadly twilight of cold war with the Russians. Warren Davis's struggle.

The scholarly quiet of Helder's library soon exploded, however, as a man who looked like a black bird appeared in the doorway screaming, "What is the meaning of this?" Obviously, Eleanora Swaim had taken matters into her capable hands and called someone. This man. "Unless you have an order from a court, I insist that you leave at once."

"I'm not a policeman," said Somerfield quietly.

"Then who the hell are you?"

Who am I? Somerfield wondered; by what legend shall I live by now? "The name's Potter and I'm a dealer in rare books."

"Are you indeed? And by what right have you

trespassed on these premises?"

"For the inventory, sir!"

"What inventory?" The birdman was in the room fully now. "I am the executor of this estate and I have not authorized any inventory."

"It was the District Attorney who authorized it, sir. I have been engaged by him to survey the contents of this library." Now he became officious. "By the way, what is your name?"

"I am Helmut von Bork. The District Attorney? What is his interest in the contents of the library?"

He was a bureaucrat now. "I'm not at liberty to disclose that information, I'm afraid."

Birdman von Bork was indignation in full fight. "Indeed! Well, I'll see about this immediately! I shall telephone the District Attorney's office."

With an exaggerated flourish, Somerfield pointed to the telephone on Helder's desk. "Feel free!" A blatant dare.

Hesitation froze the bird man.

No, of course you won't phone the DA, gloated Somerfield silently.

"Just get out," screeched von Bork. "Now."

"As you wish, sir," said Somerfield, retreating. "Good day to you."

Outside, he thought, That'll put the fox in the chicken coop! "Damn," he grunted, walking away. "Damn, damn, oh *damn!*"

At the Dorset, Lyman laughed it off. "That was mighty fast thinking, though," he said. "Coming up with the stuff about being a rare book guy. You've really got a flare for faking things, haven't you, Alex?"

"Yeah. It's legendary."

"So what did all that poking around in that library get you?"

"For want of a better word," said Somerfield. "Insight."

"Which means you're no closer to finding out who killed Helder than I am," judged Lyman bitterly.

As they left the hotel, chance assumed a significant role.

Lyman forgot his hat.

By the time he'd gone back into the bar, retrieved it and returned to the sidewalk, Somerfield had gone and was proceeding halfway toward Fifth Avenue at a slow and thoughtful pace. But on the opposite side of Fifty-fourth, Lyman noticed, there was a man obviously young and spry enough to be capable of a brisker progress, yet he was keeping up with Somerfield, although discreetly to the rear.

"Hello, who are you?" muttered Lyman. What's your game? How come you're tailing my friend Alex? Are you planning to roll him, perhaps? Is this a stickup about to happen? Or are you up to some other mischief? he wondered as he began to follow the follower.

As intriguing as the man who was trailing Somerfield was, Somerfield himself drew Lyman's curious attention as he seemed to be wandering through midtown. Straight for a couple of blocks. Then a one-block jog down followed by two up. A sudden dash across Park Avenue. Doubling back. Dawdling in front of store widows on Madison. A meander through Central Park on the Fifth Avenue side. Another reversal that brought him out of the park opposite the Plaza Hotel. Studying the toys displayed at F.A.O. Schwartz. Examining the picture of a Bunny on a billboard outside the Playboy Club. Across Madison and a beeline to Alexander's Department Store on Lexington and more window shopping. The same at Bloomingdale's. East to First Avenue and Sixty-sixth and a leisurely dinner at Maxwell's Plum. Then, at last, north to Sixty-fifth, around the corner and into an apartment house where he appeared fleetingly at a second floor window as if examining the street below.

In all this, the young follower had trailed him skillfully. And when Somerfield entered the building, the follower had slipped into a doorway opposite, silken and silent as a shadow, never having seen the follower at his back.

In a single movement, Lyman stepped into the doorway, jammed his gun into the follower's ribs and cocked it.

By the sound of it, Amnon judged the weapon to be a .357 Magnum.

Chapter Forty-Five

Word Games

Lyman was rough, turning and slamming the watcher to the wall and then searching him while Somerfield looked on from the side with a mixture of fascination and bewilderment reflecting his astonishment at being interrupted in going to bed. "I took it upon myself to watch your back," Lyman was saying as his deft fingers removed the contents of the pockets of the silent figure splayed against the living room wall. "I spotted this character trailing you." From an inside jacket pocket he produced a wallet and a pair of passports, British and French. He took a 9mm Beretta semiautomatic pistol from his coat pocket and placed it on a table, having disarmed the man on the street below. "Any idea who he is?"

I've got plenty of ideas, Somerfield thought as Lyman drew his prisoner's arms down and behind his back, handcuffing him. What sort of person carries two passports and a Beretta? One of the mob wiseguys of Dick Lomax's vivid imagination? Hardly! No mob hit man would require the intriguing falsities of the several identities in the wallet. Three credit cards in two different names. An international driver's license for one Tomas Fotash of Budapest and a New York permit for Thomas Foty. A business card belonged to J. Goldstein of a local antiquarian firm dealing in religious artifacts of the Holy Land. All the documents were excellently crafted. Where did he get them? London? Paris? Moscow?

"Which one of these legends is you?" he asked gently, waving the passports. "Douglas Porter, an Englishman from Kent, or Bernard Levalle of Paris? Are you Mr. Fotash of Hungary? Mr. Foty of New York? Are you Mr. Goldstein? Or are you really someone else using these worknames?"

You won't talk? Very well, what does your appearance say about you? You are somewhat middle-aged. Too young to have been in the Second World War but old enough to remember it. The right age to have been a combatant in the more subtle struggle that followed. Are you now or have you ever been a Cold Warrior? If so, for whom? An American? Definitely not. His style was Continental. Was he French? Swiss? Italian? Hungarian? Are you one of Warren Davis's reapings among the lush fields of double-agentry? Or might you be a suave Russian spy tutored by Misha Shilovsky? An assassin? Had Alex Somerfield's old nemesis finally put the dogs onto him? Had there been a meeting in the old czarist prison in Dzerzhinski Square at which this fellow had been given the green light for a wet job? *Mokrie*

dela, old sport? A termination with extreme preju-
dice? From Russia, with love?

"Speak up," said Somerfield. "This isn't a honey
trap." His tone was almost pleading as he stood with
his hands clasped loosely behind his back. He picked
up the Beretta. Who in the world's intelligence
community issued Berettas? "The city of New York
has very stringent laws concerning the carrying of
firearms," he went on chidingly. "Is this one
registered? I'll bet not."

While Somerfield spoke Amnon had been assess-
ing his situation and the two men who controlled it.
The cop was an open book, like cops everywhere. An
action man. Tough-minded, hard-fisted. Gun in the
ribs. "Up against the wall!" The quick, expert, and
suitably rough frisk followed by a flint-eyed Old
Hollywood B-movie glower hinting of the Third
Degree to come. The rubber hose in the back room.
Iron fist. Gestapo tactics.

The second man was not a policeman yet he had a
keen appreciation of the ways of the police, shrewdly
taking the opposite tack of the other; the Good Cop
versus the Bad. The carrot. Wielding a stick was not
this man's style. No rough stuff. All velvet in voice
and manner, he could have befriended Eichmann. As
soft as his pajamas and comfortable as his robe was
this slick smoothie. The reasonableness of maturity
speaking. Here was no amateur. These skills were
professional. You ask who am I? Who the hell are
you?

"Leave him to me," barked Lyman. "I'll sweat
answers out of him."

"I don't believe that will be necessary," said

Somerfield gentlemanly patient. "If this fellow had intended to harm me he's had plenty of chances to do so before this, hasn't he?" Had he come from Moscow with murder on his mind, he thought, it would have happened before now. "And I do think we could do without the handcuffs. We've got the guns, after all. Please, Sheldon, do me a favor and take them off."

Grudgingly, Lyman complied.

Somerfield edged to a window. "Is it possible," he said, parting the drapes, "that our friend was not alone?"

Lyman shook his head definitively. "He was all by himself."

Letting the drape close, Somerfield turned with a satisfied look. "Yes, I'm sure you're right," he said, pocketing the Beretta and turning to the man with many names. "If you don't talk to us here and now I'm afraid Detective Lyman will have to turn this into an official police matter. Somehow, I don't believe you'd want that. No, somehow I don't think that would suit you. Nor the people who sent you. Am I correct? Well, I don't want it either. It will be best for all concerned to keep this business strictly unofficial. Who are you and why were you baby-sitting me tonight?"

Strictly unofficial? How could he be in the custody of a police officer and remain unofficial? First he'd been handcuffed. Now there were none. What was going on here? Who are these guys? What sort of operation were they running? What to do? Stick to his course? Or gamble? Remain clammed up? Keep his cards to his chest? Or raise the ante?

"The game of Secret Agent is poker," he taught the

recruits at Kfar Sirkin. "But it's the sort played in the saloon in an American cowboy movie. The rules of survival are simple. Keep your eyes on the dealer. Never sit with your back to the door. Don't accuse anyone of cheating unless you're sure you're quicker on the draw than he is."

The cards he was holding were not insignificant. He knew far more about the two opposing players than they knew of him. Which was what? One was a cop, unquestionably. And quite good at his work! But he wasn't working officially. He was taking his cues from the other, who was neither a policeman nor appeared to be an official of any kind yet conducted himself as if he were. Whoever he was, he was no amateur. Whatever they were up to, it wasn't kosher.

"I ask you again," Somerfield said without a flicker of emotion. "Why were you watching me tonight?"

All right, let's play poker, thought Amnon. "Oh, it wasn't just tonight."

Years of experience pursuing his bizarre but kindred trades paid off now for Somerfield. The objective reporter staying cool and aloof from his story, the unflappable secret agent shielding himself behind a mask of inscrutable cover, the spinner of mystery yarns subtly slipping the vital clue past the reader but not his sleuth, he froze into impassivity wordless.

The leaden silence was unexpected, a vacuum demanding to be filled, unnerving in its urgency "You don't believe me?"

Somerfield shrugged. "Why shouldn't I? If you

followed me tonight, why shouldn't I believe that you followed me at other times? The question you must answer is Why?"

Amnon chuckled. "You're very good at this, sir."

"You're not bad yourself. So, listen. Why don't we just put all our cards on the table?"

Amnon grinned. "Sure. You go first."

Lyman exploded. "For crissakes, Alex, enough of this crap. I'm gonna haul his ass over to the precinct." Drawing his pistol, he declared, "You're under arrest, pal!"

Raise and call, thought Amnon. "On what charge?" he demanded indignantly. A blatant bluffing. There were plenty of charges. The game was over. It was shoot-out time in the old saloon and he was caught weaponless.

"I think you'd better come clean," Somerfield said gravely. "We want the straight dope. No playback bullshit."

Until that moment Amnon had steeled himself for the worst and vowed that if burned he would reveal nothing concerning Operation Judah. If caught he would recite a cover story and no matter how often he was questioned he would repeat it with the inflexibility of a tape recording.

The adult game of Secret Agent is laden with the childish, not the least being its imagery. Safe house. Postman. Lamplighter. Watcher. Baby-sitter. Listener. Workname. Dead drop. Cobbler. Honey trap. Black-bag job. Sleeper. Mole. Cut out. Sanitize. Turn. Inquisitor. The Take. The Target, Hard or soft. Cover. Cover story. Playback.

Amnon's inquisitor had used several of these terms

too many times to be a coincidence.

On at least four occasions that evening as he'd followed this man Alex through midtown Manhattan from the Dorset Hotel to this safe house on Sixty-fifth Street he thought he'd been spotted. On the previous occasion when he'd followed him, first from the Helder Galleries and then from New York University this man had been just as adept and wary, clearly a man with training and experience who showed every sign of being an astute, if somewhat rusty, member of the worldwide select society of secret agents—a superb tradesman.

Now he had all but announced it, demanding "no playback bullshit" with an icy certainty that he was being understood, one fraternity brother speaking the inviolate code of comradeship to another. "It's safe now," he was saying. "You are among friends."

"It's a horror story," began Amnon.

Chapter Forty-Six

Whodunnit?

While Amnon Dorot spun his tale of atrocities committed by the Nazi Grenier, how Grenier had eluded capture and become transformed into Peter Helder, how a chance encounter at the theater had exposed him, and how the steps taken by the government of Israel to track him down and bring him to justice had been thwarted by the murders of Helder and the agent Daniel Ben Avram, Alex Somerfield stood by the fireplace placidly smoking his pipe.

Detective Lyman had been slouched on the couch with his legs crossed at the ankles and thrust toward the center of the room. At the end of the narrative he was sitting up and leaning forward slightly with his hands loosely clasped and a glowering frown creasing his forehead. "Let me get it straight, Amnon. It's your opinion that whoever killed Helder also killed your man, this kid Daniel Ben Avram, and my partner because he was close to cracking the case?"

"It is the only explanation," said Amnon.

"Well, it sure explains why I never located the kid named Danny that Helder was with. My Danny was your Daniel?"

"No question about it. When the time is right I will claim his body. As discreetly as possible, of course."

Lyman's eyes shifted to Somerfield. "So who killed them, Alex? Helder's pals in the Atlantis Club?"

"It would seem so," said Somerfield. "They killed Helder because, somehow, they'd found out that he was in danger of being exposed. How they learned this is the only remaining puzzle. But they did. Then they killed Daniel Ben Avram. And when Hargreave started getting close to the solution to the Helder murder, they killed him. Proving it will be a problem. In fact I don't see how you can. My assumption is that the government of Israel is not going to be helpful. Correct, Amnon?"

"No chance."

"Too many complications would ensue," said Somerfield in an explanatory tone. "Too many risks. Israeli secret intelligence methods might be compromised."

With a mixture of incredulity and anger, Lyman said, "So whoever killed Helder, Daniel Ben Avram and my partner gets off!"

"It seems so," said Somerfield. "I don't see any other possibility."

"You knew right away about me, didn't you Alex?" said Amnon. "You had my number the

326

moment I came through the door."

"Not that soon," said Somerfield with a shrug.

"How? When? I have to know."

"Ah, Amnon," said Somerfield, throwing an arm affectionately around the Israeli's slender shoulders, "how does that old joke go? You can always tell a man from Mossad. But you can't tell him much!"

"By the way, I wasn't the only one watching you," said Amnon gravely. "When you left Professor Levitan the other day and went for that rambling stroll through the Village you had two shadows. Mine. And another."

Somerfield looked quizzically to Lyman. "One of your men?"

Lyman threw up his hands. "Definitely not."

"Oh, it wasn't a policeman," said Amnon. "After you returned to this house—with me and the second chap following you—and it was pretty obvious that you were home to stay put for the evening he broke off his surveillance. I was intrigued to know for whom he worked. So I followed him."

"To where?" asked Somerfield anxiously.

"I expected him to go to the Atlantis Club. But he proceeded to a travel agency in Rockefeller Center. I waited a long time for him to come out. But I lost him. I assume he left by another exit."

Somerfield was rigid now, expectant, holding his pipe as if it were a weapon. "What was the name of that travel agency?"

"Battersby Associates."

"Christ," gasped Somerfield, thrusting the pipe into his mouth. "Jesus Christ Almighty!"

327

Chapter Forty-Seven

The Call

"I think I see it all very clearly now," said Somerfield after a long thoughtful pause. His shining eyes danced between the Israeli agent and the New York City homicide detective. "Now I must ask both of you to place your entire trust in me—no questions, please. There may be time for questions and answers later. But not at the moment. For the time being, you must leave it all to me."

Amnon was not surprised.

Lyman was troubled. "I insist that I be your backup in whatever it is you've got in mind."

"No," exploded Somerfield. "I'll have to do this alone."

"In that case, do you have a piece?"

Somerfield was a blank for a moment. "You mean a gun? Heavens no."

"I'll get you one," asserted Lyman.

"Oh, I don't think so."

"Listen to him, Alex," interjected Amnon urgently.

"You don't have the option, Alex," declared Lyman. "Either you take a gun with you or I back you up."

"Very well," sighed Somerfield. "The gun."

The one which Lyman brought to the apartment within the hour was a nickel-finish Colt Cobra .38 Special with a two-inch barrel. "It belonged to a pimp I arrested a year ago," explained Lyman. "I salvaged it from the property room. Don't ask how."

"I shan't," said Somerfield as he laid the gun on the fireplace mantel.

"You are familiar with guns," said Lyman, almost as an afterthought.

"Oh, yes," said Somerfield. He'd been trained in weapons and always scored high in required annual tests but he'd never actually been issued a pistol and owned no guns of his own. "I'm sure I won't need it."

"I don't suppose you'd care to tell me where you're going and what you'll be doing?"

"Better you don't know," said Somerfield with a slight smile.

"You're obviously familiar with this Battersby Travel Agency and—"

"Detective," exclaimed Amnon. "Let it be. Alex knows what he's doing. Don't press! This is an entirely different world than yours! Correct, Alex?"

"A whole universe," said Somerfield with a quick smile.

Lyman slowly shook his head. "Who the hell are you, Alex?"

Somerfield shrugged, a gesture that was a question in itself.

"C'mon," said Amnon, tugging at Lyman's sleeve. "I think it's time for us to get out of the way."

Fifteen minutes seemed the right time to wait before leaving the house to make the telephone call, Somerfield decided.

Another fifteen minutes passed as he wandered the streets being certain that no one was following and deciding that he would place the call from a pay phone in a liquor store.

The woman who answered had a voice like a chirping bird. "Battersby Travel, how may I help you?"

"Mr. Battersby, please."

"May I say who's calling?"

"Mr. Deerstalker."

Chapter Forty-Eight

The Park

His trench coat was heavy in the righthand pocket because of Lyman's pistol as he began a surveillance of the entrance to the small park at the Sutton Place end of Fifty-seventh Street.

"A meeting," he'd demanded of a surprised Russ Branson on the phone. "The usual place. One hour from now."

Beyond the park lay the East River and the spiderweb steel of the 59th Street Bridge that had been seen as a backdrop in so many movies and made newly famous for the sixties generation by a Simon and Garfunkel song. A mansion that had belonged to the legendary showman Billy Rose was to the right and the apartments of Number One Sutton Place to the left.

He waited not in the park but at a corner where he was able to see its approaches. From uptown, the light slope of Sutton Place North. The steeper hill from the south. From the west came Fifty-seventh Street like a broad black river in the bed of a wide canyon whose cliffs were brick, gray, and brown stone facades of expensive apartment houses with windows alight.

One of these had to be the route for whoever would come and presently he spotted him a half-block away, a short figure, hatless, in a light spring topcoat.

A ramp slanted to the left and led down to a landing and a reverse ramp to the park itself which was a square of pavement with benches, sculptured animals for children to climb upon, high iron fences to separate it from Billy Rose's former garden and the apartment house and a long wall of black stone low enough to rest one's arms upon while admiring the view but high enough to keep a person from easily tumbling onto the FDR Drive immediately below. The view northward was of the East River flanked by the stolid white skyscraper of New York Hospital and multihued Upper East Side high-rises, the flat expanse of industrial Long Island City on the opposite shore, the river widening past the United Nations and, most spectacular of all, the bridge sparkling with strands of lights like diamonds draped along the suspending cables between its towers.

As if he were a fashion model positioning himself to be photographed in one of the most attractive spots in the city, he stood with his back to the bridge in the corner formed by the wall and Billy Rose's fence which he was hopeful he could vault if he discovered he'd made a mistake. His left hand he laid nonchalantly atop the cold rough wall.

The right he kept in his trench coat pocket lightly touching the smooth cold steel of the pimp's pistol.

Unhesitatingly, Warren Davis sauntered down the ramps and halfway across the park before he stopped and raised his arms from his sides, hands opened and fingers spread. "Alex," he exclaimed, "it is dangerous to finger loaded firearms in the pocket of one's coat." The remark was similar to a warning expressed by Professor Moriarty to Sherlock Holmes in their first meeting and Somerfield couldn't help smiling at Davis quoting it. "Now tell me what this is all about," Davis said, taking a step forward.

Somerfield drew the pistol. "Far enough, Warren."

"Alex! Really! What's going on?"

"You know, Warren."

"Yes, I suppose I do," said Davis with a grin as winning and trusting as it had been so long ago on the Iowa campus. "I owe you congratulations. Well done. And what a surprise. I never would have thought it would be you. Who'd have supposed that brainy Alex Somerfield would wind up mixed in all this mess and using muscle?" He nodded at the gun. "You were never on that side of the game, Alex."

"It's not a game, Warren."

"Oh, Alex, of course it's a game. All of a history has been a game. It's been the Power Game from Day One. Strong versus weak. Might versus might. That was fine in conventional times. Only now we've gotten to the point where it's got to be brains up against brains. The muscle is nuclear and if one side uses it so will the other and that's the end of it. The day is past, if it ever was, when the Soviet Union and the United States might settle matters the old-fashioned way with a shooting war. That's what I had in mind when I went out looking for people like you. Smart guys."

"What the hell did ex-Nazis have to do with the Cold War?"

Davis looked astonished. "The Nazis were Communism's first enemy. Their files were incredibly rich. Their knowledge was extremely useful after the war. The technical boys needed the Nazi rocket scientists; we in the intelligence community needed the data that the Nazis had accumulated."

"Including the Nazi Grenier whom you helped escape hanging and then brought here, transforming him into Peter Helder, art dealer and valued member of the Atlantis Club?"

"Yes."

"The Atlantis Club was the front."

"A very convenient one, too."

"How long had you been a member?"

Davis formed a triumphant smile. "Your investigation didn't turn up that piece of information."

"No one's perfect, Warren!"

"I've been on the club's board of trustees since the war. Not under my true name, of course."

"Of course."

"It's an organization that's done quite a bit of useful work, you know. Quite aside from the aspects that have attracted your astute but unfortunate attention."

"Why did you have Helder killed?"

"Alex, you don't know? You haven't deduced why? But of course you have! You just want to hear it from me. You want confirmation. This is to be like one of those scenes at the end of your delightful mystery books where all is explained! Very well, I'll play your game. It became necessary. He'd been found out. Compromised. The Israelis were after him. They'd sent this young man looking for him. Oh, he was excellent, for being just a kid. Had they dragged Helder back to Israel, can you imagine the trouble he would have caused spilling all that stuff about how certain men in the United States government aided and abetted war criminals in their escapes?"

"So you had the Israeli agent killed, too."

"An unfortunate necessity."

"I thought Israel was on our side."

"Israel is on . . . Israel's . . . side."

"Now you sound like von Bork! Surely, Warren, you're not a Jew-hater?"

"Not in the least," said Davis indignantly, wounded. "But I am not one of those in government who still blindly believes that America's interests in the Middle East must rest entirely upon a relationship with Israel. Why not be friends with the Arabs, too? If for no other reason, we ought to be at peace with the Arabs because it is they and not the Israelis who have the oil!"

"All of this has to do with oil?"

"Alex, it has to do with Russia! American interests lie in keeping the Russians out of the Middle East. The Cold War was destined to be a game of shifting interest, changing allies. That's just what has happened in the Mideast, you see! Right after the war it made sense for us to get behind a Jewish state. It was our ticket of admission to the Mideast! How could we exert our power and influence in that region if we had no foothold? Israel provided it. But times are changing. We have made the mistake of backing Israel to the point where we have alienated the Arabs and driven them into the hands of the Russkies. We can't have that! Arabia is stirring out of its lethargy. The Arabs are uniting! The day is coming when we will have to deal with them if we are to keep the Russian Bear at bay. You do see?"

"What I see is that you helped ex-Nazis escape, that you had one of them killed, plus an Israeli agent, and an American detective. And you tried to kill a reporter! All in the cause of what you call American interests. I don't see how murder can be in the American interest!"

Advancing a step, Davis said, "And what are you going to do about it?"

Somerfield wiggled the pistol. "Stand still, Warren. I don't want to hurt you."

"Had you really intended to shoot me, Alex," Davis said, retreating a pace, "you'd have done so the moment you saw me." He moved back two more steps. "Why didn't you? I'll tell you why. Because you had to have this little talk. You needed the intellectual confrontation. It wasn't enough to know who killed whom. You had to know . . . WHY. All your life you've chased those six big questions. Who? What? Where? When? How? Why?" Turning his back, he strode to the bottom of the ramp leading up from the park, stopped, and turned again. "Now that you know, what are you going to do about it?"

Somerfield had the gun raised.

Davis was at the landing, gripping the railing,

shadowed by a lamp. "I have told you why all this happened. Now I shall tell you why you won't do a damned thing about it. First, you have no real proof. You have only conjecture. Your famous Sherlock Holmes-style deduction! You have what I've said here this evening, but without any corroboration it's not evidence. None of it would stick in a court of law. You can't prove any of it. A second point is much more personal."

"And that is?"

"Your oath as an agent of the United States government. The one you swore on the first day at the farm down in Virginia? It's still in effect, of course. It's a lifetime vow not to divulge secrets."

"That applies to government secrets, Warren, not to murders."

"Ah," said Davis with a grin, "but suppose for a moment, dear Alex, that all that's been done was . . . *official?*"

"Ridiculous!"

"What if it was all sanctioned, Alex? What if the entire enterprise were authorized at the highest level of government and classified top-secret? It has been, of course. Now that you know the top-secret stuff, Alex, where does it leave you? And your oath as an agent? If you were to go public with any of it, who would be the criminal? I, who was carrying out an authorized action under Top Secret orders? Or you, who revealed them?"

"You're forgetting the Israelis," retorted Somerfeld. "I could slip them the whole story. I'll give it all to their man, Amnon Dorot. Then they can go public."

"Afraid not, Alex. You see, Mr. Dorot has been recalled by Tel Aviv. It happened within the hour. He's already heading for Kennedy Airport. You see, the last thing Israel will want now is an embarrassing situation between themselves and us. They've just won this stunning victory. Defeated the Arabs in six days! Astounding! Now they will need American friendship even more! Even if you could tell the Israelis the whole story, Alex, it would do no good. They'll classify all of this, as well. So, you see there's nothing you can do."

"I'll give Lomax the story."

"No good. Where's your proof?"

"The police! Lyman!"

"Again, it's only your word," said Davis, slowly ascending the ramp. "And would the police brass believe you or the person who would surely call them from Washington warning them of grave implications for national security?"

Somerfield cocked the gun.

Hearing the cold double click, Davis hesitated shoulders hunched, head bent slightly, eyes shut expecting a shot. When it did not come, he breathed a quiet, relieved sigh, adjusted the fit of his topcoat said "Go home, Alex," and sauntered away.

Chapter Forty-Nine

Last Train to Philly

In the sparsely populated and unlovable Penn Station waiting room that smelled of stale coffee in discarded paper cups, tobacco smoke, and the ammonia of wash water being sloshed onto the floor by cleaning men, Somerfield found a safely remote bench where he watched two cops banging their nightsticks on the benches and against the worn soles of sleeping derelicts and homeless women, rousting them in the manner of railroad dicks since the days of steam.

It would be an hour before his midnight train would be called, the last one to Philadelphia. Plenty of time to rehash what had happened in the park, going over the dialogue with Warren Davis again and again, replaying its cold cynicism.

He could see why Davis and others in the American government had aided and protected Nazi war criminals and their reasons for doing so. He

understood their reasoning in soliciting help from
former enemies in the fight against Soviet Communism.

He did not approve of what they did, but he could
understand.

He could follow their thinking in wanting to seek
the friendship of Arab countries in the crucible of
crises that was the Middle East.

He didn't agree with that policy, but he understood it.

He grasped the twisted reasoning as to how all of
this had led to the murders of three men—the ex-Nazi
Helder, the Israeli agent, and the New York detective.

He knew everything.

But he couldn't prove any of it.

That was his infuriating frustration as he waited,
cold with anger and fear, for his train to be called.

Listening to Davis correctly explaining why there
was nothing that Alexander Somerfield could do—in
that sickening reality—he had been pushed to the
brink of violence. In the park for one heart-stopping
second he'd been on the verge of pulling the trigger
and killing Warren Davis.

Why hadn't he? Fear of being caught?

Certainly not. He could have simply walked away
and no one would ever have connected him with the
killing, which in all likelihood would have been left
to languish like the deaths of Helder, Daniel Ben
Avram, and Hargreave.

He hadn't shot Davis for a very simple reason
which Davis must have known instinctually—
because it would have been wrong. Killing Davis
would have made Alexander Somerfield no more

han a murderer. It would have made a lie out
of everything he had stood for all his life. As Davis
had said to him long ago, he wasn't a gunslinger.
His weapon was the truth and his ammunition was
words.

But in this situation, he found himself unarmed.
Words were insufficient.

To prove that three murders had been committed,
evidence was needed. And there was none.

Neither was there any chance of providing Dick
Lomax with the story of what had happened.
Journalism, like the courts of law, required facts.
The Who, What, Where, When, Why and How of a
news report had to be backed up by verifiable sources
of information. In these three murders, he knew,
none would be found. The lid would be slapped on
tight. Lips buttoned. A top-secret stamp inked and
readily at hand. The "national security" would be
invoked. The cover-up would be complete. Nothing
could be done.

"Go home, Alex," Davis had said.

Which, promptly at midnight when his train was
announced, Somerfield did.

Chapter Fifty

Déjà Vu

Had he been younger, Somerfield would have sprinted up the long snowy driveway from his mailbox to his house, but in a year—November 1990—he would mark his fifty-fifth birthday, a slightly overweight "ex-" man with a touch of angina pain if he overdid things, so on a blustery noontime in early March of 1989, twenty-two years after his righteous anger had driven him close to becoming a murderer, he trudged slowly to his cocoonish home nestled beneath frosted pines on the gentle slope of the marshmallowed hill at the edge of Valley Forge National Park, curling in his gloved hand a letter from Professor Norman Levitan.

Going down the hill for the mail and the daily newspapers had become a ritual in a daily pattern of activities in a rigidly structured regimen—waking up at seven each morning, going down the lane for the newspapers deposited by a stalwart deliveryman whose Jeep's engine was Somerfield's alarm clock, reading the *Times* over a breakfast of English muffins and coffee, catching the latest news headlines from Philadelphia's all-news radio station and then turning to music on FM as he went to his desk at eight o'clock to write. It had been his way of doing things in all those years since Dick Lomax had summoned him to New York, a city he visited now only for the annual Baker Street Irregulars dinner each January and for book business, never staying overnight, although Wiggins had issued a standing invitation to use one of the bedrooms above his bookstore "for as long as you wish and for whatever devious purpose you choose, provided you confess everything to me, in strictest confidence, naturally!"

It had been Wiggins who'd alerted Russ Branson and Warren Davis that Alexander Somerfield was poking around in matters related to the Atlantis Club and that he would be chatting with Professor Levitan, Somerfield had deduced. He'd done it quite innocently, of course; just another juicy bit of Wiggins gossip whispered into Russ's or Warren's ear. Surveillance had begun within hours, Somerfield presumed, although the watcher whom Davis had assigned wasn't aware of Amnon Dorot's observant presence.

"The stuff of fiction," Somerfield thought as he carried Levitan's letter to the house.

A word processor had been introduced into his notes in 1986, an impetuous and dubious experiment with the new technology that revolutionized his methods and, he believed, made him a better writer because he edited more. Bathed in the green glow of its screen, he became lost in the reality of whatever fiction he was working on and surfaced around noon for another stroll down the lane, this time for the mail and this day the happy surprise of Levitan's letter.

Business letters were commonplace—his agent, editors, accountants, lawyers, and the occasional note from a reader forwarded by his publisher. Personal letters were rare, intimate correspondence among Americans, even literary ones, having been replaced by the telephone.

In the summer of 1967 a note had come from Dick Lomax announcing that because of the seriousness of his injuries and what doctors said would be a much longer convalescence he had decided to get out of the news business and return to his native New England where he'd been offered a partnership in a real estate development. "Too bad that Helder story never panned out," he'd ended, surprisingly blithely.

A letter from Sheldon Lyman had arrived at about the same time stating proudly that he'd been promoted to the rank of lieutenant, which pleased him, but moved out of homicide and into the narcotics division. "That's the area of police work that is booming and which is going to get even more important in the years to come," he wrote prophetically. Indeed, increasingly over the years Somerfield caught glimpses of Lyman on television news reports of the culmination of various drug investigations, these broadcasts from New York being scooped out of the air by an ungainly but miraculous TV satellite receiving dish that had been erected behind Somerfield's house at about the same time the work processor had been acquired. And a microwave oven.

Sandra Hargreave had written to him once—1968—a sweet letter thanking him for his interest in her father's murder, "as fruitless as it was for all of us, the case being still unresolved." The envelope also contained a clipping of a news story about her wedding, not to Lyman but to another prosecutor. The item said her husband was considering running for Congress but added "if his wife doesn't do so first." An edition of the *Times* two years later had carried a story of her attempt at elected office and a defeat but two years after that she'd succeeded and had been reelected each November thereafter.

Over the years since the murders of Helder, the Israeli boy, and Detective Hargreave when he'd had the extraordinary privilege of meeting Professor Levitan and listening to his illuminating discourse on how history was shaped frequently by bizarre beliefs, he'd engaged in a sporadic but delightful and instructive, if somewhat formal, correspondence with him. Therefore he was pleased and excited as he opened the latest.

Dear Mr. Somerfield:

I am certain that you recall our first conversation many years ago in which you expressed an interest in the group known as the Atlantis Club. I do not know if you are still concerned with it, but I thought that if you remained fascinated by that peculiar organization you would want to know that there is to be a gathering of its international chapters at the Penta Hotel in New York on April 30th of this year. As I am confined to my house by my advanced age and declining health, it is my hope that you would come and observe. I believe you will find it worth your while.

The Penta used to be called the Hotel Pennsylvania because it stood opposite Penn Station. Its telephone number had been made famous by the Glenn Miller Orchestra in the song, *Pennsylvania 6-5000*. In the 1960s when the Pennsylvania Railroad had become Penn Central, the hotel had been known as the Statler Hilton, catering to tourists and businessmen who liked its moderate prices and convenient proximity to the Garment District, Broadway theaters, Macy's and, of course, the trains.

In its large, ornate, and crowded lobby as Somerfield arrived the faces of the tourists were of a far more international cast than in the hotel's heyday in the Glenn Miller era when people with colored skin were unlikely and unwelcome. But here on this balmy last night of April 1989 were all the hues of the world's flesh.

Flowing against the gaily clothed exiting guests were scores of men and some women, many wearing the white robes of the Middle East and the flowing checkered headdress which the leader of the Palestine Liberation Organization, Yasir Arafat, had made a symbol of the Palestinian people's long struggle with Israel, all proceeding toward elevators that would take them to the grand ballroom of the hotel and what a sign in the lobby described as the Annual Banquet of the Conference of the Atlantis Clubs of the Earth and Friends United for the Restoration of the Ancient Lands. Merging with them, Somerfield ascended, unchallenged.

Long tables with white cloths lined the lobby outside the ballroom and from neat stacks upon them, the guests helped themselves to elegant programs describing the evening's menu and the events to follow the meal and a listing of guests and their designated tables. Taking one of the booklets, Somerfield made his way through the throng toward the men's rest room. There, he opened the program to the list of speakers. First, he noted, was the president-emeritus of the Atlantis Club of New York, H. von Bork, who would introduce the current president, Victor Stoessel, identified as Chairman and CEO, AmerAbCo Investments, who would in turn introduce the main speaker, Mr. Warren Davis, president of the Ishmael Society.

On a separate page appeared a biographical notation:

> Mr. Warren Davis, a longtime member of the New York Atlantis Club, founded the Ishmael Society in the autumn of 1967 declaring, "It is our purpose to seek ways to improve relations between the United States and the nations of the Arab world, the descendants of Ishmael, son of Abraham, from whom the Arab people derive a just claim to live in peace and prosperity."

A noted international businessman for more than four decades, Mr. Davis has devoted most of the past twenty years to the problems of the Middle East as an advisor to several governments and many multinational corporations

347

and global financial institutions as well as several international youth organizations whose purposes are to seek a just and equitable solution to problems of the region.

Accompanying the text, Somerfield found Davis's photograph, the seemingly ageless, puffy-faced, roly-poly and seductively smiling Pied Piper from the Iowa campus of thirty years ago.

Then, as if conjured, Davis was before him, pushing open the men's room door and freezing with as much shock and amazement as he found registered in Somerfield's face. "Why, Alex, old boy! It's you! What a hell of a jolt! Blast from the past and all that." He let go of the door and leaned against it, barring it. "You do have a way of showing up at the most unexpected places and times!"

"I see it's still going on, Warren," said Somerfield coldly.

"What's going on, old buddy?"

"The work of the Atlantis Club."

"Of course it is!" He stepped away from the door and crossed to a lavatory, leaning against it facing the door. *"Never keep your back to a door, gentlemen,"* he'd taught at the Farm. "The Atlantis Club is a fine philanthropic outfit that—"

"Save the lofty ideals speech for others, Warren. You know damned well what I mean. *It's still going on.* The nurse-maiding of the ex-Nazis. The coziness with Jew-haters. The snuggling up to the worst elements of the Arab world because of oil and in the interests of keeping the Russians at bay. I recognized a lot of the types going into that banquet room

348

Warren. You taught all of us how to spot the types, remember? What do I see out there? Aryan types. Palestinian types. Terrorist types. This meeting is about Israel and how to deal with the Jews. Hitler would be right at home here. It's April thirtieth, the fortieth anniversary of his death. But he's alive tonight, Warren! What's the agenda? The Final Solution to the Jewish problem?"

"Alex, my old and dear friend, colleague . . . *pupil*, times have changed! Look what has happened since we last saw one another back in sixty-seven. There've been a couple of new wars in the Middle East. The Arab oil embargo. The fall of the Shah. The rise of Muslim Fundamentalism. The Ayatollah Khomeini. Hostages. Lebanon. The Palestinians rising up in anger in the Occupied Territories and Gaza. Israeli soldiers shooting Arab kids. We were on the wrong side, Alex. I was right back then and I'm right now. The United States government's policies have changed. Reagan is gone. The State Department is meeting regularly with Palestinians. We're now officially friends with Yasir Arafat. The whole world is dealing with the Palestinians. It's the only way. Grow up, Alex. There's a fresh wind blowing! President George Bush says so himself! A new century is in the offing, Alex. Get in step, man!"

"The goose step, Warren?"

"You are so damned emotional and single-minded, Alex. It was your only fault as an agent. It's always been black and white. Never the gray areas for you."

"Were the murders of three people one of the gray areas?"

"Alex, that is ancient history. We settled that over twenty years ago. I thought we patched together an agreement."

"It just came unstuck."

"Ahh! And what can you do about it tonight that you couldn't do then?" He turned away, bending over the sink and running water into cupped hands but with his flinty, exploring and suspicious eyes fixed on Somerfield reflected in the mirror. "To borrow a phrase from your friends the Jews in their Passover rituals," he said with a sudden benign smile, " 'Why is tonight different from all other nights?' "

"I guess you could say that the statute of limitations has expired," snapped Somerfield, easing toward the door. "Those murders happened, as you said, more than twenty years ago. Well now I think the time has come to tell the world about them."

"The oath you swore has no expiration date save one, Alex," said Davis, drying his hands with paper towels. "It coincides with the date of your death. So, if you are telling me that you're going to write something about what happened—"

"A book, Warren," interjected Somerfield. "It will be a book that I'll write, for sure."

"I wouldn't do so were I you, Alex," said Davis, the amiable mentor from the Farm. Crumpling the wet towels and slamming them angrily into a wastebasket, he abruptly became the other Warren Davis—hard and mean—whom Somerfield had known of but had never truly seen. "Unless, of course, you are anticipating a *posthumous* publication."

Stunned, Somerfield lurched hard against the

door. "Is that a death threat?" Shaking his head in disbelief, he muttered, "God, you have taken a leaf from the terrorist's manual, haven't you? What was it you liked to quote Joseph Stalin as saying? *'Smert shpionam.'* 'Death to spies.' Now you have joined the ranks of the fanatics who say 'Death to authors!'"

"Alex, no one wants to kill you." He laughed, a hard, raspy guffaw. "But there are things that can be done short of that," he said as his eyes narrowed to knife-thin slits. "There are laws. Those that deal with the breach of secrecy, the national interest, libel, and slander." His tone was professorial now, the legendary Warren Davis lecturing the recruits at the Farm. "A book such as you're thinking of writing could easily be enjoined," he said. "Tied up in legal knots for years. Decades! And what about sources? You'll need to talk to people and look at files. Do you really believe you'd gain access to all the facts you'd need?"

"Research is not what I have in mind, Warren."

Someone was pushing at the door, banging on it, yelling, demanding to get in but Somerfield held it shut.

"I wasn't thinking of a non-fiction book," he whispered. "No. I'd never write a kiss-and-tell book. My journalism's pretty rusty after all these years. I was thinking in terms of fiction. A novel. You might call it a *roman à clef.* You know. Thinly disguised characters. A plot that has overtones of real events. I thought once upon a time that the Helder murder would make a hell of a yarn. I even came up with a title: *Death Mask.* That would have been a simple murder mystery, of course. But I've got a better book

351

in mind, a political thriller filled with all sorts of sinister types—an ex-Nazi, an Israeli agent who's on his trail, a mysterious organization with a hidden agenda, and a shrewd cop who's adding it all up. Then all of them are murdered! Who done it? To find out, I'd introduce a gutsy newsman and an old pal of his who also happened to have been in the espionage business. Whatcha think of it, Warren?"

"Don't be a fool, Alex," sighed Davis, suddenly showing his age as he slumped, arms and shoulders and legs going limp like a marionette whose strings had been severed.

"It ought to be a pretty good yarn," enthused Somerfield. "Maybe a bestseller. Possibly a movie deal! I'll send you a copy, Warren. Autographed, of course."

"You are crazy, Alex," growled Davis, the old fires rekindled.

"I've got a great title for it," said Somerfield, easing away from the door. *"Secret Orders."*

"Alex, listen to me!" thundered Davis.

"Sorry, Warren," said Somerfield, letting the door open and edging outside as several angry and impatient men rushed in. "I'd love to stay and hear you talk to your friends, old pal, but I've got this book to write!"